Without the strings of bulbs to light the way, the trees appeared like rows of giants with pointed heads and outstretched arms. I brushed through the clawing branches that snagged my coat and reentered the fair grounds. None of the stall workers were around. Everyone had left. No music touched my ears. No alluring aromas tickled my nose. No scent of sugary pastries or gingerbread cookies or warm, yeasty bread or sizzling sausages. It hit me that I was starved, having skipped a few meals in the craziness of the day. The ever-present pine scent lingered on my clothes, and the image of Meredith's dead body crept into my consciousness.

My feet had just trod over the spot where she'd died. My heart clenched, and fear fluttered in my chest. My courage drained away like coffee dripping from the brewer.

Friends Come to Call

by

Karen C. Whalen

Tow Truck Mysteries, Book 4

Friends Come to Call

COPYRIGHT © 2023 by Karen C. Whalen

Cover Art by *Diana Carlile*

The Wild Rose Press, Inc.
PO Box 708
Adams Basin, NY 14410-0708
Visit us at www.thewildrosepress.com

Publishing History
First Edition, 2023
Trade Paperback ISBN 978-1-5092-5021-9
Digital ISBN 978-1-5092-5022-6

Tow Truck Mysteries, Book 4
Published in the United States of America

Dedication

To family and friends, evergreen trees, candy canes, holly and ivy, a first noel, and a Merry Christmas.

Chapter 1

"What can I do to make this your best Christmas ever?" Sheriff Ephraim Lopez swooped down and touched his lips lightly to mine. Strands of "All I Want for Christmas is You" played from hidden speakers.

Whoa boy. I leaned in, closed my eyes, and let my imagination take over. The holiday music surged stronger, the twinkling lights brightened, and the mixed bouquet of potpourri, evergreens, and mulled wine intensified like someone had turned my senses up a notch. Our first Christmas as a couple. What would it be like? What memories would we make together? Nostalgic? Romantic? The perfect holiday memories?

I opened my eyes to look dreamily into Ephraim's, but my former boyfriend walked past us and distracted me. *Jeez.* Not what I wanted to see. Not right now. Not in this winter wonderland moment. The vision of Ephraim and me holding hands beneath a star-filled sky took flight and was replaced by Tanner next to his flatbed in front of a booth selling cheap Christmas decorations. Tanner must've just finished delivering the shed, like he had the other wooden stalls at the *Spruce Ridge Annual Christkindl Market.*

Ephraim followed my line of sight. "Oh, there's Tanner. Let's go say hello." He grabbed my hand and tugged me along with him.

My face heated with embarrassment,

although…why should I be embarrassed? Spruce Ridge, Colorado, is a small town, and I was bound to run into my ex, especially being in the same vehicle recovery business.

Yes, you heard me right.

Me, Delaney Morran, all of twenty-eight years, five foot two, and redheaded. *I* was a *badass* tow truck driver. And that ex-boyfriend of mine, Tanner Utley, was the one who taught me everything I knew about hauling cars.

I stopped at the side of his truck and looked down at my high-heeled boots. "Merry Christmas, Tanner."

He greeted us, "Merry Christmas to you."

This *gorgeous-head-turner* at six foot one, with hard muscles, dark-blond hair, and dark eyebrows, his shirt sleeves folded up to expose his tattoos, shook my boyfriend's hand while I shook off my awkwardness. With the two men standing next to each other, it was obvious Tanner's height topped Ephraim's six feet, but the sheriff had more pounds of pure muscle. My gaze darted up to my old boyfriend, who was certainly good-looking, to the new man in my life, who was no slouch either.

Let me tell you about the sheriff. He's older than me by ten years and has the bronze complexion of his Mexican heritage, with black eyes and hair. His smile showcased his dimples. No woman in her right mind could hold out against this hot Latino. Today was Ephraim's day off, so he was not wearing the light-blue uniform of the Clear Creek Sheriff's Department. Instead, he had on a tan suede jacket, blue jeans, and cowboy boots, with a cowboy hat to keep his head warm.

"What are you doing here?" Tanner slid the tailboard chain into the pocket hole on the back of his flatbed with a loud clunk. "The market doesn't open until tomorrow. I've still got more of these huts to bring in." All the wooden sheds were the same size and didn't have the usual double doors. Instead, they had a hatch with a roll-down shutter at the front, and the door to get inside was at the back. At this booth, a man barked out orders while a woman gave him an impatient eye. Ah, the stress of the season.

"Some of the stalls opened early." Ephraim pointed down the walkway between the sellers, each booth festooned with pine boughs and blinking lights. The path wandered through tall plastic snowmen, Santa Clauses, toy soldiers, and compact mounds of snow.

"I'm looking for a Christmas tree." I peered in the other direction toward the lot with rows of stacked trees and wreaths that gave off a Christmas-y fragrance. "You ready, Ephraim?"

"Yes. Let's go."

"But first, Kristen's coffee stand, then the tree lot."

The coffee kiosk was at the opposite end from the booth that sold trees. My best friend, Kristen Guttenberg, had opened in time for the morning crowd, and it was now afternoon. She'd probably racked up tons of sales already. I crossed my fingers and hoped she had. Kris was counting on good end-of-year sales to put her balance sheet in the black.

"See you later, Tanner." Ephraim once more took my hand in his. My faux-fur-trimmed boots kept my toes toasty, while Ephraim's hands kept my fingers warm.

A brawny guy, showing off his muscles in a tight, long-sleeve shirt and bib overalls, hosed out garbage and recycle bins. A woman sporting a Santa Claus hat held a clipboard tight under one arm and muttered to herself.

We sped past both of them, then proceeded through booths filled with ornaments, candles, soaps, woolen goods, knick-knacks, and mouthwatering food. Several of the best restaurants in town rented booths at the market, and their cooking aromas assaulted our noses.

We sidled up to Kristen's booth, and Ephraim said, "Good afternoon, Kris. How about some coffees?"

"Hey, you two." Kris and her younger cousin, Axle, stood inside the cozy hut. Her booth had a counter made from a two-by-six plank with several stools tucked underneath, and the sheriff and I each took a seat.

The kiosk was equipped with an industrial-sized espresso machine from Kristen's shop, Roasters on the Ridge, along with several coffee makers and milk frothers. All things necessary for every kind of specialty drink. The only type of machine she didn't bring was her bean roaster. Kristen was a purest who experimented with her own blends, making her coffeehouse a popular place around town. Promotional coffee cups crowded the shelves at the back. The red mugs were similar to the mulled wine mugs sold by the local winery's booth next door. Kristen's were embellished with the name of her coffee shop, and I was proud of the fact that her souvenir mugs were my idea. Her booth also sold beans in soft packages and Christmas tree ornaments stamped with the name, Roasters on the Ridge.

She pulled two cups from the shelf. "Do you think I'll be able to sell all these mugs? I can't use them next season because, you know…" She rubbed her finger across the year stamped on the back.

Kris had widely spaced gray eyes, dark shapely brows, and shiny, smooth shoulder-length brown hair, unlike my curly red hair. And she's tall. I always wanted

4

her straight hair and height. Not that I was envious…well, maybe a teensy bit. She's my fierce friend who always encourages and defends me against the world, and I want to do the same for her.

I answered, "Sure you will. Customers will flock to your booth for hot coffee and cocoa. And they'll love the mugs." At least I hoped so. I was well aware the ceramic cups would be outdated after this season due to my suggestion to include the year.

Kristen and her cousin exchanged worried looks. I gulped. "What?"

"What do you know?" Axle said. "Maybe you will sell out, Kris." He turned to Ephraim and asked, "What's your drink?" Ephraim told him, and Axle got busy making his nonfat latte and my double shot espresso. He was an expert mechanic and had quickly learned to master the espresso machine so he could help his cousin during the holidays. Axle didn't usually make the drinks, but since he was an automotive genius, he was a natural.

When Axle handed us our mugs, I said, "Thanks, little cuz." That's what I called him. Since he's Kristen's cousin, I considered him my cousin, too, or even the brother I never had. He also rented the spare bedroom in my apartment to help me out with finances. In his late teens, he didn't have his usual earbuds in place, but he was sporting his typical gray hoodie with the logo of an Indie band, and his dark hair was covered by a black stocking cap.

Kristen aimed her eyes at the mulled wine booth. "I found out I ordered the same number of commemorative mugs as they did." She'd ordered five hundred. "I wonder if they're worried. They look deserted right now."

"You'll sell even more than they will. Everyone loves coffee and cocoa, but not everyone drinks wine." Especially mulled wine, but that's just my opinion.

Another customer grabbed the stool next to me and ordered three coffees in the coffee shop's logo mugs. See? I was right. Her mugs were a big hit.

"We're headed over to get a tree, so we'll see you later." I indicated to Ephraim we should get going. Kris said goodbye, and Axle gave us a hand flap.

"So, back to my question." Ephraim tightened his grip on my fingers as we skirted around a giant wooden toy soldier and continued down the path.

I asked him, "What question?"

"What's your perfect Christmas?"

Oh, that question. The one that came with a kiss.

I said, "Well, for Kristen's Christmas booth to be a success. And Kris is also on a quest for the perfect picture for her Christmas cards, so I guess I want that, too, since we're sending cards out together. Let's see, Axle is saving up to buy a car…"

Ephraim halted and stroked my face. "I mean you. What do *you* want for Christmas, *mi amor*?"

I laughed. "You can help me find a tree."

We swept past the booth Tanner had set in place a few minutes ago. He was gone, but a sign now hung from the roof, Jennings Christmas Emporium, and the man and woman team had unpacked boxes of glitzy trinkets. Beyond that was a stall with colorful scarves, mittens, wool blankets, and Christmas-themed aprons and pajamas. I definitely needed to come back and check out those pajamas, but at the moment, the Christmas tree stand urged us forward.

I looped my arm in Ephraim's as we ambled through

fragrant trees of various heights. The blue spruces were too tall, but the Douglas firs were ideal with their full pyramid shapes and soft, shiny needles.

Ephraim held a fir tree up with one arm. "How about this?"

I walked around to get a good look from every angle while "It's the Most Wonderful Time of the Year" blasted from the speaker.

It's the hap-happiest season of all…

Yes, the tree was perfect.

When friends come to call…

It would look excellent in my apartment window.

I could picture my friends around the tree singing Christmas carols. *Yeah, right. As if.* I had to laugh at my sentimental self.

Something caught my eye. A black knit cap under one of the cylinder trees a few steps from the booth. The knit cap was on the head of someone wearing a gray hoodie. A someone whose body landed underneath the pine boughs, face down, arms akimbo, legs crossed as if tripped. That's what Axle was wearing—a black beanie and a gray hoodie.

Axle? How did he get here ahead of us? And what is the matter with him?

I yelped, put a hand over my heart, ran past Ephraim, and pushed the tree aside. I did a deep knee bend to get closer, but Ephraim slid his hands under my arms and pulled me away. "Hold on, Delaney, let me."

I regained my balance as Ephraim rolled the body over, and dark hair fell across the face. Something was horribly wrong here. I stepped back to take in some deep breaths of cold pine-scented air that iced the inside of my nose. Once the sheriff returned the body to its face-down position, he stood up.

"It's a woman."

Oh my God! It's not Axle. I blinked back hot tears, feeling both relief and shame, the shame causing my cheeks to burn like hot espresso on my tongue.

I asked, "Is she dead?"

He nodded once, his stony cop face on.

Everything went completely still and silent and dizzy. I couldn't even hear the music over the buzzing in my ears. "Who is she? What happened?"

Ephraim held up a hand. "Give me a second." He keyed into his phone and turned away, likely calling the sheriff's department. After he hung up, he took me by the arm and propelled me across the lot to the tree seller's hut. "Wait here." He had a few quiet words with the vendor, who nodded with wide eyes, visibly shaken. After one more firm nod of the man's head, the sheriff sprinted back toward the body.

I sat down on a stump, and the tree seller slouched onto a stack of wood next to me. He was bundled up in a plaid peacoat, heavy scarf, and a hat with earflaps. Only his face was uncovered, his skin tanned and rough from the elements, obviously someone who worked outside. We exchanged *what-the-hell-just-happened?* looks.

I held out my hand. "Delaney Morran."

"Kane Quigley." His coat sleeve rode up his arm when he shook my hand, exposing skin marred with red welts, probably scratches from the sharp pine needles. "You found a dead body on my tree lot?"

I nodded wordlessly. We must have been shocked into silence because we both stared vacantly ahead. Within five minutes, a Chevy Silverado pickup, four-wheel drive, with *Sheriff - Clear Creek County* written on the side, careened into the lot with lights flashing. Two sheriffs exited the truck, and Ephraim assisted them in erecting a yellow-tape perimeter as a handful of curious spectators stopped and gawked before moving on. A silent ambulance showed up next and blocked everyone's view.

After a while of anxious waiting for Ephraim to return and realizing he wasn't going to anytime soon, I left the tree seller on his own and made my way back to Kristen's booth to announce the news. "Someone died over there"—I tossed a thumb over my shoulder—"on the back side of the Christmas tree lot."

The blood drained from Kristen's face. "*Whaa?*"

Axle gave a startled bark of laughter. "You're joking."

"I wish."

"Get the heck out!"

I gave him the shush sign and looked around to see if anyone was listening, but no one was close by.

Kristen said, "Good Lord. Are you okay?"

"I'm fine." Which I didn't believe for a minute. I sniffed and dabbed at my face with my sleeve and went on to provide the few details I knew—a dead woman in a black knit cap and gray hoodie under a Douglas fir. "That's it. That's all I got."

Axle made me another espresso. Yes, it was a two-espresso kind of day.

I retold the story several times because they kept asking the same questions, then I hung around the kiosk nursing my drink as various customers stopped in for coffees in souvenir mugs.

Another hour passed before Ephraim caught up with me. "You ready to go?"

"Sure. What's happening over there?" I jerked my head in that direction.

"Forensics are still working the scene. I'll take you home, then I need to go into the station."

I slid off the stool. "Forensics?"

"Just routine." Not a single muscle moved on his face, so I knew, if I had any doubt before, that this wasn't only a tragic death but something more complicated.

After telling Kris and Axle we were leaving, we walked through the archway where a banner proclaimed: *Welcome to the Christkindl Market! Artisan craftsmen and authentic food vendors from around the world!* We hustled over to where he'd parked his black F250, a rear-wheel drive truck.

He drove me to my apartment above Roasters on the Ridge at the corner of Pine Street and Eagle Avenue. The building where I live is a two story with an outdoor staircase in the back attached to the dark wooden clapboards. Kristen lived across the landing. The coffee shop took up the first floor, and our apartments occupied the second floor.

"Do you want me to come up?" Ephraim asked.

"Can you? For a couple of minutes anyway?"

After unlocking the door and closing it behind us with a thud, I left my boots on the rug and barefooted it to the couch. Boss, Axle's Rottweiler, ambled out from Axle's room down the hall and sniffed at my feet before plopping onto the floor.

The word art above my sofa spelled out "Family," and the mismatched floral pillows on the two facing loveseats shouted out "shabby chic," the style I loved. Kristen had given me the plaque because she was like a sister to me—another reason that made Axle almost my cousin. Or a close relative, anyway. Close enough to share the apartment.

Ephraim eased down beside me and snaked his arm around my shoulder. "Are you okay, Delaney? How are you doing?"

"I'm doing all right, but I'm glad you're here." I sagged into him. "Did you determine what happened to her? Any idea who she is?" As my boyfriend, the sheriff would share a few details, but not many; I had to be satisfied with that.

"She didn't have any identification on her, but a witness came forward and informed us she was with the local winery. One of my deputies was heading over to the mulled wine booth when we left, so I might get an ID soon."

"A witness?"

"Rory Rearden, a friend of yours, right? He only said he recognized her, that's all."

I bobbed my head up and down. "I know Rory from the coffee shop. He's a regular customer, a good guy." Because I'd worked for Kristen before taking on the tow business and since I hung out there all the time, I knew her frequent customers. I asked, "Do you have the cause of death?"

"Not yet. Until then, we're treating this as a homicide."

The icy clutch of dread hit my gut. Homicide. Deliberate murder by person or persons unknown. Not a heart attack. Not a stroke. Not even a freak accident. Not hit by flying reindeer. There was a killer at the *Christkindl Market*...where everything was supposed to be joyful and merry, not scary and dangerous. I snuggled closer to Ephraim and could feel his steady heartbeat. He smelled like citrus, jasmine, and musk—fresh, clean, and calming. I took several deep breaths until they came out even.

"Are you sure you're all right?" When I nodded, he brushed my hair aside to put his hand on the back of my neck and draw me into a deep kiss. Once he released me, he said, "I'm sorry we didn't get you a tree."

"I forgot all about it." Especially after that kiss. But, in truth, I didn't want to think about the scene of the crime. Finding a dead woman had a way of ruining the romance. *Amiright?*

"You want to go back? The site is still cordoned off, but I can go in and bring out a tree for you."

I withdrew from his arms and shook my head. "No." Not just no, but hell no. The memory of the body was too fresh.

"Okay. Maybe tomorrow, then." He stood up and stretched. "I need to get to the station anyway."

"You'll be in charge of the investigation, right?"

"Yes."

All homicides are investigated by the county sheriffs, and Ephraim was the homicide detective for the county. The Spruce Ridge Police Department had only a small force, and the Clear Creek County Sheriff's Department was better equipped. In the past, the city police did not like handing their cases over to the county but grudgingly cooperated anyway.

Ephraim said, "I'd like to see what forensics came up with, not only from the tree lot but from the wine booth, too. It's been shut down."

I asked, "Just the wine booth, not the whole Christmas market, right? The grand opening is tomorrow." I knew I should be concerned about the poor woman who died, but what I was most worried about was how her death would affect the market and whether Kristen's booth would be a success. Yup, I'm not too proud of myself for that thought.

"That's what I need to discuss with my team. I'd better get going." He was anxious to take off, I could tell, and he'd be working late tonight.

Why did I date men who were always on call? Before this, Tanner Utley in the towing business, and now Ephraim Lopez in the law enforcement business. But then, I'm in the towing business, too, and calls for tows interrupted everything from meals to sleep, especially sleep, although my phone didn't ring as much as Tanner's. I hadn't had a job in a couple of days now.

I walked Ephraim to the door. After he kissed me goodbye and left, I threw the deadbolt and wished Axle was home. I stared out the window to the empty parking lot below, pulled the band from my braid, and raked my fingers through my red corkscrew curls. Not only was I uneasy about Kristen's booth, but my mind also questioned how I could get a Christmas tree and celebrate the holiday with this kind of distraction. I wanted to be free of thoughts of murder and enjoy Christmas! That's how selfish I am. I'm so bad.

After fifteen minutes of beating myself up—which I was shockingly good at—I gave myself a mental slap. Enough, already.

Note to self: Show some respect, but give yourself some slack. Wanting a wonderful Christmas is okay, too.

But this new homicide dredged up all kinds of unsettled feelings. Like life disrupted, unanswered questions, and how to move on from death. You see, my dad was killed by an unknown driver in a hit-and-run accident. The mystery of his death was something I had yet to come to grips with.

I hadn't known my dad at all. After my parents divorced when I was seven, my mom relocated to Denver, taking me with her. My dad remained in Spruce Ridge, and I never saw him again. When my best friend, Kristen, scouted for locations to open her coffee shop, I suggested this small, upscale town halfway between Denver and Vail, surrounded by rugged beauty and known as the gateway to the mountains. That Dad still lived in Spruce Ridge was a draw, but Del Morran died before we'd had a chance to reunite.

Dad had owned a reputable autobody shop with a towing business on the side. And—you won't believe this—when he died, he left me his tow truck, a self-loading Fulcan Xtruder, the best in the industry. The letter I'd received from the estate attorney with news of my inheritance was a shock to me, too.

The enigma of the man who fathered me, left me his name, his Irish red hair, and his tow truck, but no fond memories, was *a thing* with me. A significant event, totally unreal, and I was struggling with it because I never had the chance to get to know him. I didn't have cool memories of Dad and me at the circus. He never taught me how to ride a bike, drive a car, or any of that, like other Dads did with their kids. And I had so many questions, including what caused his accident and why he had to die when I still had so much to figure out. I pushed that fatherless little girl inside me to the back of my mind, but that little-girl-lost was still hoping to get to know her father.

Somehow driving his self-loader gave me a déjà vu kind of feeling, a connection to him I never had when he was alive. So, after I'd learned to operate the truck, I left my barista job with Kristen at Roasters, painted the truck red, and added the outline of a black stiletto with the name, Del's Towing.

And that's how I became known as the high-heeled tow truck driver.

Chapter 2

Today was the official opening day for Spruce Ridge's *Christkindl Market*, which drew international crowds to this small town.

Kristen, Axle, and I met at the twenty-foot-tall Christmas tree in front of the ice skating rink, the centerpiece of the marketplace. The Edison lights strung on wires from booth to booth were not lit this early in the day. The tree wasn't glowing either because the lighting ceremony was tonight. The professional photographer I knew from the Chamber of Commerce was here to take our picture for Kristen's Christmas cards.

Kris and I had on green winter coats and mittens that were *matchy-matchy*. She wore a pair of brown rubber boots with plaid trim, and I wore my faux fur ankle boots with heels. My long red braid that curled at the end fell over my right shoulder. Axle, however, sported his usual baggy jeans, a black hoodie with a skull and crossbones, and dirty oversized sneakers. His earbuds were in, and he was tapping his knees and bobbing his head to his music.

"Ready?" asked the photographer. "I'm going to count to three, then all of you say 'candy cane' with a big smile. Okay, one, two, three." She snapped away as we made cheesy smiles in her direction. After five or so minutes, she lowered her camera and walked toward us.

"Delaney, I'm going to upload the photos and email

you a link as soon as I get back to my studio. It won't take me long. You'll have the images in half an hour."

"Wonderful." We shook hands and she left.

I took a moment to enjoy checking a task off my list. "That's done, Kris. You've got to be happy."

Kristen opened her arms wide. "Come here, you two." She pulled us both in for a group hug.

Axle extracted himself and hitched up his baggy pants. "Where to next?"

The heat of the sun blasted our faces, but the freezing winter temperature made me shiver, a typical clear day in the thin Colorado air. "Coffee? Or mulled wine?" I joked.

Looking into the sun, Kristen shaded her eyes with one hand. "How about we check out the ice sculptures?"

"Let's do that." I was looking forward to the ice sculpture contest along with everyone else. The competition was the highlight of the festival, with artists coming to Colorado from across the globe and a nice prize sponsored by the nearby ski resorts.

My friend kept up a bright chatter as we turned in that direction. She was all bubbly because she had a space of extra time on her hands. Normally she ran the booth by herself, and that meant long hours. How any of the businesses in town managed to keep their restaurants and stores open and still operate a stand at the marketplace was a conundrum. They must've hired extra help, while Kristen was making do with only her usual staff. Axle and I promised to check on her from time to time so she could take bathroom breaks—providing me a great excuse to visit the marketplace—but today her booth was manned by one of her best baristas from Roasters, an English lit major by the name of Guy.

She led the way, and Axle and I trailed after her past the maintenance man emptying the trash and groups of tourists clutching packages. Calliope music overloaded my ear drums when we came to the charming old-fashioned carousel, and the sweet smell of pastries from the *Christstollen* booth tickled my taste buds.

The carnival music went silent when the merry-go-round came to a halt, but a *ding-ding* noise took over as Tanner's flatbed reversed into an open space between two mammoth ice blocks. We stopped to watch while he lowered another frozen chunk onto the snow-covered grounds.

"Tanner's really busy with this market." Axle attempted to catch my eye, but I ignored him. He nudged me with his bony elbow.

I forced a smile. "Yup."

"You want to talk to him, say hi?"

"Nope, I'm good." I gave my lil' cuz a push. "Move on, buster."

Kristen said, "Yeah, there's not much to see here until the artists start working on their sculptures." There was an apologetic tone in her voice. "The contest isn't for a few days yet."

"No worries. It's still fun to see." My cell gave a loud ping with a text received, and I rooted around in my bag for my phone. "Let's go sit down somewhere so we can look at the pictures. I think I just got the link."

"There's a bench over there." Axle brushed past us to lead the way to the sunny spot.

I sat in between my two friends and accessed the cloud storage site to scroll through the images.

In every single solitary photo, Axle's face was blurred. In one picture, his black sweatshirt blended in with the dark evergreen background, and it looked like his fuzzy face hovered in the air above a skull and crossbones.

Kristen and I pulled our eyes away from the screen at the same time and glared at him.

"Way to go, Axle." I bumped him with my shoulder.

He said, "These photos aren't so bad."

I rolled my eyes. "They are, too."

"Are not."

Kristen leaned across me to poke Axle in the chest. "These pictures won't work." I gave him an *I-told-you-so look*. She added, "Is this the kind of photo you want to see on a holy holiday? The Lord's birthday? Do they promote good tidings of joy and peace on Earth?"

"I guess not." His mouth twitched in amusement, and we all laughed.

"I'm not going to ask that photographer again. She took these for free since we're on the Chamber together, and she didn't do a very good job. I guess you get what you pay for." I shook my head and tucked my phone back into my purse. The photographer really should've made Axle turn off his music.

"You two"—Kris pointed between me and Axle— "keep thinking about a good photo op. We need another idea."

My phone rang, so I pulled it back out. "Excuse me," I said to Kristen and into the phone, "Hello, this is Del's Towing."

A man said, "I need a tow. I went off the road, and I'm stuck in the snow."

I had a customer. Someone had slid into a snow bank. *Tres cool*. I mean, *that sucks*. For them. Not for me, though.

Kristen headed to her coffee booth across the fairgrounds, and Axle and I took off to get my tow truck. I kept my truck parked at Oberly Motors, my dad's old autobody shop that had been sold to his top mechanic, Byron Oberly. This is where Axle worked, although he wasn't working today. I'd gotten to know Byron fairly well since starting my towing business. He often acted the role of my father better than my actual father ever did. No kids of his own. Never married, as far as I knew. And I called him the *Old Man* just like his nieces and nephews did. Axle was my lil' cuz; Byron was the Old Man. And, not to honk my own horn, but I'd gotten Axle a job with Byron.

When we alighted from my Fiat—the car I drove when not driving my truck—in front of the three-bay garage, Byron let out a low whistle between the gap in his two front teeth. "I heard about the body ya found, Delaney." He stuffed a red rag into the pocket of his paint-splattered coveralls. "You're not in any danger, are ya?"

I didn't want to alarm the Old Man, but I also knew he'd be disappointed if I didn't tell him what happened. "No, no. I don't even know who the woman was." I gave him a brief rundown, then added, "I'm sorry I can't stick around, but I've got to go out on a tow."

"Sure, sure. You get goin' now."

"You coming, Axle, or do you want to hang with the Old Man?" I beeped the key fob to unlock the truck.

Axle shrugged. "No offense, Byron, but I'll go with Delaney." He nodded at his boss. Today was Axle's day off. "I'll see you Monday morning."

I gave my wingman a smile. "Okay, good. Get in the truck, cuz." He saluted me and got in.

I slipped into the pair of red high-heeled boots I kept stored under the driver's seat.

Red for the Christmas season.

Customers expected me to show up in the trademark heels that set me apart from the all-male tow truck drivers in town. Plus, did I say the heels were cute? I mean, come on. They're *adorbs*.

I set my foot on the pedal and my hands on the steering wheel and breathed in the faint smell of motor oil, combined with a woodsy scent, clinging to the upholstery. I imagined Dad leaning back in the same seat, his hands on the same wheel. It was almost like he was here with me, as if the tow truck held me safe in Dad's arms. I fired up the motor, and the rumble of the engine made my heart glad as it always did.

I took Fifth to Columbine, Columbine to Main, then cut across town toward the highway. The customer who'd called had spun out his Hyundai Santa Fe, front-wheel drive, on the icy service road. I rolled to a stop in front of his vehicle and stepped down from the cab. My heels hit the ground, then I carefully navigated across the snow-packed road to the man with crossed arms next to his car with its rear wheels embedded in a snowbank. He was of middle height, wearing a long wool overcoat with a plaid scarf tucked in the collar, a fedora, and leather gloves, when everyone else around here wore puffy coats, knit caps, and mittens, including me.

"I'm Delaney." I shook his gloved hand with my mittened one.

"Noel Yarborough." He looked at me through his close-set eyes.

I let go of his hand. "You just need pulling out of the bank, right?"

21

Helping people stranded in winter made my job satisfying and put me in a happy place. Being appreciated for coming to the rescue was one of the perks of the profession. I'll admit I had the white-knight syndrome. That's why, upon graduation from college, I got a job in social work at the Department of Social Services. But after five years, I decided that was not what I wanted. I was the tender-hearted type, tearing up at every dire situation, of which there were many. Those five years were hard ones. I left social work behind to help Kris open her coffee shop, and after that, I inherited the truck and started my towing business, but I hadn't shed the sympathy gene—I still had that going for me. It was gratifying to respond to simple car accidents and breakdowns. An essential service like this one.

I thought social work was difficult, but hauling cars was not always easy either. Believe me.

"No, I need a tow. My rear fender is bent into the wheel well, damn it to hell, and I don't know a mechanic in this shitty town. I'm from Palisade. We don't get much snow over there." He shut his close-set eyes while speaking. Then, he opened them, stomped around, and repeated a choice word that began with *f*. I can't bring myself to say that word in front of a customer, but you know what I'm talking about.

So…this was one of those *not-always-easy* situations.

And, hey, he insulted my town! I loved Spruce Ridge and felt lucky to live in this beautiful location. Spruce Ridge is split by the I-70 highway, with mansions climbing the forested south slope and shopping centers sprawling through the narrow valley below the north slope. Old town was quaint and touristy, and winter was miraculous and breathtaking, with the unparalleled elegance of the snow-topped mountains looking so different in the winter light. Right now the sun was high, warming the air, puffy white clouds banked against the sapphire peaks, and the only sounds were the incessant wind and the cawing mountain blue jays. But I needed to quit admiring the view.

"Actually, Axle here"—I pointed at my sidekick—"he's a great mechanic and works at Oberly Motors."

Axle was making a *no-no* fanning motion with his hands, and I shot him a *not-helpful* look while the man frowned at me. Yeah, I didn't really want him as a customer, either, but I had to take what I could get.

I asked him, "Do you want me to tow you to Oberly's?"

The man shouted some more obscenities. I took that as *I'm not happy, but yes*.

This modern-day Scrooge needed to learn a lesson, so I said, "It's Christmas. The tow is free." I didn't work for nothing very often, but that sympathy gene of mine had kicked in. Besides, it was the sort of turn-the-other-cheek thing Kristen would do, and maybe a bit of kindness would rub off on him.

The man had the grace to look ashamed. "Okay, thanks."

I recorded the VIN in my phone for my records, then climbed back into my truck. I drew in a deep, steadying breath and rolled my shoulders to relieve the tension. I reminded myself this was the part I liked best. This was when the magic happened. My Fulcan Xtruder, a self-loading tow truck, had an integrated lift—that's a wheel-lift system controlled hydraulically from inside the cab. The button on the wireless remote operated the T-bar that lowered to the ground. The scoops, which those of us in the industry called "claws," would go under and around the tires, and the boom would lift the vehicle off the ground.

When I first began in this business, all cars looked alike. Now I paid attention to the vehicles on the road. I'd learned when the gear is in Park on a front-wheel drive, the drive shaft locks the front wheels so they can't move. But if you lift the front wheels, the back wheels will roll. Just the opposite with rear-wheel drive. Newer cars are front-wheel drive, but plenty of older rear-wheel vehicles were still on the road. And, of course, with all-wheel and four-wheel drive, all the wheels are locked, so all the tires must be lifted in order for the vehicle to be towed. My self-loader only captured one set of tires, the front or the back. That's why a tow truck driver, like myself, needs to know whether a vehicle is front-wheel, rear-wheel, or all-wheel drive. Got it? Yeah, it took me a while, too.

I punched the buttons, the front of the Santa Fe swung into the air, and I was ready to haul ass. My truck was amazing!

Axle folded himself into the compact back seat, my customer climbed into the passenger side, and I towed the vehicle to Oberly Motors. The whole time, the man stared out the window, and Axle listened to his music. This customer did not compliment my red high-heeled boots or utter any words resembling gratitude. What an *asshat*. What an understatement. Usually at the least, I got a comment on the heels.

Ten minutes later, Axle and I were parked outside Roasters on the Ridge, glad to leave our difficult customer behind. Coffee had a way of grounding me with a sense of calm, plus I'd promised Kristen we'd check on the coffee shop while she was busy at the Christmas market. So here we were.

I spent a long moment outside, taking in the look of the place. Around the coffee shop's entryway, fragrant pines and clusters of aspen trees glittered with strings of holiday lights, the white aspen trunks contrasting against the needles of the evergreens. This chilly late afternoon had emptied the outdoor bistro tables.

A couple came out the door with coffees in hand and another walked in. Axle went through the door next. When I stepped inside after them, charming signs greeted me with the messages, "Coffee makes everything possible" and "Humanity runs on coffee." Antique skis and poles, snowshoes, and ski boots mounted on the walls provided a themed ambiance. Distressed-wooden shelves held beans, mugs, and syrups, and Christmas music played at low volume. Today Kristen's barista, Guy, managed the counter, but there were only a few customers in the seating area since most people were headed to the opening day ceremony at the *Christkindl Market*.

So, after a quick look around—everything was hunky-dory—Axle and I climbed the stairs to our apartment. I headed to my closet for the soft cream-colored sweater that went well with my skinny jeans and the red boots I still had on my feet. I finger-combed my long red waves of hair and touched up my lipstick.

Axle returned from walking Boss, both of them stomping their feet and shaking off the snow. The Rotty arranged himself on the sofa pillows, and Axle headed to his room to emerge a minute later, shuffling down the hall with his hands in his pockets. The strong scent of aftershave followed him into the kitchen.

I pinched my nose and made a wafting motion with my other hand. "A bit much, Ax."

He shoved his hands deeper in his pockets. "What?"

"You have a hot date or something?" I wiggled my eyebrows. He gave me a sideways glance but kept his mouth buttoned up. I asked, "Is Shannon going to be at the opening ceremony tonight?"

"Yeah, she's one of the angels," he admitted.

He did have a date.

Shannon was Byron's teenage niece, who worked part time at the autobody shop and was addicted to all things vintage—bell-bottom jeans, cat-eye sunglasses, and music from the '60s. Byron and I had always wanted Axle and Shannon to get together, but Axle had resisted our matchmaking attempts until recently—at least so it seemed because it was hard to know. Getting information out of a teenage boy was more difficult than towing a heavy semi. Pretending not to care was his go-to response for everything.

I dampened a paper towel under the kitchen faucet, then touched it lightly to Axle's neck and cheeks. He endured my ministrations with a stiff face.

I said, "That's better," and gave an air kiss to the tips of my fingers. "I'll make an adult out of you yet, and remember, less is more." I should've said, ditch the beanie, but that would've been going too far. Instead I said, "It's go time." I grabbed my green puffy coat that coordinated with my green knit hat, scarf, and mittens.

Nightfall descended by five this late in December, and the lighting ceremony was scheduled for six. Even though we had plenty of time, Axle urged me to drive faster, and I did have trouble finding a parking place, even in my Fiat, a subcompact that fit just about anywhere. The streets were full, no empty spots for two blocks. After I maneuvered into the tight space we were lucky to find, Axle trotted off, earbuds dangling from around his neck, and I hurried to keep up.

A throng was already crowded around the roped-off area in front of the twenty-foot-tall Christmas tree. The audience was jammed tightly against the ropes, and everyone behind the first row was craning their necks for a better view. Before this, I'd never set eyes on so many people in Spruce Ridge at one time, but it was no surprise since the *Christkindl Market* attracted international shoppers, just as the ski resorts drew international travelers.

I scrunched my forehead. "Wow, Axle, I guess you were right." He did have a good reason to hurry over and get a place to view the angels.

"Say what?" He cupped a hand behind his ear, teasing. I never admitted he was right.

"You heard me." My gaze took in the mass of people. The babble of voices seemed to grow louder by the minute, and I recognized some German words from my high school language classes.

Soon, the last of the daylight disappeared behind the mountain peaks, and the temperature dropped even more. The two of us bumped shoulders as we pounded our feet on the pavement in an effort to keep warm. People vying for better positions tried to forge a path between us. Axle shifted his stance and clutched his phone to his chest, then said, "I need to move closer to get a picture of Shannon when she comes out."

"Okay, Axle." I looked away for a moment, and when I looked back, he'd disappeared.

Should I attempt to follow him or just stay put? I tried to inch forward, but there was no space to move. The decision was made for me. I was sticking to this close-packed spot.

The noise of the restless crowd increased, so I went up on tippy-toes to unblock my line of sight, but my view remained hopeless. Elbows jostled me on both sides, and someone poked me in the back. I sighed in acceptance that I would miss seeing the performance but still experience the moment.

The master of ceremonies spoke into a squawking microphone to announce the Queen of the Festival, and I caught a glimpse of a woman in a red evening gown, her shoulders draped in a white fur cape, entering center stage. Her hair was a golden yellow, framing her heavily made-up face. He handed her a bouquet of white roses. The moon slid out from under a cloud at the same time the lights switched on, and the high-reaching tree erupted in thousands of white lights. *Oohing* and *aahing*, the crowd split for a moment and I caught sight of white-clad angels dressed with fairy wings and golden halos that appeared to float above their heads. Music trumpeted from the speakers, and the words of "O Holy Night" floated on the air.

It was a Christmas-y moment, a feel-good moment that made my heart swell, evoking strong feelings of childhood, happiness, and excitement.

But as soon as the song ended, the spectators rushed forward, and I was caught in the press of bodies. And I'm talkin' a bone-crunching wedge of humanity here. It was gridlock. *Yowza*. Since I'm vertically challenged, even in my heels, I couldn't see anything other than the dark-blue coat of the man I was shoved up against. Another strong push from behind squished my face deeper into the wool, and a sharp bump to my shoulder sent a bolt of pain down my arm.

I could sense a stampede attempting to funnel through the narrow passage between the outdoor stage and the massive evergreen tree. People were in full-on panic mode now, like fans at a soccer game crammed up against a closed gate, a reactionary crowd shoving and pushing to get out of a dangerous situation. I was about to be trampled! My heart raced faster than a high-speed chase through the Eisenhower Tunnel.

Disoriented, I didn't know if I was going backward or forward. One second, the breath was squeezed out of me; the next moment, I could suck in air, then the pressure returned. I couldn't move my feet, blood whooshed in my ears, and the scene blanked out for a moment. I was losing it. I looked up to try to find the North Star to guide me through.

That's when someone clapped a hand on my shoulder.

Chapter 3

Ephraim had the back of my jacket in his fist. He tucked me under his protective arm and weaved me through the packed horde. The mass of people parted before his imposing figure. Once we were in the wide open space near the ice skating rink, I sat down hard at the curb, taking deep breaths in and out, heaving big mouthfuls of air. Calm descended and my quivering limbs steadied.

"You saved me. Thanks, Sheriff." I gave him a feeble laugh.

He was wearing his light-blue sheriff's uniform under his heavy coat. He had to work tonight, which is why we hadn't come to the ceremony together.

"I lost Axle." My voice sounded faint, and I cleared my throat. "Have you seen him? Is he all right?"

"Yeah, I bumped into him and Shannon. He told me where to find you. He tried to get back to you but everyone was scrambling in opposite directions."

"I was so scared."

Ephraim pulled me to a stand. "You had reason to be. Injuries caused by human crush are well known, and you had a right to be afraid." His hands lingered on my shoulders and then slid down my arms. "You okay?"

My hand went to a tender spot in my back, and I wiggled around. "I am now." I budged my head against his chest and felt his heart pulsing against my forehead.

"What caused the panic?"

"Someone shouted out something about the marketplace not being safe, that there was a killer on the loose, and that's what started it."

"No. Really?" I stepped back and tipped my face up. "I didn't hear that." A lump lodged in my chest, and I had a pain in the pit of my stomach. I'd felt endangered tonight. The market didn't feel safe to me either, but the audience's reaction was even more frightening than a murderer.

"The sheriff's department made a decision to keep the market open except for the mulled wine stand. We locked that one down, but we should've cancelled the opening ceremony, too. I see that now." He held onto my elbow.

"So the wine booth is still closed?"

"Yes, and we haven't eliminated more closures."

Despair settled on my shoulders like a heavy wool coat. "I hope you don't have to shut anything else down." Kristen was counting on the seasonal income, and a lot of other local venders were expecting their booths to do well, too. Kristen had been hoping for the best sales month yet.

Soft strands of "Where Are You Christmas?" touched my ears. Where had the holiday spirit gone? It was here a little while ago, but it'd been pounded out of me along with my breath in that crushing crowd.

But it's Christmas…when there's supposed to be peace and joy. That inner peace. That blessed joy. And don't forget about Kristen's picture-perfect Christmas photo and my picture-perfect Christmas tree. This crime needed to be solved, the killer apprehended, and the market allowed to proceed without fear and mob-panic, that's all there was to it.

Ephraim stared down at me. "Your eyes just clouded over. What's on your mind?"

I fixed him with a serious look. "I don't want the festival to be cancelled."

He assumed a wide-legged stance and folded his arms. "Let's hope that won't happen."

"It can't happen." I inspected his face. "Let me help you. I know you can't discuss an ongoing investigation, and I'm not asking you for confidential details or anything, but let me nose around. I might pick up useful information here and there. You know I hear stuff at the coffee shop, and sometimes my towing customers tell me things. This is a small town where everybody knows everything, except they might not tell it to you."

He made a small side-to-side motion with his head, and I could see his thoughts shutting me down. *Like that's ever deterred me before*. It wasn't going to this time, either. I was in the middle of talking myself into solving the Mystery of the Marketplace Murder.

I held up my hand. "Stop. Just stop. Don't go shaking your head like that."

It looked as if he was going to protest some more, then he sighed and nodded in grim resignation. "I know you'll investigate anyway, Delaney, and I have to admit you have great intuition." *Yes!* I wanted to jump into his arms, but then he added, "You have a way of making an accurate guess."

"Guess! Guess! Humpf!" I groused, punctuating each word with a fist pounding into a palm. "More like an accurate assessment."

"All right." He rubbed his eyes with the heels of his hands. "But you have to stay out of danger. I'd never

32

forgive myself if something happened to you. And don't get all bent."

It's true, I was starting to get in a state, but I wasn't interested in a lecture to play it safe, and—even worse—more patronizing words that whatever I uncovered would only be the result of guess work.

Snow began to fall, jumbo flakes dancing on ice-chilled air, and the Christmas tunes rolled over to play "It's Beginning to Look a Lot Like Christmas." The music was so appropriate that we both laughed.

He said, "I'll tell you what you want to know."

Ephraim and I approached a bench and took seats. He said, "Here goes. This is what we have so far. The victim's name is Meredith Yarborough. Her family owns a vineyard on the western slope, and she operated a tasting room in Spruce Ridge, in addition to the wine booth here at the Christmas market. We're considering letting the booth reopen in a day or two. The owners will object to remaining closed if everyone else is allowed to stay open."

"Wait!" I practically levitated off the bench. "Did you say Yarborough?"

"Yes. That's her name, Meredith Yarborough. It's in the press release, so it'll be in the news."

"I towed a Santa Fe for a person named Yarborough this afternoon. Noel Yarborough."

"That's her brother. He drove over from Palisade today to ID the body. He has an alibi since he arrived after the victim died. We've already questioned him, so you don't need to." He gave me a nudge, obviously trying to lighten the mood.

"Funny." I attempted to pin him with a *not-funny* look. "So, go on."

"Means of death is poison." He took a moment to let that sink in. "A fast-acting poison, probably in the wine."

"That's why you closed the wine kiosk."

He nodded. "We took all the bottles into evidence."

I stared over at the ice rink where a couple laced up their skates. The old-fashioned lights shone down on the woman pushing the man out in front. He teetered around on weak ankles before grabbing the railing. Skaters talked and smiled, their laughter carrying over in the crisp evening air.

My mind wandered to the question of *when the victim's brother actually arrived*. Could he have gotten here earlier? Like yesterday morning before his sister was poisoned? He could've faked a later arrival by making a pretense of going off the road and needing a tow. He may not have a solid alibi after all. And he was a prime murder suspect in my book. Remember, he spewed profanities. And he hated Spruce Ridge. How do you explain that? He wasn't a nice person, that's how.

Ha! Did you see what I did here? I figured out my first suspect. Everyone knows the victim is usually killed by someone close to them, like friends or family. Did she have a significant other? I would need to find out.

The opening ceremony crowd had dispersed, spreading out over the length of the field that served as the rodeo grounds in the summer and the *Christkindl Market* in the winter. Strings of lights reflected off glittering snowflakes, as if tiny jewels danced among the shoppers bundled up in hats and scarves. The *Christstollen* booth, with the mouthwatering pastries, and the next booth over, with ornaments from around the world, were doing a brisk business. The lights twinkled, the music played, and snow twirled across the night sky as far as I could see.

The romantic feelings of Christmas were making an effort to return.

Ephraim entwined my fingers in his tight grasp. "You want to pick out a tree?"

My face broke into a smile. "Yes, but let's walk over to the coffee kiosk first to check on Kris."

"Surprise. I wouldn't've guessed that," he said with a grin of his own.

"You got it." I squeezed his hand.

We made a beeline for the coffee kiosk, and Ephraim purchased two hot cocoas in the red commemorative Christmas mugs. I'd probably end up with a dozen of these before the season was over, but that was okay with me. Kristen said she didn't need a break, so we continued on, wandering through the food stalls, stopping to stare at the chocolate desserts on display. The scent from our hot drinks, the same chocolate scent as the yummy desserts, was rich in our noses.

I tried to pull Ephraim away to move on, but he tightened his grip. "I have a gift for you."

"Now?" *Uh-oh.* I didn't have his gift yet. Instant panic!

His brown eyes twinkled. "I was going to wait, but I can't." He shoved his hand inside his jacket and came out with a small box. Jewelry? *Yikes!*

I know what you're thinking. A lot of couples get engaged at Christmas, a sentimental time that's all about love…and when you add in the mistletoe…but no. No, no, no. We hadn't been going out that long, not that long at all, so banish those thoughts. Even though I considered us a couple because we were dating, I hadn't actually called him my boyfriend yet. Not to his face, anyway.

And he hadn't called me his girlfriend. We hadn't said the "L" word!

I asked, "You want me to open it or put it under the tree?" The tree I didn't have.

"Open it."

Okey-dokey. I tore into the paper. *OMG*. Silver hoop earrings with dangling stilettos that had red gemstones for bows. I plucked one of the earrings from the satin lining, revealing a corner of a piece of white paper.

"What's this?" I snagged the paper out with my fingernails.

Ephraim's eyes went wide. "That's not the receipt, is it?" He jumped to grab it, but I held the box behind my back. He feigned left and right as I swiveled one way, then the other. He chuckled with a deep sound in his chest, then hooked an arm around my neck. Hugging me to him, he reached down behind me and snatched the box. My arms were short, his were long. No way I'd be the victor.

He let me go, examined the paper, then handed it back to me. "You can have that."

I scanned a certificate for a genuine ruby in each earring. "Ephraim! This is too much. You shouldn't have done it."

"I couldn't let these stiletto earrings get away. They had your name all over them." His fingers rubbed the strands of my hair together. "And ruby red's definitely your color."

If my cheeks grew any hotter, I could ignite an engine without any gas. I *did* have the flaming red hair of the Irish, actually a little more orange than red. Normally I kept my long hair in a wide plait down my back, but tonight the corkscrew waves tumbled to my waist. As a typical redhead, tiny, dark-brown freckles covered my face. I have pale-hazel eyes, equally pale brows, and easily blush. All the things I disliked about my appearance were the very things Kristen said were my best features. She could say that, having smooth and shiny dark hair like the models in shampoo commercials. Notice there's never a little-orphan-Annie type in those ads?

I said, "Ruby is my birthstone, too." I was a July baby.

"I know."

"Thank you."

He tipped his cowboy hat in acknowledgment. "You're welcome."

I rested my hand against his cheek, and he captured my fingers, placing a kiss on my palm. A flash of heat shot through my entire body. *Whoo-hoo!* He held my face in his hands and gave me a kiss that yanked my breath into non-existence.

I would need an extra-special gift for this romantic cowboy Casanova. One just as thoughtful, just as meaningful as the earrings with my trademark stilettos and birthstone. How in the world was I going to top that? I didn't think I'd be able to do it.

****

Monday morning, I padded out to the kitchen in my long sleep shirt and wool socks and filled the coffee machine's reservoir with filtered water. After I hit the start button, I sprinkled kibble into Boss's dish and topped off his water bowl.

While the coffee brewed, I took a long shower. One thing about curly hair, you can't brush it when it's dry or the curls turn to frizz. It needs to be combed when wet, so while under the water, I applied conditioner and ran a wide-tooth comb down its length. After rinsing, I stepped out and pressed a towel against the dripping strands. I can't braid my hair when it's damp, either, but if it's dry when braided, the curls turn into soft waves. So, while I let my curly locks air-dry, I scrambled into a pair of high-rise wide-legged jeans, a black sweater, and black ankle boots with three-inch platforms.

By the time I was ready, Axle was in the kitchen with a bowl of soggy cereal in front of him.

"How was your date with Shannon last night?" I asked, trying to keep a straight face.

"Wasn't a date. We just hung out together." He shoved in another spoonful.

There was no reason for Axle to deny his long-standing crush on the vintage girl, but there he was, doing it again. Deny, deny, deny. He always did. I guess he was a normal male teen with a normal male teen attitude. Although at eighteen, you'd think he'd be a bit more mature. I reminded myself once more that his silence might have something to do with his crush being his boss's niece. Axle felt he had to tread lightly when it came to Shannon.

He finally finished his cereal and placed his bowl and spoon in the sink. Then he leashed up his dog and they took off down the stairs. After they got back and Boss settled on the couch, Ax and I descended the steps and entered the coffee shop through the back door. I inhaled the aroma of the fresh brew; entering the fragrant coffee shop was like coming home. Guy was running the place with the help of another barista, Sierra, the blue-haired punkette.

Axle and I stepped into line behind one of the café's

regulars. I said, "Good morning, Rory."

"Morning, Delaney, Axle. How are you two doing?" Rory fished out a five, then waited to the side. Guy poured a steaming dark stream of coffee into a mug and handed it to him.

After I placed orders for Axle and myself and dropped a tip in the jar, Guy pulled shots for our drinks. Sierra came out from the backroom to spritz the empty tables with vinegar water and scrub the tops clean. Two customers sat at the west-facing window and three at the long counter under the pair of north windows. A group in winter coats was outside on the patio, braving the elements. There would be more customers occasionally throughout the late morning, then another crowd around noon. The shop closed at four every day except Sunday, when it was closed all day.

When our *wake-me-up* espressos were ready, I handed Axle his and wrapped my hands around my own to-go cup. We paused to take long swallows, then I sauntered over to Rory. A lucky coincidence to run into him since Ephraim had told me Rory knew the murder victim, but then the whole world seemed to pass through Roasters on the Ridge. At least everyone in this town.

I said, "You know the woman who was found dead at the *Christkindl Market*?"

"I sure do. I was walking through the Christmas tree lot, and I saw the police all over the place, so I stopped and talked to them." Rory threw me an uncertain look. "How did you find out? How did you hear?"

"Ephraim and I were the ones who discovered her body." I raised my cup to my lips and observed him over the rim. "How did you know her? I was told you helped identify her to the police."

Rory dropped his head in agreement. "Yes." His pale face was covered in freckles like mine, poor soul. He wore high-end jeans, an untucked shirt, and hiking boots, like the stylish and rich local he is. There were many trust-fund kids in the affluent City of Spruce Ridge, and since he'd once told me he worked in his dad's company, I suspected he was one of them.

"How'd you know her?" I glanced at my lil' cuz, but Axle just hiked up his jeans and looked bored.

Rory's gaze shifted to look out the window. "From the wine tasting room in town."

"So, you bought wine there?"

"Once." He nodded in a vague way.

"Well, it's too bad what happened."

"Yeah," he repeated.

I opened my mouth, about to launch into an interrogation, when Axle broke into my moment.

"Delaney…" Ax twitched his head toward the door.

"Right." I shrugged my purse higher on my shoulder. "We need to get going. See you later, Rory."

In the Fiat on the way to drop off Axle, I said, "Rory wasn't himself. Don't you think he was quieter than usual? I mean, after I asked him how he knew the murder victim."

"True, that. It's normally verbal vomit with him." Axle plugged his earbuds in for the remainder of the short ride, setting the volume to ear-splitting. His reticence was typical for him, unlike Rory.

Once at Oberly Motors, Axle lunged out of the car and crossed the parking lot to the auto bay. I pulled the key from the ignition and went inside, too.

"Morning, Byron." I did a double take. "Morning, Shannon." Axle's love interest was working today. My gaze darted from Byron's niece in a tied-dyed sweatshirt at the counter to Axle in his greasy beanie in the auto bay. He nonchalantly picked over tools in the big red chest in an attempt at a laid-back, cool look. Not wanting to cramp his style, I yelled over, "I'll see you later," and stepped back outside.

No calls had come in for a tow, so my morning was free. A public scooter was parked at the corner, and I'd wanted to try one out. Dozens of these electric skateboards with handlebars had been brought to town for the *Christkindl Market*, and I'd already downloaded the application. I scanned the barcode with my phone to unlock the machine, then sidled forward for a closer look, not sure what to do next. I'd never ridden an e-scooter before.

How hard can it be? I slung the long straps of my hobo bag over my head and across my chest. Standing to the side, I squeezed the handlebar. But when the scooter jumped forward, I let go and it fell over. I cringed, hoping no one saw that.

But somebody had. The sound of hard boots clomped on the macadam behind me. Axle asked, "You gonna ride this?"

I turned around to give him an eye roll. "That was the plan."

"You need to actually be standing on the board before hitting the throttle, brainless."

"Excuse me?" I feigned indignation. "I know what I'm doing." That was a complete lie, of course, and he gave me a disbelieving snort. "Hey, now." I swatted his arm, then lifted the scooter off the cement, climbed on, my left foot on the board, my right on the ground, and looked at him expectantly.

He cracked his knuckles like some cartoon bad guy. "First, raise the kickstand. Then lean forward, holding the handlebars with both hands, then press the throttle." He pointed at the handle. "And here's the brake lever to stop. Now go on." He gave me a push.

Easy peasy. I hit the throttle and shot down the sidewalk. I yelled at Axle, "This rocks."

He shook his head and headed back inside the garage.

I cruised the bike path along eastbound Fifth Avenue until I reached the marketplace. The frigid two-mile ride in the brisk winter air took about ten minutes and went without mishap. Ha! I'd have to tell Axle later. I left the scooter where it wouldn't block traffic and tapped the button on the app that I was finished, so the electric skateboard would be available for other riders. If a call came in for a tow, all I had to do was find another one and whisk back to Byron's where my truck was parked. No driving around forever trying to find a parking place. *Am I good, or what?*

It was still early but the market was bustling with activity; vendors unloaded morning deliveries and called greetings to each other and to me as I walked by. The woman in the Santa hat holding the clipboard flitted from booth to booth, while the Queen of the Festival, with a beauty pageant-type sash crisscrossing over her warm coat, followed in her wake. I rubbed my arms up and down and hightailed it over to Kristen's coffee stand. She popped open the back door, and I dashed inside where she'd plugged in an electric heater.

I said, reporting in, "I stopped at Roasters this morning. Guy's doing a good job. The place is clean and there were a couple of customers."

Kristen said, "I think Guy's really turned the corner." My friend hired people who had trouble finding work, including the one-year-sober college student, Guy, and the blue-haired, formerly homeless, Sierra. Kristen's good like that. She was what everyone aspired to be. She lived her beliefs and helped those in need. I was proud to call her a friend.

"So there were customers?" she asked.

"A good number." I gave her an encouraging nod, but she was looking at her row of mugs, her lips moving, like she was counting them. "You're pretty busy here, right?" I asked.

"I'm not getting that many people. My best day was the soft opening. I thought a lot more would buy coffee after the grand opening last night, but it's been slow."

"Ever since the murder, then." It didn't help that the booth next to hers was closed. It was no longer busy at this end of the fairgrounds.

Her gaze retracted back to me. "That's right."

I offered her my most hopeful smile. "That'll change."

She folded the wet bar rag, then carried two empty mugs to the plastic tub that served as a sink. Customers had the option of purchasing the mug or staying to drink their coffee at the kiosk and returning the mug. These used mugs had been returned and would be thoroughly washed and disinfected.

I said, "Look what Ephraim gave me for Christmas." I pulled the jewelry box out of my purse to show Kris, and she gasped. I put a little sarcasm in my voice when I said, "It's earrings. Ephraim got me *earrings* for Christmas." *Jeez, people!* I prized open the box and held it out for her to see.

43

"Oooh. Pretty," she crooned, then glanced at her left hand. She and her boyfriend Zach—a City of Spruce Ridge police officer—were courting. I'm not sure what that means, but I think it's something we called "going steady" in high school. Not engaged. But it looked like maybe Kristen wanted to get engaged.

"Where's Zach?" I asked. "I haven't seen him in a while."

"He's working overtime because of all the tourists in town. I guess there's been a lot of pickpocketing going on."

"Really?" My jaw dropped. Spruce Ridge had very little crime, other than the recent murder, that is. "Is he working on crowd control, too? I got caught in the stampede during the opening ceremonies last night."

She patted my arm. "I heard about that panic. You okay?"

"I am now." I nodded. I'd put it behind me and had forgotten the fright of the crowd. There were other things besides frightened fairgoers and murder to stress me out now, like Christmas shopping. What can I say? Presents are important. I asked my friend, "So, I still have to get Ephraim's Christmas gift. He gave me these great earrings. Now I have to find something for him just as cool."

"Yeah, let me think." She put a thumb and finger to the corners of her eyes for a second, then dropped her hand. "Give me a little time and I'll come up with some ideas."

"Good, 'cause I don't have any."

"Have you looked at all the booths here at the fair? You might find something unique that you wouldn't find at the mall."

"I haven't yet, but I will." I'd be here often enough because I planned to relieve Kris as many times as I could. Working ten-hour shifts in the small hut by herself was not going to be easy, but the rest of her staff's time would be taken up handling the coffee shop in town without her. As my own boss, I could always pop in at the market to check on Kristen and get some Christmas shopping done. Win-win.

"We still need to think of an idea for our Christmas picture, too," Kristen reminded me. "I already texted Axle to meet us here when he has a chance so we can give it another shot."

"I'm down with that." I stared at the closed booth next door. "Did you happen to see the woman working Friday? She's the one who died, you know." The victim's name was in the morning news and everyone in this small town would have heard by now.

Kristen's face fell. "It's so sad to think about. I was already open for a while when she started unpacking her booth. I went over and asked her how many Christmas mugs she stocked. She told me and that's when I figured out I ordered the same amount."

"Did she say anything else?"

"No, she was too busy setting up. I did send Axle over with a free coffee. You could ask him."

"I will. I wonder why he didn't mention that. He should've said something." The little twerp. "Had you ever met her before?" Small business owners in this insular community seemed to know each other, especially those in the food industry.

"No."

"Hunh." Nothing to be learned there. "What time did you talk to her?"

Kris chewed on her lower lip. "Probably around nine in the morning because that's when I had a short break between customers. Axle went over right after we spoke."

"And Ephraim and I found her sometime after one." That brought back the memory of the body in the tree lot. The person in the knit cap and hoodie so like Axle's that I feared for a moment it was him. I needed to push aside that punch to my gut.

"She finished getting ready and opened up at noon." Kristen placed a hand over her heart. "I wonder what she was doing on the other side of the market an hour later. What was she doing at the Christmas tree lot when she should've been waiting on customers?"

I asked, "Was anyone helping her?"

"I didn't see anyone else over there."

"The victim's brother is in town. Noel Yarborough."

"I met him. He came by for a coffee yesterday, and I asked his name to write on the cup."

"So, he didn't want a mug?"

"No, just a to-go." Kris made a pouty face and glanced at the wall of souvenir mugs.

"I hope the wine booth opens as soon as the police release it. That will draw customers in your direction." And I'd be able to question him if he was at the adjoining booth. A prime suspect, only feet away. I tapped my chin with a fingernail, thinking I really should write down my list of suspects, even if I only had one name at the moment. I rummaged around in my purse for my spiral notebook and a pen.

I told Kris, "Tell me everything Noel said. Did he mention his sister? Did he say anything about her death?"

Just then a customer hopped onto a stool on the other side of the counter and asked for a caramel latte in a commemorative mug.

I drummed the pen on the paper and tapped one high-heeled foot with impatience. My questions would have to wait.

Chapter 4

"So, did Noel mention his sister?" I asked as soon as Kristen finished filling her customer's order. I poised my pen over the paper.

"No. That may not be significant, though, because I'm a total stranger to him, and he probably didn't feel like sharing with me." She shook her head and leaned on the counter. "What clues do you have so far?"

"Let's see. Just that you talked to Meredith and that Axle brought her coffee, and that's it." I scribbled a side note, *question Axle.*

Kristen scratched her temple. "I remember that man who empties the trash was at the booth, and he bought a mulled wine. You know, the guy who looks like he spends a lot of time at the gym. He came over to my booth afterward to tell me he'd be back later for a coffee, but he didn't come back. Maybe he got distracted after the news was out about the murder."

"What time was that?"

She shrugged. "I don't know. Right around twelve?"

I jotted down the new information and the question, *ask Ephraim if he talked to the maintenance man.*

I told Kris, "I'll check with Ephraim for the exact time we found her because he'd know when that was."

Kristen's text dinged. She read her screen, then told me, "Axle said he can take an extended lunch today. He's going to ride a scooter over and meet us here, and Sierra said she'd swing by from the coffee shop to watch the booth for me. It'll be picture time."

The sound of knuckles rapping the hard ledge caused us both to jump.

Zachariah Bowers greeted his girlfriend, "Morning, Kris." His prominent chin stuck out, and his stiff handlebar mustache covered his upper lip. His premature salt-and-pepper hair—he's only in his thirties—was longer on the top and buzzed on the sides. The city police officer was an all-round good guy whom my friend had met at church.

Kristen returned his smile. "Glad to see you this morning."

While they visited, I made his usual drink, a nonfat latte. After I handed it to him, I told Kristen, "I'll be back for the photo shoot," then quick-stepped away with my notes hidden in my purse.

If Zach knew we'd been discussing the murder, he'd warn me off investigating on my own, even though the county sheriff's department, not the city police, was heading up the homicide case. Despite the fact Ephraim had basically given me the go-ahead, Zach would tell me to mind my own business, and I didn't need that grief.

I slogged past the trash bins where the maintenance man was showing off his muscles while emptying the containers, then I doubled back.

"Hello there!" I called.

He looked to be a few years younger than me, possibly midtwenties, with a cheeky smile and a shock of hair over his eyes. He'd be sorta cute in a way if he wasn't so concerned with watching his reflection in the shiny trash can. I ran toward him, but after glancing in my direction, he hopped into a golf cart with garbage cans strapped to the back and motored out of sight.

I shrugged, knowing I'd have another opportunity, and began working my way through the crowd over to a park bench. I sat and looked at my notes, then added, *speak to maintenance man, talk to victim's brother, and talk to other vendors*.

So…where to begin?

I aimed straight for the booth that sold the colorful scarves. Might as well get in a little shopping while I was at it, and I'd spotted a perfect scarf for my mom there earlier, black with a tan design woven through it. The colors would go well with her beige sweater sets. There was a long line at the cash register, so after I paid for the scarf, I left without questioning the vendor. I'd seen nothing at this booth that looked appropriate for Ephraim—I checked—so I went to the booth selling matching Christmas pajamas for the whole family, which seemed to be a thing lately.

The *ugliest-ever* onesie, an elf costume, made me chuckle to myself. When I handed the cashier the money for two matching sets for me and my lil' cuz, I chuckled again. I couldn't even begin to picture Axle wearing this. He always slept in his clothes, and as far as I knew, didn't own any pajamas. The couple behind me snickered at the PJs, too, and the three of us burst out laughing. "Have a Holly Jolly Christmas" belted from the PA system. Perfect.

Clutching the bagful of pajamas, I turned and bumped into a man carrying a miniature wooden carousel with a rotor at the top that spun by candle power. "Oops, sorry."

The man blew out his cheeks and yelled, "*Pass auf, wohin du gehst!*" All eyes in the crowd shifted toward me and the man. He wore a blazer with elbow patches and a Bavarian type of hat with a feather, a mix of academia and Alps, and his voice was loud.

My face flushed scorching hot. "I'm sorry, what'd you say?"

"*Pass auf, wohin du gehst!*"

"Pass what? I don't understand German." I wish I knew the language. Why didn't I study harder in high school?

"What *unhöflich*."

I planted my hands on my hips. "What the what?" But another customer jostled me, and the alpine man tromped off.

A woman in a red wool coat with curly blonde hair poking out of an adorable hood patted my back. "Don't worry, hon. He's the one who runs the booth with those yummy German pastries. But he's a grouchy sort. I heard him yelling at someone else the other day." She rolled her eyes. "Actually, he was yelling at another vendor, the one who runs the mulled wine stand."

I gasped. "Meredith Yarborough?"

"You know her?"

"Yes. I mean, kind of. Do *you* know her?"

"I know who she is because I saw her at her booth, and I'd seen her at the wine tasting room in town a few times, too, but I don't know her." The woman's gaze darted around, then settled back on me. She said in a low voice, "She's the one who was murdered, you know."

I clutched my shopping bags to my chest and whispered back, "I heard that, too. So, who do you think did it?"

"Do you think that angry man could have…" She pointed toward the alpine man at the *Christstollen* booth.

I tried to keep the excitement out of my voice. "What were they arguing about?"

"I don't know, hon, he was yelling at her in German." *Darn! We Americans should really learn to speak other languages.* She added, "Actually, the lady, umm, Meredith, was here with another woman I'd never seen before. They were all three yelling at each other. Some kind of argument was going on." She lifted her shoulders and let them fall. "Well, Merry Christmas, dear." She strolled off toward the ice rink.

So, I went back to the bench and added the alpine man to my suspect list. Okay, I agree, it wasn't much to go on. He yelled at me, too. So what? I also scribbled down a note that there was another woman in the argument. Was she a suspect? Now I had all these witnesses to question: *Victim's brother, maintenance man, alpine man at Christstollen booth, and the other unknown woman who was in the argument.* Were they just witnesses or was one the killer?

My notes were growing longer, but I was not growing closer to an answer. I had two gifts purchased, but no nearer to a gift idea for Ephraim.

I rose from my seat and followed the crowd of fellow shoppers down the fairway.

Axle slouched against the coffee kiosk with a bulging bag tucked under one arm, intent on his cell phone. I cuffed him upside the head with a gentle upsweep of my hand. "Hey! Look alert!"

He returned a hard shoulder bump and called over to the coffee stand, "Kris, you ready? I've only got an hour."

She came out from around the side wearing her Roasters on the Ridge apron embroidered with a swirl of steam over a coffee mug. Realizing this, she tugged the apron loose and tossed it across the counter. "Sierra, can you put that away for me?"

"Sure will, Kris." Her helper swooped up the apron and stuffed it out of sight.

Kristen stabbed a finger in the vicinity of the main drag. "Let's get some food and take a selfie of us at the table with the market in the background."

Axle gave her a thumbs up. "Good idea. I'm starved." Sweeping past the two of us, he led the way, and we followed him to the kiosk set up by the local brew pub. He plopped his overstuffed sack on a high-top table. Kristen asked us for our orders and went to the vendor to place them.

I dropped my packages under a stool and climbed on top. "Axle, I've got a question."

"Yeah, what?" His eyes were on a nearby pair of teen girls, laughing and shoving each other.

"Kris said you took a coffee over to the mulled wine booth. Did you talk to the woman there?"

He flicked a glance toward me. "Well, yeah. I told her to enjoy her coffee."

I said, "Wow. You came up with that on your own?" which he ignored. "You know she's the murder victim."

"Oh, that." He waved me off. "I know."

"So, you didn't talk about anything else?"

"That'd be a big no."

I sighed, and we both watched the laughing girls sashay away.

Kristen returned with a cardboard tray holding three steaming hot polish sausages and two local ales, one for me and one for Axle, and a mug of root beer for herself. Axle took a big bite and followed it down with a swig of ale before I even had my napkin open.

"This food's going to be gone before I get that photo." Kristen hovered her hand over Axle's sausage. "Let's take the picture now."

The three of us crowded together and raised our mugs and sausages in the air, and Kristen captured a dozen images. She passed around her cell phone so we could pick the best one.

I said, "Did you notice the Festival Queen photobombed that last picture? She made a face and waved peace signs with both hands right behind Axle."

"Not my fault this time," Axle said around a full mouth. "I got an idea. You could write something on the card like, we're drinking hot buttered rum. Nobody will know it's ale. Isn't rum a Christmas drink? I've never had one myself." He took another big sip of his pale ale.

"You can tell it's beer," Kristen argued.

Something wasn't right here. Something was bothering me. What was it?

I had it. "Wait! Axle is only eighteen. He's not supposed to have alcohol."

Kristen set down her sausage. "You're right. And I bought it for him. My bad. I need to pay more attention from now on. Those photos are out."

Axle groaned. "You mean we can't use one of these pictures?"

"No," Kristen insisted. Her perma-smile faltered, and I was disappointed, too. She tossed up a hand. "They were good photos, but I'll need to delete them."

She reached for his beer, but he moved the frosty mug closer to his elbow. Axle looked up at the sky and shook his head. "Unbelievable." He wolfed down the rest of his lunch and got up to leave.

Before he could, I snatched up his shopping bag. "Anything in here for me, Axle?"

His eyes widened in surprise, then he shifted his feet around. "No."

"There is, too. What is it? What'd you get me?" I'd hidden my packages under my stool and hoped Axle wouldn't notice and hassle me back. His pajamas were in one of my sacks.

He tried to grab his bag, which tore open, and a dozen boxes of earbuds spilled out.

I quipped, "Oh, you bought presents for yourself, I see." I picked one up and read the box. These were some high-quality noise-cancelling wireless earbuds. "How much did you pay for the buds?"

He paused for a moment, then looked pleased with himself. "I got them for fifty apiece at that Jennings Emporium booth. They usually go for two hundred bucks each."

Kristen said, "Good job, Axle. Those make great gifts." She stood up and gathered her purse.

"Do you think I should get Ephraim a pair of these?" I shuffled the boxes back into his sack and folded it closed over the tear. I handed the bag to Axle.

Kris crinkled her nose. "No, earbuds aren't personal. They don't leave a message."

She always gave good advice. "You're right." I collected my purse and my bags from under the table.

"I'm heading back to the coffee stand. See you two later." She bounded off.

"Did you ride a scooter here?" I asked Axle as we followed after Kris but at a slower pace.

"Yup. All on my own. Nobody showed me how to do it." He gave me an elbow to my gut.

"Ow. I'll take a scooter back, too, because I need to pick up my truck. I probably should drive around looking for stalls."

We hoofed it down the concourse toward Fifth and Prairie Falcon Drive, a busy corner certain to have several of the rides available. I gulped in a deep frosty breath and caught whiffs of fudge, scented candles, and candied chestnuts. I was getting so used to the holiday music I hardly even heard it now, but my nose couldn't ignore the strong aromas.

"So, how many friends do you have that you need so many earbuds?" I asked.

"They're not gifts. I'm scalping. I figure I can make a hundred profit on each one and still undercut the prices at the stores."

I halted my steps. "Axle, how can that booth afford to sell those so cheap? Are they fakes?"

He walked a few paces past me, then stopped and turned around. "No, they're the real-deal."

"They could be stolen."

A wary look came over his face. "You think I hadn't thought of that?"

"Axle! No!" I grasped both of his hands in mine. "You could go to jail for selling stolen goods."

"Then don't tell anybody." Axle shook me off. "Especially not Ephraim."

I threw my hands in the air. "No shit? I mean, really?" And I'd thought about getting Ephraim a pair. That made the heat rise to my face.

Axle walked backward a few steps. "Hey, I really do need to get back to work. Let's keep going." My high heel caught in a crack in the pavement, and I almost went down. Axle came back to hold my elbow while I bent over to free my shoe. He said, "I don't know how you can walk in them things. It must be your super power."

"I don't do a very good job of it, evidently."

"Maybe you just want to commit *shoeicide*."

"No, you're the one killing me." I hurried to catch up with him as he strode away. "Back to the subject. Please find out if the earbuds are stolen before you sell them."

"Not doing that." He tapped his cell phone at the first scooter we came to.

Twirling in a circle, I looked around for another one. By the time I came about-face, Axle had taken off and was halfway down the block.

He threw his words over his shoulder, "Do not tell the sheriff!"

I shook my fist at his departing back. "Really? Really, you twerp?"

A sharp pang of disappointment hit my chest. My lil' cuz was letting himself in for a heap of trouble.

Chapter 5

Using my phone app, I located another scooter, rode the vehicle to the truck, and drove the truck to the highway. My truck and I chugged out of town and up the canyon where the pines scented the air and the cold breeze shook the snow off the bare aspen trees. White-topped mountains towered in the background.

A while back, I'd landed a city contract to remove abandoned vehicles from the side of the road. Sometimes I received a call from Code Enforcement, but other times I simply searched for the orange-tagged vehicles. Once I found them, I hitched up the cars and delivered them to the impound lot, preferably unharmed. So…yes, I used to have a problem jackknifing when in reverse, but I'm over it now. Almost, I swear. This was a good income source and supplied me with business between calls on the Del's Towing line. Plus, it made me feel good. Owners appreciated having their cars hauled out of harm's way, and removing the vehicles made the roadways safer.

I spotted a tagged monster truck on jacked-up wheels but kept going because my self-loader was for light-weight towing only. After a few passes east and west, I got off on the frontage road, connected with Industrial Lane, then headed east toward town where I maneuvered through the north–south grid of streets. I pulled the visor down to block out the glare of the winter sun, my seat rumbling underneath me. I didn't bother entering the golf course community but stuck to the older, working-class section of town. Sometimes junk cars were tagged by the city for removal from public rights-of-way.

Sailing down Main, I spotted Tanner's black flatbed ahead. He motioned with his arm out his window, indicating I was to follow him. After turning off on a side street, he stopped at the curb. I nicked my truck in behind his and forced myself out of the cab.

I jerked open his passenger door and looked inside at the man behind the wheel. "Hey, Tanner."

"Got some news for you." This ambitious, self-made man, with a business degree from night school, had built up his towing company from scratch at a young age and is singlehandedly raising his two younger siblings. I'd dated him not long ago, emulated his business plan, and tried to be as professional as him, but we'd broken up after I'd figured out Tanner's first priorities would always be work and family. I understood it had to be that way, but it wasn't what I was looking for in a relationship.

"What's up?" I ran my hand down the length of my braid and gazed everywhere else but at him.

He ducked down so he could see through the open door to where I stood on the curb. "The shops on Main Street don't want us to monitor the towaway zones during the *Christkindl Market*."

After a moment of astonished silence, I said, "They don't?"

His head lumbered side to side.

Tanner held contracts with the downtown businesses to keep their loading docks clear. He subbed

Tuesdays and Thursdays to me, and he covered Mondays, Wednesdays, and Fridays. Parking was not restricted on weekends because there were no deliveries then. In spite of warning signs prominently displayed that if anyone parked there, their cars would be towed, Main Street patrons left their vehicles there anyway. And we towed them to impound lots. This was another piece of business that I counted on.

"Why not?" I asked.

"Most of the shops have a booth at the market and they're getting deliveries there. All their customers are going to the fair so there's plenty of available parking downtown. No one's bothering to park illegally in the alley."

"Well, if someone does leave their vehicle there, I guess not getting towed is an early Christmas gift. Thanks for letting me know." I began to shut the door.

"Laney, wait." Tanner reached out his hand, so I paused with one high-heeled foot on the running board. "How are you doing?" He gave me the old once-over and blood rushed to my face.

I could see Tanner's pulse thumping in his neck, and his body heat radiated across the short distance. It took me a long moment to remember I was with Ephraim now. I labored to breathe but managed to answer, "Fine. I'm fine."

The hot tow man was as great-looking as the cowboy sheriff, what can I say? It wasn't easy being around two such hunks, but hey, I managed to make it work for me.

I asked, "How's Tate and Annie?" Those were his brother and sister.

A smile cracked his lips open. "Good."

"You seem pretty busy with the market. Are you done setting up the booths?"

"Yeah, they're all in place now. And the ice blocks for the sculptures, too, so I've got a break."

"Did you know the woman who was killed?" I might as well ask. Everyone knew everybody in this minuscule town, especially the small business owners.

"Not personally, but I heard about her."

"Huh. No one seems to have known her. I'm surprised at that." At least Kristen hadn't known her, other than meeting her at the market, and now Tanner didn't know her either.

"She just moved here last month to open the tasting room. Her family owns one of the vineyards in Palisade, and the wine is supposed to be good. That's all I heard." His sky-blue eyes were intense and amazing. "You investigating?"

I laughed. "Just curious. So, she's from out of town. That explains why no one knows much about her, I guess. Well, I'll let you get back to it."

He gave me a parting smile. "See ya."

I felt his gaze burn my back as I shut the door to his cab and made my way over to my truck.

After driving around for a while more, I didn't spot any stalls, so I texted Ephraim. He texted me back, agreeing to meet at the market at six when he got off duty, and it was almost that time now. Not wanting another frozen scooter ride, I exchanged my truck for my car and managed to wedge the tiny Fiat into a tight spot a block away from the fairgrounds.

Yes, I was back at the market. Yes, I couldn't seem to keep away. Ephraim was already tired of the place and complained most of the booths sold the same wares—

cinnamon-scented pine cones, colorful quilts, hand-carved nativity sets, and sweet pastries—but it would take a lot for me to get tired of it. I love Christmas, and this was all so *Christmas-y*. Plus, I needed to check in with Kristen.

After crossing through the gate, I followed a man in a long wool coat and fedora. I knew that coat and fedora. That had to be Noel Yarborough walking ahead of me. I trudged after him, hanging back a little, to watch as he unlocked the mulled wine stand and lifted the wooden shutter, exposing the almost empty interior. The hidden speaker outside his kiosk broadcasted "The Little Drummer Boy."

I stepped forward. "Are you open?"

He closed his eyes in a long blink. "No, not yet."

"Remember me? I'm Delaney. I gave you a tow, Noel."

"How could I forget?" He tugged off his leather gloves and switched on the portable heater. The shelves were bare of consumable goods but did hold other items for sale, like commemorative mugs, wineglass charms, and bottle openers. "I was told I could open in a day or two if you want to come back later. I'm only here to restock." The door to the back of the stand was cracked open, revealing cases of wine stacked two and three high.

"Do you need any help? I'm here to relieve one of the other vendors"—I pointed over to Kristen's stall—"but I can help you for a few minutes."

He slid the fedora from his head and hung it on a hook, giving me a quick side-eye. "No, that's okay." His hair was dark brown in a trim cut, parted on the side.

I shrugged but tried again. "I work with Kristen Guttenberg at the coffee booth next to yours. I towed your Santa Fe. I'd think you can trust me, but if you'd rather not have any help…"

He yanked his scarf from around his neck with a deep sigh. "Okay, sure. Go around back."

I scurried around the side and met him at the door. Brown cardboard boxes containing groceries crowded the narrow space next to the wine cases.

He said, "You carry in the food and let me get the wine. It's heavy."

"Okay." I lifted one of the grocery cartons and followed him into the booth. "Where do you want these?"

"Under the counter." He poked the wine bottles into racks. I arranged bags of oranges and bundles of cinnamon sticks on the low shelves. The job didn't take long between the two of us.

After the last item was put away, I dusted my hands together. "I never thought about this before, but there's a lot of product in these booths. Is everything safe overnight?" My gaze darted over to Kristen's kiosk where she had expensive coffee-making equipment.

"I wondered about that myself. When I was talking to the sheriff, I asked him how good the security is. He told me the grounds are patrolled twenty-four-seven and that there'd never been a break-in at one of the stalls, although there is a pickpocket on the loose."

"I heard about the pickpocket." And we all knew about the murder. I said, "Security has probably been beefed up after what happened to your sister. I'm really sorry for your loss. I was the one who found her, me and the sheriff."

"That was you?" His close-set eyes held an intense look.

"Yeah." I flushed warm and saw the tip of my nose turn red. "Like I said, I'm sorry, Noel."

He reached up to the top shelf and extracted a bottle of wine. "Hand me an opener, would you?" I placed the opener in his hand, and he pried the cork out of the bottle. He poured red wine into two mugs and gave me one.

"Thanks." I smelled the bouquet and took a sip. "Gosh, this is good. I would've expected you to use cheap table wine for the mulled wine." Yikes! Was that an insult? Heat rose to the roots of my hair to complete my red flush.

He closed his eyes and took in the bouquet, then filled his mouth with the wine. He appeared to swish the fruit of the grape around over his tongue, then swallowed and opened his eyes. "Oh, no. We're using our best blends from this season."

I studied him over the top of my mug. "Tell me about your winery."

He looked eager to explain. "The vineyard has been in my family for three generations. My parents retired last year. They wanted to travel, go see other vineyards, and enjoy their golden years, right? So they took off for Italy this Christmas. They tried to get an early flight back, but at this time of year they couldn't get tickets until next week."

"That must be awful for them. And you're here, having to handle everything by yourself."

He swirled the wine around in his mug. "It sucks that Merry was killed."

"This must be hard for you. You called your sister Merry?"

"Yeah, and she spelled it M-e-r-r-y. I hate this town. How dangerous is this place?" Only he added a swear word to describe my beloved city.

"Unfortunately there's crime everywhere, not just here." I tried to tamp down the irritation. This man lost his sister, I reminded myself.

"Merry did say she liked living here."

"See, Spruce Ridge is a great place to live. I like it, too. Not only is it beautiful with views of the Rocky Mountains everywhere you turn, surrounded by these fantastic pristine forests, and the shopping, but we also have some pretty upscale eateries—"

"Okay, okay," he interrupted, holding up a hand, palm out.

"Sorry, but it's a friendly city, too. I stopped what I was doing to help you, didn't I?"

"I thought you had time to spare. You practically begged me to let you help." He poured himself another measure. "But, okay, I guess it's a friendly enough place. Though Merry said the tasting room was struggling. I have to decide if I'm going to close it."

"Really?"

"I don't need the aggravation. I opened the tasting room for Merry because she wanted to tell me how to operate the vineyard. I thought if I gave her something else to do, she'd leave the vineyard alone. The tasting room was her deal, not mine."

"What was Merry like?" Look at me. Being so bold. The wine couldn't have gone to my head already.

"Bossy. She wanted to make changes, had all kinds of big ideas." He barked out a laugh, then drained his mug and reached for the bottle. "You want more?"

I peered into my mug. "No, I'm good."

"I'd like to sell out these mugs and all the product from the tasting room so I can recoup some of Merry's losses. I really hope I'm allowed to open this booth soon."

"Why are you stocking the place if you don't know when you'll open?"

"So I'll be ready when I get the all-clear." He glanced at his rows of souvenir mugs.

"Kristen's worried about selling all her Christmas mugs, too. She doesn't want anything left over." I took a last swallow of my drink. "Did you get your car back from Oberly Motors?"

He nodded. "They were able to pop the fender back in place. At least I'm not stuck here waiting on a *f-ing* part."

The woman chosen for Queen of the Festival and the woman in the Santa cap walked up to the counter. Queen said, "Hey there, Noel." She wore the same Queen sash and sported a ginormous diamond ring on her left hand. Some fellow paid a lot of money for that cluster of ice.

Noel gave her an appreciative smile. "Hi."

Santa Hat asked him, "Are you open tonight?"

His smile turned into a frown. "No, damn it."

Santa Hat held out her hand to me. "I'm Belle. I'm the fair organizer. And this lovely lady is the Festival Queen." She squeezed the pretty blonde woman's arm and looked at me expectantly. "And you are?"

"Delaney Morran."

Chimes rang out over the PA system and the twinkling bulbs on the market stands lit up all at once, signaling six o'clock. We gazed at the glittering scene, lights strung from booth to booth above the walking path, and listened to Bing Crosby sing "White Christmas."

I needed to get over to Kris's booth and meet Ephraim. "Where should I put this?" I jiggled my mug.

"I'll take it." Noel grabbed hold of the mug and placed it in a plastic tub. "Thanks for your help."

"I'll be back as soon as you open," I promised. I ducked out the door and texted Ephraim:

—are you here?

My phone pinged with a reply:

—look up.

Ephraim was waiting for me a few feet away at Kristen's coffee stand. His eyebrows were raised in a question, but his arms were wide open. I ran over into his embrace and teetered on my heels, but his hands around my waist held me to him.

"How was your day?" I asked, my face nestled against his neck. The pine scent was everywhere from the freshly cut trees. Even Ephraim smelled like pine, but the fragrance reminded me of finding Meredith's body and that wasn't a pleasant sensation.

After his arms tightened for a squeeze, he released me. "Good. Let's go to my place for dinner. But before we leave, do you want to pick out a tree?"

"Let's check on Kris first."

Kristen went on a quick break while I took care of customers. The booth was busy, but she wasn't gone long. After she returned and assured me she was good until closing, I told Ephraim, "We can go now. I'll get a tree later."

He held my hand as we walked to his sheriff's truck parked behind the last booth. One of the perks of law enforcement was getting a close parking place. As he pulled into the stream of traffic on Fifth, I cast a look at the booths selling toys, poinsettias, and chocolates, all doing a brisk trade.

"Is the mulled wine booth going to reopen?" I asked.

I hoped for Noel's sake he could resume operating soon.

Ephraim glanced at me, then back to the street. "Is that what you were talking about with Mr. Yarborough?"

"Wouldn't you like to know," I teased.

His eyes opened wide before narrowing down to a straight line. "You'll tell me what you found out, right?"

"If you tell me what you found out."

"Gosh, let's see." He rubbed his chin. "Not gonna happen. But you'll still tell me, right?"

"You gotta give me something."

"Oh, I will." His deep voice made my insides quake.

Ephraim lived in a townhome that backed up to the forest. After he pulled his truck into his garage and we climbed out, an Uber turned in to his driveway. Ephraim sprang over to the driver's door and extracted his wallet. He handed the driver some money, and the driver passed him a bag of food. Ephraim unlocked the front door, and I entered ahead of him. He set the fragrant bag on the kitchen counter and took my coat.

His townhome was brand new and had all the new home features. Open concept, kitchen island, granite countertops, gas fireplace, vaulted ceilings. I liked the outdoor patio with a firepit best. Ephraim bought the place a couple of years ago but only had the basic furniture—a worn leather couch and club chair, a television that hung on the wall, and a bare minimum bedroom set. The rickety dining room table and chairs were hand-me-downs from his mom. The walls remained pristine white. No color. No pictures. Not even family photographs. His home lacked personality.

"You don't have a Christmas tree." I pointed out the obvious as I stood at the counter. He didn't have any counter stools, either.

"What about you? You don't have a tree. We should've gotten yours tonight."

"There's still time to get one." I didn't want to explain I was putting it off because the pine scent reminded me of the dead woman...which is why we needed to solve this crime and get on with life.

"Okay. Dinner's ready and I worked really hard on this." Ephraim reached into the bag and brought out cartons of Chinese, his favorite take-out meal. He might have a gourmet kitchen, but he never cooked himself.

I plucked some plates from the cabinet and silverware from the drawer. "Napkins?"

"In the bag." He carried the food to the table, and I followed with the plates and forks. We dug in to the chow mien and Peking roasted duck.

I began, "Have you talked to the maintenance man?"

"The groundskeeper? Yes, we questioned him, along with a lot of other people. Why?"

"Kris saw him order a mulled wine from Meredith." I kicked one eyebrow higher than the other in a questioning way. Was this news to him?

"We know. He didn't lead us anywhere."

I tried to hide my disappointment. "Okay. Then there's this. Noel told me he took over the Palisade winery from his parents but that Merry, that's what he called his sister, wanted to run things. So he opened the tasting room in Spruce Ridge to get her out of his hair. He said she was bossy." I stabbed a piece of duck with my fork. "Now your turn."

"Mr. Yarborough said she was bossy, huh? He never mentioned that to me and we grilled him pretty hard."

"See, I can get witnesses to tell me things. And call him Noel."

"And how did you get *Noooooel*," he exaggerated the pronunciation of his name, "to tell you that?"

"I batted my eyelashes and made kissy sounds, how do you think?" Then I gave him a smile. "No, really, people will tell you things if you listen."

He grabbed my hand, turning serious. "I know that. And you're a good listener."

I squeezed his hand back. "Noel has a motive. His sister was interfering, and he wanted her out of the way so he could be in charge. I think he might have some anger issues." I felt Ephraim stiffen in the chair beside me and hurried to add, "Not directed at me or anything. It's just that Noel swears a lot. But it could be that's just the way he talks." Maybe I was exaggerating the angry attitude. It was probably nothing.

"That's common. People use language." Ephraim rubbed his thumb against my palm.

"Quit that." I drew my hand back. "We have to finish our food."

"All right." He gave me a smoldering grin. "I do have information for you. You'll want to hear this."

Chapter 6

"Tell me," I squealed and jumped up for my purse. I found my notes and ran back with my spiral.

Ephraim said, "Your friend Rory Rearden was acquainted with the victim."

I was about to write that down but looked up. "Right. He recognized her from the tasting room."

"No, he knew her before."

"*Reeeally.*" I covered my mouth with my hand.

"Yes. It's odd he didn't disclose their connection up front. I had to find it out for myself. Mr. Yarborough explained that his family knew the Reardens when I asked him if the victim came into regular contact with anyone in town. That's how I learned about it."

"That *is* news. The fact he didn't mention it right away is important, isn't it?" Rory hadn't said anything to me, and he hadn't informed the police, either.

Suspicious, much?

"So the families knew each other…but that doesn't mean Rory had anything to do with Meredith's death, right?" I was looking for an out for my friend.

"Mr. Yarborough said they grew up together. Rearden knew the victim well."

"Please call him Noel. It's weird you calling him Mr. Yarborough. You're not in a briefing or whatever you call your meetings at work. And the victim is Meredith or Merry."

He only grunted. "So, let's see your notes."

"I need to add the info you just gave me, plus what Noel told me today, but here you go." I slid the pages across to Ephraim, and while he tried to read my handwriting, I folded up the cartons of leftovers and put them in the fridge.

After I came back to the table, he pointed to my notebook and said, "I didn't know about this argument Meredith had with the man at the *Christstollen* booth. Good job, Delaney."

"And good luck to you. I'm not sure the guy speaks any English." I returned to my chair. "Have you talked to any of the other vendors yet?"

"Sure. We're working our way through them. There are over fifty booths and not all of them are local. I'm not sure the out-of-towners will be helpful, but maybe someone saw something. We haven't found out much yet from the ones we've covered."

I glided the notepad back in front of me. "What time did we find the body?"

"One thirty-five."

I knew he would know. "Do you have the time of death?"

"It was close to the time we found her. In fact, the body was still quite warm. It would've cooled quickly outside in the cold."

I jotted that down on the page. "Was her body moved from someplace else?" That seemed like a reasonable question to ask.

"No. We have a witness who saw her walking through the tree lot."

"Who?"

"Delaney, I can't give out his name."

Okay. This was still a lot of good information. Plus, the witness was a man. "Was there any DNA evidence? Skin under her fingernails?" Thank goodness for television crime shows where we learned this kind of stuff, like when the victim scratched the killer and DNA provided the smoking gun clue.

"The labs aren't back yet, but she was wearing mittens anyway."

I made a note to follow up. "The poison was in the wine, you said. Do you know what kind of poison?"

"Sodium fluoroacetate. A rodenticide, rat poison. It's illegal now, has been since the 1970s, except for limited use. We're trying to track down the purchase, but it might prove impossible if it was bought years ago."

"How did her body end up under one of the Douglas firs?" I had a brief thought that someone had tried to hide her body.

"The poison caused convulsions. She may have thrashed around after collapsing."

Rat poison sounded like a horrible way to go. I couldn't help but shudder. "Have you released the information about the poison?"

"Yes, but not the type."

"Why didn't she have identification on her?"

"She left her purse in the wine booth. She had her car keys, though."

"Meredith grabbed her keys but not her purse, proving she was in a hurry, maybe not even thinking straight. She just wanted to get home because she felt so sick."

"It's time to put work aside." Ephraim tugged on my elbow. "Come on, you want to watch a Christmas movie? How about *It's a Wonderful Life*?"

One of my favorites.

We snuggled up on the couch, and I wondered how much of the movie we'd actually watch.

****

The next morning after Axle and I locked up our apartment, I noticed Kristen's Prius still parked in the lot, so we hiked back up the stairs and knocked on her door.

She cracked the door open. "Oh, good morning, you two. Come on in."

"Why haven't you left yet?" I asked.

"Guy is opening the booth, Sierra is opening the store, and I get to take my time this morning. I'm heading over to the market pretty soon." She turned toward her kitchen. Her apartment was the mirror image of mine, but she'd decorated it in all black and white. The monochrome scheme worked for her.

"You're not in any hurry, are you, Axle?" I flicked him a glance to catch his reply, but he had his earbuds in.

Kristen asked, "So, what else have you found out about the murder? You're still investigating, right?" She knew me so well.

I extracted my notes. "Meredith's brother is my number one suspect." I explained what was, in my mind at least, a competition between the two siblings for control of the vineyard. Major motive. If it's true, anyway. "And I have a timeline." I plopped my notebook on the table with the chronology I'd put together. Kristen and Axle read through the short bullet points.

Friday, 9:00 a.m., Kristen talks to Meredith, Axle takes her a coffee.

Friday, noon, wine booth opens and maintenance man buys mulled wine.

Friday, 1:35 p.m., body found, still warm.

Suspects: Noel Yarborough, maintenance man, alpine man with the Christstollen booth, unknown other woman involved in argument.

Means: poison.

Motive: Noel wants to be in charge, sibling rivalry. Unknown motives for others.

Kris looked up. "Poison?"

"Awful, I know." I gave a solemn nod. I didn't mention the poison was for rats. I trusted Kristen to keep it to herself, but Ephraim said it was not yet public knowledge.

"And who's the *Christstollen* vendor-slash-alpine man?" Kristen's eyebrows pinched together.

"The man who had an argument with Meredith, he and another woman." I pointed to my notes. "That's why the unknown woman is also on my list."

Axle asked, "What's going on between the *sibs*?"

"Sibling rivalry. Families are complicated. There's probably so much more to it." I asked Kris, "Do you know anything about the Yarboroughs' tasting room in town?"

"No, but I can ask around." She had a lot of contacts in the food service industry, and somebody had to know something. "I hope they solve the murder soon so that poor family can have resolution."

I nodded, tucking my list back in my purse. Kris may not say so, but she was worried about her booth, too, and unlike me, she would put everyone else first and her concerns last.

"You dug up a lot, Delaney." Axle directed his palm at me. "Gimme a five." We slapped hands. "But, we gotta book."

I slung my purse over my shoulder, and we said

goodbye to Kris. It only took minutes to buzz over to Oberly Motors, and just as I pulled the Fiat into the lot, a call came in for a tow.

"I can't stop to chat with Byron, so tell him *hello* for me," I explained to Axle as I gathered up my purse and red high-heeled boots with the white fringe from the Fiat's back seat.

"I can go with you. Let me tell Byron." Axle beckoned me to wait for him, so I parked the Fiat and pulled my truck up to the door. I fiddled with the radio until I found a Christmas music station.

"You sure Byron doesn't need you this morning?" I asked my lil' cuz when he boosted himself into the cab.

"He's not that busy, and I don't want him to pay me for sitting around." Axle braced himself on the dash when I took the corner too sharp pulling out of the lot.

"Not busy? First Kristen and now Byron!"

"It's okay. Byron warned me that people don't want to pay for expensive paint jobs right before Christmas. It'll pick up after the first of the year."

"Okay, well, it's nice to have you along, Ax." I gave him a sweet smile, but he pinched my arm. "Ouch!"

"That's so you don't think I care."

"If I didn't know better, I'd think you do care."

"Good thing you know better." He popped his earbuds in.

The stalled vehicle was a Jeep Cherokee, four-wheel drive, and the young driver told us after we arrived at her apartment that she thought her battery was dead. Axle found the jump charger under the truck bed and got to work, but the charger would not power up her battery.

Axle said, "I think your battery's too dead to take the charge. Or you could have an electrical problem.

That can be figured out with a diagnostics test."

The girl's shoulders slumped. "Maybe I should have my car looked at. Can you tow me over to my mechanic?"

I said, "Of course, but don't you want to buy a new battery and try that first?"

"No. I don't want to call you to come back if the problem's not the battery. I'd just as soon get this taken care of right away."

I gave Axle a roll of the eyes, but the customer is always right, and besides, this was money in the bank for me. I told Axle, "We need the tow dollies," and we both reached under the truck bed to roll them out.

Axle attached the first dolly to the front driver's side tire, and I attached the second to the front passenger's side. We pumped up the dollies so that both front tires were off the ground. The dolly wheels were *kickin' kewl*. I brought out the remote control from the truck cab and pushed the magic button. The T-bar extended out from the back of my truck with a groan and a whiff of hydraulic fluid, and the claws connected to the rear wheels, closing around the tires. The boom raised the Jeep Cherokee's back end. All four tires were lifted from the pavement. We were ready to roll.

"Wow, that's impressive," said my customer.

I told you, didn't I?

"And I love your red boots. Real cute." She actually smiled when she handed me her credit card. "Put a twenty percent tip on there. And Merry Christmas."

"Merry Christmas to you, too!" How I meant it.

She gave me the directions to her mechanic shop and told me she would let them know I was on my way. After I'd recorded the VIN and delivered the Cherokee to the shop, "Baby It's Cold Outside" came on the radio. I sang along and made up the words I didn't know.

Axle groaned. "Haven't you gotten sick of this crap music yet?"

"No."

He inserted his wireless earbuds, but I swiped the one out of his left ear. "Are those the stolen buds?"

"Let it go, Delaney."

I gave him the evil side-eye. "Do you think that booth has more stolen goods? Is this a clue to the murder?"

"Why would this be a clue?"

"Stealing is a crime. Murder is a crime."

Axle twisted at the waist to look at me. "Pickpocketing is a crime. So, is that a clue?"

"*Ohhhh yeah*, it could be." I gave him an excited look. "Maybe the market pickpocket is the murderer."

"*Pffttt*." He fluttered his lips in dismissal.

Both our phones pinged at the same time with an incoming text. Axle checked his phone and said, "Oh boy. Kristen has another dumb idea for the Christmas photo. She says here, what about a picture of us at the ice rink?" He thumbed something into his phone and mine dinged again.

"What'd you tell her?"

"I sent a vomiting face emoji. You're on the text, too, so you'll see it. I love that emoji." He stared at his phone screen. "Kris just replied that we'd better show up or else."

I laughed. "Or else, what?" I couldn't imagine my friend threatening anybody. The most severe thing she'd say is, "Can't you please be there?" Axle was busy tapping on his phone while mine pinged and dinged. I asked him, "What in the world?"

"I convinced Kris to ditch that plan. You can catch up with the texts later. Just drive."

Axle got out of the truck at Byron Oberly's. After I left him, I kept my eyes peeled for orange-tagged stalls and ended up by the marketplace. When I spotted a parking spot near the fairgrounds that was big enough for my truck, I couldn't pass it up.

That's the only reason I stopped, I swear.

That and to check on Kris, of course.

Okay, okay. I'm pathetic. I can't keep away from the *Christkindl* marketplace.

Anyhoo, as I passed the Christmas tree lot, I noticed the tree seller, Kane Quigley, helping a woman tie a tree on the roof of her Ford Escape, front-wheel drive. She gave him a side hug before climbing into her Ford and exiting the lot. A smile spread across his face when I walked up to him.

He said, "Hello, Delaney."

"Hi, Kane. Your customers must really like you, the Christmas tree man, giving you hugs and all."

He laughed and shuffled his feet. "Well, you know. It's the season."

"You the man, you." I nudged him with my elbow. "This job is probably a good place to meet singles."

"It is." He chuckled. "You looking?"

I laughed, too. "No. I've got a great b-b-boyfriend." I said it out loud! I'd never called Ephraim my boyfriend before out loud. "But how come a nice guy like you isn't taken?"

His eyes did a shifty thing. He said, "Well…" and I caught the hesitation in his voice.

I had to ask, "Are you married?"

He blushed. "Yeah. My wife's the market organizer."

"You're married? You don't act married." *Oops.* This was awkward, like I'd shoved my stiletto-clad foot in my mouth. I fumbled around for something else to say. "She wears a Santa hat? Carries a clipboard?"

"That's her. Belle."

"I know her. Well, I've run into her over at the wine booth. She's very efficient, a good organizer." Like I knew. I'd only spoken a couple of words to her. And now I was blabbering to him. A scowl crossed his face so he must think I'm an idiot. "Anyway, I'd better get going. Bye now."

I power walked away, glad to make my escape. I headed toward the Emporium booth where Axle had bought the stolen goods. Not that I would find any gift ideas there, but I had to get away from Kane and this cringe attack.

Snow globes, music boxes, small plastic toys, gadgets, penny candy, Russian nesting dolls, nutcrackers, costume jewelry, refrigerator magnets—all possible stocking stuffers, but nothing I'd want for Ephraim, the number one person on my gift list. I twirled the display of personalized key chains and miniature license plates looking for my name, which I could never find anywhere. Was Delaney that unusual? Behind the counter, under lock and key, were gold bracelets with initials. At least I could always find an initial bracelet, I guess, if I really wanted one. I moved on to the toy rack.

The well-dressed man behind the counter said to the plump woman in a Christmas sweater climbing a ladder, "Watch what you're doing. You almost put your foot in the fudge." His nostrils pinched white in irritation, and he moved a box out from under her.

"Sorry, Frank." Her eyes looked puffy like she'd been crying.

"Ma'am, I'd love one of those potpourri ornaments." I pointed at the twisted ball of twigs with cinnamon sticks and dried fruit in the center. "While you're up there, can you hand me one?"

"Sure, miss. Here you go." The ladder tottered when she leaned toward me in her worn-down shoes, and I steadied it with one hand.

"Thanks. You're so helpful." I smiled at her, then gave the man my best badass tow driver glare. "And I'd like two boxes of the red and silver ornaments, too, plus this toy." The label on the box indicated the undercover-agent kit contained a spy glass, tiny binoculars, and a plastic periscope. Only nineteen bucks.

The man said, "I can ring that up for you."

I handed him my debit card. "I don't see any wireless earbuds. Didn't you have a bunch of those?"

The man handed my card back. "Some kid bought me out."

"Oh." I'd looked over the other goods, but the prices for everything seemed about right to me. I had no idea what might be stolen, if anything.

"I'm bringing some more earbuds over from my other booth. Should have them up here by this afternoon."

"Where's your other booth?"

"At the Denver Flea Market, pretty far for you to go. Do you want me to hold one here for you?"

"Sure." Why not? That way I could buy them to show Ephraim without involving Axle. If Ephraim said they weren't stolen, that'd be for the best. If they were stolen, there was no need to involve my lil' cuz.

I stopped by the gingerbread booth and took a moment to open the toy spy kit and examine the pocket-sized scope. Too cute. I held it to my eye and trained it on the *Christstollen* kiosk ten or twelve yards away. It worked amazingly well for just a toy. Through the lens, I spied the Festival Queen talking with a woman at the cash register while the alpine man inserted a mouthwatering pastry into a sack. I turned the scope for a sharper focus to look into the depths of the booth. Amazon boxes stacked floor to ceiling blocked my view.

I tucked the spy glass in my purse and breathed in the fragrance of ginger, clove, and molasses, making me think of gingerbread lattes. I wonder…should I sign up for the gingerbread house competition? Would that make a good Christmas gift for Ephraim? Couples always decorated these things together in cheesy Christmas movies.

Kristen would know, so I steered a course for her coffee kiosk. I slipped through the hut's back door and positioned myself in front of the space heater. Guy, her barista, unpacked soft bags of coffee beans from a cardboard box, while Kris stood at the counter. Since Guy was helping out today, Kris probably didn't need me to give her a break after all.

"Kris, what would you think if I entered Ephraim and me in the gingerbread house contest?" I moved out of her way as she stretched across me for a container of raw sugar.

She stopped and appeared to consider a polite answer, then said, "No." Guy let out a loud snort.

I held up two palms. "Why is that such a bad idea?"

Her forehead wrinkled. "While that's a cute

couple's thing, would Ephraim really enjoy it? Is it for you or for him?"

"Well…"

"Does he bake?"

"No." His oven was so clean, there wasn't enough grease inside to oil the needle on a fuel gauge.

She raised her eyebrows to give me a look like, *duh, isn't-the-answer-obvious?*

"Okay, got it." I waved my hands all around, as if I was waving a white flag in submission. Ephraim didn't even like the Christmas market that well. I knew he was tired of the place already. But I needed the perfect gift. Come on, universe, give it to me. He's a cowboy, but I can't give him a cowboy hat or a horse or a buckle. He's a sheriff, but what good did that do? What does a sheriff need? What does a cowboy want? More importantly, what would be personal and send the right message?

"Can I leave this sack here, Kris, so I don't have to carry it around?" I held up my Jennings Emporium bag.

"Sure. There's room under the counter." She directed me to the spot.

Outside the coffee stand, the muscle-bound maintenance man yanked a full garbage bag out of the recycle bin and climbed into his golf cart. As he pulled away, I said to Guy, "Quick, give me a to-go cup."

"Not a commemorative mug?"

"No." I snapped my fingers. "A paper cup. Hurry."

He gave me the thousand-yard stare, so I shoved him out of the way and grabbed one myself. Then I bolted out of the coffee stand and dashed between the booths over to the next set of trash bins. Yes, these were still full. The man would eventually show up here, and I'd wait until he did, then casually throw in this empty cup and pin him down with a few questions.

Pretty good plan, huh?

And I only had to wait a few minutes before his cart came to a stop in front of me. He flexed his muscles as he extracted himself from the cart.

I made a show of tossing the paper cup into the recycle bin. "Thanks for all you do. You work so hard, always picking up after everyone."

"Yeah?" He lifted a full can out of the bin with ease.

"Hey, since you're always around, did you happen to see Meredith Yarborough on Friday? She ran the mulled wine booth."

He lifted his chin, nose in the air. One of those jerks who was good-looking and knew it. I pictured him owning an old souped-up muscle car, rear-wheel drive, and racing the engine while he drove down Main Street.

He probably thought I was hanging around here on purpose to talk to him. *Ew, ew, ew!*

Actually, I was, but not for the reason he thought.

"Didn't you buy one of those mulled wines from her?" I asked.

"Uh, yeah." He gave me a cocky smile as if tossing me a crumb.

"So, what'd she say to you?"

"Nothing." He tugged a plastic bag from the second trash container, and the lanyard around his neck flew up. I read the name on the ID, Jack Frier.

This strategy wasn't working, so I'd try another tactic. "Jack, have you heard about the pickpockets? Seen anyone suspicious?"

"No. Look, I'm kinda busy here. I haven't got time to chat, girlie." He slid his muscular legs into the golf cart, pressed the pedal, and roared away as fast as the little buggy could carry him.

He couldn't get away from me fast enough.

Was it because he was guilty? Or just plain arrogant? Calling me *girlie*!

Should I be offended? Ya think?

Chapter 7

—I'm here. Just parked and will meet you in five minutes. Your Mother.—

Like I wouldn't know the text was from her.

I caught a glimpse of Mom and Will before they saw me. Mom's blonde hair was styled in its usual short bob. She had on a fashionable wool coat with a faux fur collar and wrap-around belt. Her husband, Will, at five-foot-ten with thinning brown hair, wore khaki pants and a leather jacket. Will was okay for a stepdad. As a lawyer, he helped me out with the legal side of my business.

They were holding hands and looking into each other's eyes. The romantic holiday season must be affecting them like it had me at the beginning. You know, before the murder…

"Hello, dear." Mom pressed me to her chest for a hug, and Will patted me awkwardly on the back.

I gave them a smile. "What do you want to see first?"

"What do you recommend?"

"Are you looking for Christmas ornaments, stocking stuffers, or…"

Mom plucked a tiny spiral from her pocketbook along with her reading glasses. "Let's see. I need gifts for the neighbors, Will's secretary, and Will's nieces and nephews."

Crikey. I couldn't think of a gift for Ephraim, who I

cared a great deal about. How was I going to come up with ideas for people I barely knew? I suggested, "Let's walk around and see if you spot anything." That was my plan for Ephraim. It was the best I could do.

We roamed past booths selling Russian crepes, scented candles, and international chocolates in the shape of toy trains. The Queen of the Festival bumped into Mom and said, "Excuse me," before hustling to catch up with the market organizer in her Santa hat toting her clipboard. Belle was her name. I stared after them, but Mom pulled me to the next stall to buy a jar of Colorado honey and a can of roasted nuts. She ticked two people off her list, and I breathed a little easier.

Will said, "How about something to eat? Are you hungry, Delaney?"

"How about German food?" I pointed my parents in the direction of the *Christstollen* kiosk. I wanted to try some authentic German food since this was a *Christkindl Market* after all. And I wanted to spy on that alpine man some more.

When it was our turn in line, Will ordered each of us a *flammkuchen*, a thin flatbread covered with cheese and bacon. While we waited for the food, Mom and I looked over the ornaments from Germany. I bought two Santa gnomes, each slightly different, one for Byron, one for me, and Mom purchased a miniature wooden carousel ornament. Once we were handed our food, we stood around a high-top table and noshed away, and as much as I stared at the alpine man, I didn't spot him doing anything suspicious. *Dang it.*

After Mom dabbed a napkin to her lips, she reached into her purse and poked her hand in every corner. Then she held the bag open with both hands and stuck her nose inside. "My change purse is gone."

Will said, "Did you look in all those pockets?"

"Of course I did. It's been stolen." Her voice went up a couple of octaves.

"No!" Rage reared up inside me. Mom had been pickpocketed. I stood there fuming, angry at myself for not warning my mom about these recent thefts.

Will rubbed a hand across his forehead. "What credit cards were you carrying?" He pulled his phone out of his pocket. "I'll call them first."

Mom laughed, and we stared at her in shock.

"Mom, are you okay?"

"I didn't have any plastic in my change purse. I left my cards at home because I didn't think these vendors would be equipped to take a credit card." There was a giddiness in her voice.

"Everyone's equipped. Even me." I had a card reader for my smart phone so customers could pay for tows on the road. "How much cash did you lose?"

Her smile dropped, and she quickly sobered. "Well, I'm sorry, Will, but I brought three hundred dollars with me. Minus the thirty I spent, I lost quite a bit."

He clasped her hand. "It's okay, Eve. Could've been worse."

I dialed Kristen. After saying hello, I told her, "Mom's been picked. Is Zach at the market? We need to report this."

She made sympathetic sounds, then told me to head over to the coffee kiosk and she would let Zach know to meet us there. I scanned the crowd as we hurried over, but no one had criminal eyes or looked like they had fast, sneaky hands.

I stowed my additional shopping in the coffee booth

next to my other bag from the Emporium. A moment later, the city police officer in his tan uniform strode up to us. He pointed his big chin at my mom. "I understand your wallet's been stolen, Mrs. Sharpton?"

She had on a tight smile. "Just a change purse, Zach. I had a little under three hundred in cash."

He went on to fill out a report, then said at the end, "It's very unlikely we'll recover your money, but we'll let you know."

I said, "Thanks, Zach."

He gave me a weak imitation of his usual happy grin and stopped for a few words with Kristen before departing. I walked Mom and Will to their older Nissan Infinity, rear-wheel drive, where Mom embraced me with promises to call soon to make more plans. Saying goodbye was always a long process with Mom and Will, but finally their car took off down the street, and I watched until they turned the corner.

Darn, darn, darn! I silently scolded myself.

Note to self: Watch out for Mom the way she watches out for you. She still worried about me like I was fresh out of high school.

Just as Mom had her list to check off, I had mine, and today was family day. Ephraim's extended family was up next.

I spotted his cowboy hat near the giant lighted Christmas tree where a band was playing jazzy Christmas tunes. When I caught up to him, he introduced me to his pint-sized nieces with similar names, Luciana and Mariana, and his nephew, Maximiliano, whose name I loved. The cold temperature must have infused the kids with energy because they zoomed around as if their shoes had race car engines.

Ephraim held my hand in his and said to his mother, "You remember *mi novia*."

"Yes. Good to see you, Delaney." His mom had a slight accent.

"You, too, Isadora." I said to his dad, "Hello, Alan."

Isadora and Alan Lopez were on grandparent duty. Isadora held two of the grandchildren's hands, and Alan had kid-sized superhero backpacks slung over his shoulder. Maximiliano rushed toward Ephraim, jumped on his back, and hung by his hands around Ephraim's neck.

His uncle made a gagging sound and croaked, "Careful, Max." Once the boy let go and his feet smacked the ground, Ephraim said to me, "If I want to avoid being tackled again, I'd better get you out on the dance floor."

"What?" I stifled a laugh.

"Let's dance." He led me to the empty area in front of the band performing "Santa Tell Me." He placed his hands on my waist, and I slid my hands up to his shoulders. My cowboy Casanova twirled me around in the country-western two-step style, him in his cowboy boots, me in my red boots with the three-inch heels. Several other couples joined us. The band played, the lights cast long shadows, and the fragrance of Christmas trees wafted through the air. My Christmas spirit was restored, even though the pine scent reminded me of finding Meredith's body beneath the boughs. Like I could ever forget it.

Abuela and *Abuelos*, as the grandchildren called them, swept the kids down the main thoroughfare with promises of hot cocoa and cookies.

"I love your family," I told Ephraim when we were

alone. As an only child, I came to life when I was around big families. I had no siblings, but at least I had Kris and Axle, who had adopted me as their own.

"My mom likes you a lot." Ephraim pulled me in closer. "And she loves Christmas. I have memories of Christmas trees loaded with so many decorations we couldn't even see the branches. And the outside of the house. She had my dad stringing lights for weeks."

"That sounds nice, Ephraim."

"Yeah, my mom makes holidays magic, especially Christmas."

That's what I wanted as well, but what my heart wanted, my mind was not having. No wreath on the door, no candle in the window, no decorated tree. I needed to get busy, but whenever I pictured a tree in my living room, I pictured the dead body underneath.

As if reading my mind, Ephraim asked, "You want to get that tree now?"

A pit opened in my stomach. "You'd think so, but no, not tonight."

The song ended and the band left the stage to take a break. The booths and Christmas trees were all aglow, so we left the band behind, strolled among the crowd, and listened to the piped-in music that took over the airwaves. The night was frigid with the sun long gone, and our breaths came out in vapors.

"Are you ready to leave?" he asked. "I'm about done with this place."

I tucked my purse under my free arm. "Sure, but first I have to run by Kris's booth. Oh, and I have a crime to report. My mom was pickpocketed earlier."

He halted and twisted me toward him. "Did she call it in?"

I tugged his arm to keep walking. "Yeah. Zach took down the information." I glanced around at all the happy faces. "It's such a shame. Everyone is having a good time, and it's Christmas, the season of giving, but someone is taking. My mom can absorb the loss, but what if the thief hits up someone who's relying on that money for their Christmas gifts." I tried to shake the idea out of my head. "What's happening? There's a killer at this fair, there's thieves…what's next?"

Ephraim took both my hands in his. "There's only one pickpocket, we're pretty sure, and we have our eye on someone. And the murder may've had nothing to do with the Christmas market or the pickpocket. We'll apprehend the perpetrators. Please, don't worry, Delaney."

I blinked at him for a long moment. "Have you talked to that alpine guy at the *Christstollen* booth? He's the one who had an argument with Meredith, plus…" I hesitated for emphasis "…that's where Mom was picked."

"I did. He claimed he didn't know the victim. His wife gave him an alibi, said he was in the booth with her the whole time. He's not our killer," Ephraim said, dismissing the idea.

"Humpf." I rubbed my eyebrows to keep them from shooting to the top of my forehead. Wives lie for their husbands all the time on television crime shows. *Amiright?* "What if the killer put the poison in the wine days before she drank it? No one would have an alibi."

"We thought of that, but the brother told us only unopened bottles were taken to the booth. The contaminated bottle was from the tasting room, so it had to have been opened that morning." He added, "The sheriff's department has decided to cancel the ice sculpture contest."

My mouth dropped open. "Cancel the ice sculpture!" Ephraim nodded with pursed lips. "By the sheriff's department, you mean *you* decided? Right? It was *you* who decided this?"

He rested his hand on my shoulder. "I had a say in it, yes."

I took two steps back and his hand fell away. "How is cancelling the ice sculpture contest going to help anything? How's it going to help catch the killer?"

He whooshed out a steamy breath. "There were several reasons we called it off. We received the news that a couple of the big name artists were concerned about coming here. The artist who won last year withdrew. It seemed logical to vacate the contest, and it will assist with crowd control because it will keep the number of attendees down. It'll help the pickpocket situation, too."

"Are you going to call off any other events?"

His chin sank to his chest, and he stayed like that for a long moment. "Maybe. But I hope we'll have closed the case by the next event."

I paused to think. "The next one's the gingerbread house competition. It'd be a shame to scrap that, too, or anything else, Ephraim."

"We need to make the decision that's best for the community's safety." He touched my face and caressed my cheek with his thumb.

"You aren't going to close down the whole market, are you?" I asked in a pleading tone. My gaze drifted over to the nearest booth with candles and fancy soaps, then ran down the rest of the fairway, the booths all crowded with happy shoppers.

"We haven't ruled it out."

My stomach muscles squeezed tight. "Ephraim, you can't. Kristen has boxes and boxes of coffee mugs she's trying to sell. And all those ornaments, too." Moisture formed in my eyes, but the cold air wicked away my tears. Imprinting the year on the Roasters on the Ridge ornaments as well as the mugs was my idea. If she didn't sell them this year, they'd be surplus merchandise she would never be able to sell.

"Come here." He wrapped an arm around my shoulder. "Apprehending the killer is my first priority so the town council can put the homicide behind us and assure everyone the marketplace is safe."

I sagged against his coat, my eyes still pricking with stinging needles. How was I going to explain to my best friend her booth was in danger of being shut down if the murder wasn't solved fast?

I looked up. "We need to tell Kristen. I still have to collect my shopping, anyway. I left my bags with Kris."

"Okay. The vendors are going to receive an email blast first thing in the morning, so it doesn't matter if we tell her now. We can give her a heads-up if that would make you feel better." He rubbed the back of his neck, nudging his cowboy hat forward. There was a note of frustration in his voice, and I could understand that.

We walked head down into a cold breeze, my heels clip-clopping, to the coffee kiosk. A family was lined up at the counter, so while Kristen handed each of the children a hot chocolate, I nabbed my bags of merchandise from the bottom shelf.

After doling out the last drink, Kris said, "Your parents just left with their grandkids, Ephraim." The looks on our faces must have told her we had bad news because she added, "What's wrong?"

Ephraim said, "The ice sculpture contest is cancelled."

She bounced glances between me and the sheriff and the rows of mugs that dominated the back wall. "I was hoping for a bigger crowd during the event tomorrow."

"I know you were." I stood a little taller. "But I have an idea. Give the other vendors coupons to pass out for twenty percent off a coffee drink in a souvenir mug. I bet sales would pick up then."

Her eyes narrowed, and she chewed on her lower lip. "I'll think about it."

There had been a moment like this before when Kristen first opened her coffeehouse. That was over a year ago. The monthly rent on the building was due, and she hadn't yet built up her loyal, daily customers, so her bank account was low. The only employees were Kristen and me. She didn't have the earnings to purchase the expensive triple-shot espresso maker or the bean roaster that now graced her shop. It was touch and go whether the café would be a success. And here she was again, back in the same risky situation. And I was the one who suggested the customized mugs and ornaments. Maybe she shouldn't listen to any more of my advice.

"Delaney, we're taking pictures at the ice rink tomorrow morning. Axle's on board finally. So, plan on being there." Kristen turned her back to us. "I have to get back to work." She went silent as she began to scour the industrial-sized coffee pot.

It was my turn to fall silent. There was nothing I could say to make anything better.

****

I arrived the next morning before anyone else. Axle told me he'd catch his own ride, so I had a few minutes to myself. I held my phone in my hand with the timer on and walked briskly from the mulled wine stand to the Christmas tree lot, dodging wooden Santa and Rudolph figures, plus giant, plastic snowmen, then I walked back again, this time more slowly. I added to my time line the note: *it would've taken Meredith seven to ten minutes to walk from her booth to where we found her.*

When I looked up, Belle swished past me, and I caught the end of her Santa cap with a light tug. "Belle? Belle Quigley?"

She turned with a smile as her hand went to straighten her cap. "Yes. How can I help you?"

"I just thought I'd say hello. I sometimes work with Kristen Guttenberg at the coffee kiosk."

"Sure, I remember you. We met at the wine booth." She lifted her clipboard. "We're going to need more mulled wine booths next year. Signing up only one was a mistake. It's not enough." She inhaled a deep breath as her gaze took in the fairgrounds, then her eyes found their way back to me. "What did you say your name was?"

"Delaney Morran."

"That's right." She sucked in a breath. "Jack Frier told me you've been chasing him down."

"*Whaaa?*" Did I hear that right? That muscley maintenance man thought I was after him?

"He's taken, honey. Don't get your heart broken." She pivoted away. "Call me if you need anything. I'm here for you."

Before I could defend myself, she was already gone. No offense to maintenance men the world over, but I could do better than that. I was with the sheriff. The cowboy Casanova. He's my b-b-boyfriend.

What's with that Jack? Talk about conceit.

I was enveloped in the sound of "Silver Bells" as I made my way over to the ice rink, deserted this early in the day. The flat circle of ice sat in the center of the marketplace, which sat in the center of a wide valley surrounded by rising peaks that soaked in the morning sun. The sky was the bright cerulean blue only seen at altitude. The breeze ruffled my hair not yet wound into my usual braid. This was a pretty place for a picture.

Axle sidled up next to me. "Here I am."

"There you are." I tagged his arm.

He popped out his wireless earbuds. "Man, I don't want to do this."

"But Kristen said you were on board."

He snorted. "That's a hard no."

"What's the matter, you wuss? Can't you ice skate? Are you chicken? *Baak, baak.*" I gave him a flick to the ear.

He rubbed his ear between his fingers. "Good one. I haven't heard that since third grade."

"Come on, Kris will be disappointed if you don't do this." I plopped down at the curb to toe off my high heels. I shoved my feet into the skates I'd brought from home and pushed the men's speed skates, which we'd borrowed from Zach, toward Axle. "Get these on your feet, buster."

Axle popped his eyes wide like a teenager in a sulk. "Where is she? I'm not putting them on till she gets here."

"She's coming." I finished tying my laces and stood. "Kris is pretty depressed about the ice sculpting contest.

Just do this one thing for her without complaining, okay?"

"This sucks."

"Yeah, deal with it."

"I'll twist my ankle in these skates. I'll look like an idiot," he griped, his gaze darting around like he thought someone was watching.

"Oh, cue the music. Whine, whine, whine."

"I'm here!" Kristen sang out from the other side of the ice rink. She raced over to us and asked, "You ready?" Hope was clear in her voice.

First thing Axle said to his cousin was, "Do you really need me in this Kodak moment?" Kristen's face crumpled, and I glared at him as if to say *see what you've done?* He threw up his hands. "Y'oh-kay. Fine."

I applied lip balm while Axle rammed his feet into the men's skates. I zipped my jacket to my chin and threw my scarf over my shoulder. With the smile returned to her face, Kristen skated out onto the center of the ice, and I followed her. Axle wobbled over, his ankles both turned in.

I clapped a hand over my mouth, but "*Muahahaha!*" came out anyway.

Kristen took hold of one of his arms, and I took hold of the other. Between the two of us, we managed to position ourselves for the picture.

"Just try to keep your balance," I warned Axle.

Kris held up a selfie stick in her red-mittened hand and clicked the remote button. She retracted her camera and flicked through the images. "Let's try for some snaps at the railing." So we did that next.

After Kristen took half a dozen more shots, she showed us the pictures. In every image taken on the ice,

Axle's ankles were turned, and in the ones taken at the railing, he was holding tight to the bar, his face pinched in pain.

I beat my forehead with the heel of my hand, but Kristen put her head in her hands and giggled. She said, "I think I'm going to use these pictures."

"No way." Her cousin gave her a *yeah-right* look.

Kristen laughed so hard she needed to hang on to me. Then she pulled off her skates and tied them together, still chuckling. "Come by for coffees, you two." She set off for the coffee stand.

I cuffed my lil' cuz in the shoulder with a playful punch. "Thanks for making her laugh."

"It's not like that's what I was going for." He had his skates off before I did, so he waited for me to slip into my heels. "Do you think she's going to put one of those pictures on her Christmas cards?"

"Maybe." I straightened to a stand.

"Oh well, I don't really give a rap. No one I know will see them anyway."

I thought about that. "I'll make sure Shannon gets a card."

"Don't care."

"How's it going with her?"

He shrugged, but the tips of his ears not covered by his beanie turned red. "As if I'd tell you."

"Dude, that is so cold. I'm so crushed."

"And I care, why?" Again with the shrug.

"Okay, fine."

Soooo, Shannon must like him back. They must be hitting it off.

Yeah, I can't explain it either.

Chapter 8

My cell phone rang, and I answered to a customer needing a tow from a service road in the state forest. After the customer assured me the vehicle was not a heavy-duty truck and all four wheels were on the ground, I inserted my feet in my snow boots—not heels this time—my arms in my puffy coat, and my hands in my mittens. I'd already dropped Axle at work and picked up my truck, so I was ready.

I turned off the main thoroughfare onto a dirt road only discernible from tire tracks in the snow. A sign indicated the area was off-limits unless you had a permit for tree cutting. Each Christmas, the Forest Service issued a limited number of permits in order to thin the pines for new growth. I entered into the virgin forest with towering mountain peaks covered in white. Gentle snowflakes hit my windshield and quickly melted.

A fresh-cut blue spruce rested on the roof of a Honda Odyssey minivan, front-wheel drive, lodged in a snow bank, and a family of five stomped around in the snow. Two of the children threw snowballs at each other.

I rolled down the driver's side window, and the almost-edible aroma of woodsmoke and wet pine needles scented my cab while the frigid air stung my cheeks. "Looks like you're stuck in that drift?"

The dad answered, "Yeah. We tried rocking the van, but the wheels kept spinning out. No one else has come along to help, so I called you."

The mom added with a broad smile, "We're so glad you came." Busy playing, the kids didn't seem to care.

What a contrast to the last vehicle I extracted from a snow bank. This was the kind of tow I liked. This is what kept me in the business.

"Everyone stand back, please." I reversed up to the front end, while Mom gathered her brood off to the side. I hit the button…*presto, changeo*…the miracle claws swooped down with that metallic groan and the boom lifted the front of the van into the air. I snapped the gearshift into drive and punched the gas, but the dad waved frantically for me to stop. I leaned my head and shoulders out the window. "Yes?"

"Before you move the van, can you take a picture?" He passed me his phone and gestured to his family to get in closer.

I climbed out of the cab, glad for my snow boots, and snapped some photos. The scene was somehow festive and *Christmas-y*, with the family all bundled up in matching red and black plaid scarves, the green van on the back of my red truck, the tree strapped to the roof, the snow falling…all included with the winter mountain scene in the background.

"Stay right there, I'd like to take some pictures, too." I handed Dad his phone and captured a few images on my cell.

Mom laughed, tipping her head back. "Look, everybody! Look at this! There's a deer in the photos. I'm going to use these for our Christmas card. It's perfect." Her voice sounded elated.

Dad pressed a straight hand to his forehead over his eyes and peered into the pine trees. "Here we were stranded, but it all worked out. As luck would have it, we got the perfect picture." The rest of us gazed into the forest, but the deer had already vanished. Pine branches creaked as globs of snow fell to join the snow on the ground.

I asked, catching the excitement, "Can I post the photo on my website?"

The whole family laughed, even the kids. Dad said, "Yes," and the little girl said, "That'd be cool," and Mom nodded.

I motioned for them to stand to the side one more time, then hitched myself back into my truck cab. Foot to the pedal, I pressed gently, then harder. The van remained cemented to the spot for a couple of beats before the truck lurched forward and the van escaped from the pile of snow. The kids whooped and cheered while I lowered the car and retracted the claws.

I stuck around for a minute to make sure the van's engine fired up and the vehicle moved forward onto the gravel road, then I started to go ahead of them, but the Dad stopped me. "Wait, what do I owe you?"

"Nothing. Merry Christmas!" I started to take my foot off the brake.

Mom yelled, "Not on your life. You saved us from freezing out here and you took our Christmas photo." She nudged her husband, "Clark, pay the woman." He stepped up to my cab to hand me a credit card.

I charged my minimum rate and gave the card back. "Thanks."

"Merry Christmas!" they all shouted when I took off.

Singing to Christmas carols on the radio, I wondered if Kristen had considered cutting down a tree. It'd make a perfect photo op, but I'd told Ephraim I'd pick out a tree with him…even if I wasn't feeling the vibe. Maybe that feeling was coming back.

Before another call came in for a tow, I might as well stop at Kristen's booth to check on her, and I could also ask about cutting down a tree for her picture. I could do both, cut down a tree with Kristen and pick out a tree from the market with Ephraim.

Her boyfriend, Officer Zach Bowers, and one of her regular customers, Rory Rearden, were perched on stools in front of the coffee kiosk with drinks in hand. The three of them listened to my story about the stranded—but happy—family.

Once Kristen heard my suggestion, she said, "Not a good idea."

"Why not?"

"Because we'll never get Axle to go."

Yes, that's what I thought, too. "But other than that?"

"We either do this without him, use one of the photos we've already taken, or think of something else Axle would agree to do."

"Fat chance."

"I suppose." She shot a glance at Zach, and her boyfriend acquiesced with a shrug.

She asked her other customer, "What do you think, Rory?" He usually had a lot to say.

He hunched forward, resting his arms on his knees. "Take a picture of just the two of you. You could take it here at the coffee booth, or on the pathway with a row of lighted booths behind you, or just about anywhere. The whole market is pretty. Right? Am I right about that?"

He was right, but Kristen and Axle and I were a

three-member team. I hated to leave my lil' cuz out. "Did you decide not to use the photos at the ice skating rink?" I asked Kristen.

"Yeah, I can't do that to Axle. He looks pretty ridiculous." She shook her head. "So, I'm not using those."

Rory swallowed the last of his coffee and pushed off his stool. "Well, I should be getting back to work. Gotta work for a living, you know. So, I'll see you all later."

"Wait, Rory." I grabbed his sleeve. "I heard from the sheriff that you knew the murder victim, Meredith Yarborough. You never told me that."

His gaze skirted around. "Okay. I knew her, sort of."

"Why didn't you say anything?"

"I didn't know her that well. Not well at all. We weren't close or anything. No, we weren't *that* close."

I held up a finger like *hold-on-a-sec*. "You were close! Her brother said you all grew up together."

"Just a minute, Delaney." Zach rapped on the counter, and we all turned to focus on him. "You're not investigating, are you?"

I stared at Kristen for some support, but she was studying her nails. *Jeez*, I was doing this to help her out by preventing the market from being shut down. But Zach was important to her, and as a police officer, he didn't want me investigating. Rory gave me a wide-eyed gaze as if waiting for my answer, and Zach's eyes drilled into me as if he already knew the answer.

I said, "I'm not actually investigating." As if anyone would believe that.

"You aren't?" Zach raised one eyebrow.

"I would never." I totally would. "It's just that Ephraim mentioned to me that Rory knew the victim, that's all." I threw Rory a hurt once-over. "And I was surprised my buddy here hadn't told me about it."

"Nothing to tell. Nothing to it at all," he said without looking directly at my face.

It felt like a lie, and I eyed him with suspicion. "If you didn't know the sister that well, how about the brother? Did you or did you not hang out with Noel when you were kids?"

He expelled a long breath with a puff of steam and seemed to relax a bit. "Yeah, but I don't see Noel much anymore. He's been real busy ever since his parents retired and started traveling. He's never available, so like I said, I haven't seen him much lately."

"What do you know about the winery?"

"Only that his folks split the business between Noel and Merry, but Noel was doing most of the work."

"But he preferred it that way. Noel wanted to be the one in charge. He said Merry wanted to change things, and he didn't want to." I waggled a finger in the air. "And just think, he doesn't have to worry about that now his sister's dead. Now Noel gets to control it all." I sneaked a peek at Zach to find him rolling his eyes.

Rory shrugged. "That's true, I suppose, but Noel was in Palisade when Merry died. He has an alibi, he told me."

"I hope you have an alibi, Rory." Blunt, but I was trying to needle him into giving me more info.

His head snapped up. "Why would I need one?"

"Because you knew her. About that alibi?"

He sputtered, "I, I was home by myself, then I drove alone across town. I have no proof that I wasn't anywhere near the market. But I wasn't. Near the market, that is. I arrived after the fact. That's when I spotted

Merry going into the ambulance, and I gave Ephraim her name."

I chewed the inside of my cheek, reminding myself he is a friend of mine and friends give each other the benefit of the doubt. So, I let it go. For now.

"Sorry, Rory. I didn't mean to sound accusatory."

Zach asked, "How are your parents, Delaney?" effectively changing the subject. "Did your mom recover from her ordeal with the pickpocket?"

"Sure, she's a tough one."

Note to self: Call Mom and find out how she's really doing.

Kristen asked Zach, "Any progress on catching that pickpocket? Some of my customers have mentioned they got picked, too."

The officer swiped his head side to side. "We haven't apprehended anyone."

Christmas music from the hidden PA system filled the empty moment. "Carol of the Bells."

Rory said to Kris, "Thanks for the coffee. I'm off for real this time." He pulled on a pair of leather gloves, then shoved his hands in his pockets.

I asked my friend, "Do you need a break, Kris? I'm here if you do."

"Axle stopped by to watch the counter ten minutes ago, but thanks for checking. I appreciate it."

"Then I'm leaving, too." I jumped from the counter stool and buttoned my jacket against the cold. I said, "Wait for me," hurrying to catch Rory.

He stopped suddenly, and I almost barreled into him. "Yes?"

"I really am sorry, Rory. Are we okay?"

He gave me his lopsided grin. "We're cool."

"I'm curious about the Yarboroughs' wine tasting room. Go with me?" I blew on my hands while he gave me an up-and-down look. "Come on. There's something you're not telling me," I teased. "If you won't spill the beans, you can at least go with me and help me find out things on my own. Do you really need to get to work this minute?"

He extended an elbow, and I tucked my hand under his arm. "All right, Delaney. I can go with you." There were several scooters on the corner. "You want to take one of these?"

"No!" I shuddered. "The last time I rode one, I just about froze."

"Okay. My car's only a few blocks from here."

I walked with him to his older model Lincoln Aviator, rear-wheel drive, and we climbed inside.

The building on the corner of Tall Chief Road and Bald Eagle Way had housed a gas station before the winery took over the space. The garage doors were designed to be rolled up during warmer temperatures, but they were pulled all the way down today, with condensation obscuring the glass. Rory parked nose-in and asked, "Are they even open?"

Noel's Santa Fe, front-wheel drive, was parked to the side. "Noel's here, so they're probably open." I scrambled out of my seat, and we walked to the front.

Rory caught hold of the tasting room door, and it swung free.

"See, not locked," I pointed out.

He shrugged, and I gave him a thumbs up.

"I'll be right out," a man called from the back. A half-a-mo later, Noel strode out from around a corner. "Hello, Rory. Good to see you." His eyes flicked to me.

"And you, too, uh…"

"Delaney Morran. I drive the red tow truck. I helped you in your booth the other day." I speared him with an *I-don't-believe-this* look.

"Yeah, yeah, I remember you." He set two empty wineglasses on the counter. "What would you like to sample?"

Rory asked Noel, "What bottles do you have open?"

While Noel and Rory discussed wines, I stored my purse on the floor under my chair and let my gaze wander around the room. Many of the items on display were the same as what was in the mulled wine booth: bottle openers, bottle stoppers, and wineglass charms. Ephraim wasn't really a wine drinker. He preferred beer to wine, so no gift ideas jumped off the shelves onto my Christmas list.

Noel said, "The sheriff told me I could open the booth tonight. I'm going to close up here and go over there in a little while." He filled the bottom of our glasses and plonked a bowl of pretzel sticks in front of us.

"That's great. Good news." Rory lifted his glass to his lips.

"Yes, it sure is."

"How are you managing both places?" I asked, honestly wanting to know. I took a swallow of the red.

"The tasting room here will be closed when I'm at the market." Noel turned to Rory. "Do you know anything about the guy Merry was seeing?"

What? This was news. News to me. Merry had a boyfriend. I stuffed a pretzel in my mouth and chewed the heck out of the hard stick, spellbound.

Rory placed his wineglass down. "No. She never told me about a boyfriend, and I was going to ask you the same question. I wondered, too. I thought she was probably seeing someone."

"She was, but I don't know who. Why was Merry keeping that a secret?" Noel raised an eyebrow.

Rory said, "Good question. So, you didn't know him either. She didn't tell her own brother. That's weird, huh?" He glanced my way as if to ask, *are you paying attention?*

"The police asked me over and over about a boyfriend. They don't believe me when I tell them I don't know who he was." Noel let out a string of cuss words. "They've had me in for questioning three times now."

I spoke up. "They're just doing their job."

Rory patted his friend's elbow. "Hey, I'll take a couple bottles of that merlot." He indicated the red from the first sample. "It's always been my favorite. I like all your varieties, but that one's the best. I really like that one," he rattled on in his usual way.

After Rory paid for his wine, I grabbed my purse, and we stepped out of the tasting room into the frigid air. It was cold enough I could see my breath, as if it might snow again. "Thanks for helping with the intel. Why didn't you tell me she had a boyfriend?"

"I didn't know for sure. And I don't know who he was."

"You really don't know?"

"Sorry, I don't. Turns out Noel doesn't, either. Not much to go on, I suppose." He unlocked his Aviator with his fob.

"It's more than I had before. Can you drop me back at my truck, Rory?"

"Sure, I can do that." He held open the passenger

door as I got in.

Five minutes later I was back in the cab of my tow truck. First, I updated my investigation notes. Second, I stared at my phone to figure out if there was anyone else to question. There was not. Third thing then, I checked messages, but there weren't any of those, either, although winter weather usually brought in more calls for tows.

I threw my phone down, rode Main to First, then cut across Front Street, and six blocks later entered I-70. The highway took me across the divide where I turned around and came back. Then I repeated the route a couple of times. No one had stalled their vehicles and no one had trouble navigating the pass—uncommon for this time of year.

Well, I'd made an attempt. I was done for the day.

So, I called Ephraim since he'd be off work by now. It didn't take any convincing for him to agree to get together.

After he picked me up, he said, "Zach told me he ran into you and Rory Rearden. Did your friend give you any information?"

I gave him a head shake as I buckled my seatbelt. Small town. No secrets. Of course, Zach would let the sheriff know about our conversation. "He probably told you Rory and I left together."

Ephraim nodded. "You found out something?"

"Of course I did." I grinned.

"Go on."

I wanted to give him a hard time but checked myself. We had the same goal here. "We went to the tasting room and talked to Noel. I found out Meredith was dating someone, but neither Noel nor Rory knew who he was."

I gave him an excited smile. "A mystery man. How about that?"

His lips thinned. "Nobody seems to know the identity of the boyfriend."

Okay, so he knew about the boyfriend already, but he didn't have a name. Just like I didn't. "You probably have other leads, though?"

"Not really."

I raised a brow. "That's all you've got?"

Ephraim stared forward, idling his truck at a traffic light. He wore his cop face again.

Alarm bells went off in my mind, and a flush crept up my neck and face. The sheriff pumped me for information but would not reciprocate. Was he using me? "Did you only tell me that Rory Rearden and the Yarboroughs were childhood friends so I would ask him about it? Did you trick me into doing your interrogation for you?"

He whipped his gaze toward me, surprise registering on his face. "Didn't you want me to tell you that Rory and the victim were friends?"

"Yes, but you fed me information with the intent that I would act on it. I don't want to wonder if you have a hidden agenda every time you tell me something. I want us to be honest with each other and not play games."

His eyebrows drew together. "I wouldn't ask you to question a witness. I can't ask you to participate in the investigation. Besides, you would've asked around anyway, I didn't need to manipulate you."

"But you knew I would question Rory. So what's the difference?"

He smiled and his dimples showed. "You're right. I

did know you'd dig deeper. You're a stubborn redhead. But, Delaney, if I think it will be dangerous for you, I won't pass you any info."

I gave him my best *what-the-hell* glare. "That blows."

He reached across the gearshift to place his beefy hand on mine. "I can't have you walk into a risky situation like you've done before." There it was, the lecture I expected, the sermon I'd just gotten from Zach warning me to keep out of trouble...but the way the sheriff looked out for me was one of the many things I liked about him, not just his good looks and the fact he made me warm all over.

And then he said, "Don't you know you've stolen my heart, *mi amor*."

I flushed with pleasure. What a great holiday in the making. It's wonderful to be in a relationship at this time of year.

"So, you'll be careful."

"All right," I said on a sigh. I couldn't expect anything less from the sheriff. He was willing to discuss the case with me and that was progress. "Noel mentioned he's opening the mulled wine booth tonight, so that sounds like the *Christkindl Market* isn't going to be shut down."

"We had no reason to keep Yarborough's booth closed once we processed the scene. He had every right to open as long as all the other booths are open. But that might change. We haven't found the source of the poison yet, you see. It was in the wine, but how did it get there? Where was it purchased? Until we can pin down those facts, there is always the possibility the market may need to be shut down. We have to make sure everyone's safe, you know that."

"Yeah." I guess Kristen still had that to stress about. And me, too, on her behalf.

"But the gingerbread competition is going forward tonight." The light still red, he took his hands off the wheel and removed his cowboy hat to run a hand through his hair.

"I'm glad." Wrinkles creased the corners of his eyes, so I asked, "How are you doing? You're all worried about me, but what about you? I have a feeling you're not getting much rest."

The light turned green, so he took hold of the wheel and cruised through the intersection. "I'm fine but hungry. How about pizza for dinner?"

"Pizza would be good." I was starved.

We grabbed a pizza at the pizza place and headed to my apartment. Boss appreciated a slice of his own while we ate at the counter. Ephraim didn't stay long, explaining he had to get back to the precinct to work on reports.

I closed the door behind him. I couldn't count on him to tell me much more, but the one thing he didn't say, what I heard loud and clear, was that he would not keep me from investigating on my own.

He had not given me the entire quit-investigating speech.

So, green light it is.

Chapter 9

A half-hour later, I opened my apartment door to Kristen. She asked, "Can you help me?"

I motioned her in. "Sure. What do you need?"

She hesitated at the threshold. "It's a big favor."

"Oh, stop." I made a flapping motion with one hand. Normally Kristen was the one who jumped in to help others, the one who never said no when asked for a favor, even if it meant sacrificing her own well-being. She volunteered at the women's shelter, hired transients in the coffee shop, and helped out at her church. Kris was the most giving person I knew. Whatever favor she asked I would try to accommodate. And she probably wouldn't ask for much.

Her eyebrows squished together in a worried look. "I have to work on inventory at the store. Can you take over the booth from Sierra? She's there now, but her shift is about to end. The rest of the staff aren't available, and I can't ask Axle because he doesn't know how to close by himself. And the gingerbread house competition is tonight." Her shoulders drooped, and she looked worn out.

"No problem. Of course I can do it. I can head over now." I'd been loading my dishwasher, so I dried my hands on a towel and replaced it on the rack.

She squeezed the back of her neck. "Really? Are you sure? Cause maybe I can do both…"

"Slap yourself!" I pushed her out the door. "This is a little thing. Go…and don't worry about the kiosk. I'll have everything under control."

"Wait, you need the key to lock up." She pulled a keyring out of her jeans pocket but paused before handing it to me. "You're sure?"

I just gave her a look, like *you've got to be kidding*. You'd think I didn't know how to pull a shot or create latte art. I'd worked almost a full year as a barista for Kristen when she first started up her business. I only left the coffee shop after I'd inherited my dad's tow truck. I could do this!

"I totally trust you, but I don't want to impose."

"This is nothing," I insisted. She gave me a smile of thanks along with the key and went back inside her apartment with a little more perkiness in her steps. "Don't worry about a thing," I called after her. I threw the key up in the air and caught it.

I twisted my hair into a long braid, pulled on a clean pair of jeans and a bulky sweater, and stuffed my feet into warm, lined boots. I patted Boss on the head and told him to be a good boy, then went for the door but returned for a pair of fingerless gloves and a warm scarf. The kiosk had a space heater, but the open hatch would expose me to the cold night air.

I dialed up Axle, and he answered with a grunt. I asked, "Where are you?"

"I caught a scooter to the market." He couldn't keep away just like everyone else in town.

"I'm on my way over there now. I'm manning the coffee booth tonight, so stop by and see me, okay? I'll train you in closing."

"Yeah, fine. Whatever." He hung up.

Since Ephraim had driven me home, I was without my truck or Fiat. I'd left both my vehicles at Oberly Motors. I had no choice but to take one of the frickin' scooters, too, and luckily there was one parked outside Roasters on the Ridge. My face and fingers were frozen by the time I glided into the fairgrounds. After Sierra took off, I made myself a steaming hot double espresso, then sat and drank it with my palms hovering over the space heater.

Because the hot chocolate was running low, I placed pieces of milk chocolate bars in a large saucepan, added organic whole milk and creamer, turned on the hot plate, and whisked until everything was well blended, which only took a couple of minutes. Customers soon lined up requiring hot drinks. For the hot chocolate orders, I stirred in cinnamon and topped the mugs with homemade whipped cream. For the lattes, I pulled the shots of espresso and frothed the milk. Kristen's commemorative mugs were moving fast and for that I was thankful. The customers gushed about the gingerbread houses, and I made up my mind to check out the winning entries.

While continuing to fill orders, I stared across the aisle at the mulled wine booth where Noel was doing a brisk business, too. The Festival Queen hung around Noel's booth most of the night. She was wearing the crown that fitted over her halo of golden hair along with the Queen sash. A bit much, *dontcha* think? Playing the princess role to the max? But maybe the ambassador of the festival was trying to help draw customers to the mulled wine booth, and if so, she was doing a great job. The queue was long but moved at a fast pace.

After a while, the queen left, so during a break in customers, I poured a hot chocolate and quick-stepped it over to Noel. "Hello again. This is for you."

"Oh man, thanks." He took a sip. "That hits the spot. You want a mulled wine?"

"Sure, why not? *Swapsies*." I grabbed the mug when he handed it to me. "You're glad to be open, I'll bet?"

"Yes. I can see we're both doing a damn good trade tonight."

I flicked a glance at the coffee booth, but it remained free of customers. "I'm having a lull right now, but it was busy earlier because of the gingerbread competition."

"Yes, that drew a crowd."

"Kristen is doing inventory at her store tonight. That's why I'm here." I took a long draw of my hot drink, which warmed my stomach and sent a tingling sensation to my toes.

"I know how hard it is to keep up with inventory. I had to bring in new supplies, as you know, even the food."

Replacing the esculent items seemed wasteful, but the police had to be thorough. They couldn't take a chance anything else had been contaminated. I asked, "The poison was in the wine, not the food, though? Right? That's what I heard."

He bobbed his head in agreement. "The police tested everything but only found the one empty bottle with traces of poison, and it was in the trash."

Interesting fact. But where did it get me? I eyed an open bottle near Noel's elbow. "You know it was some kind of poison that's illegal now?" He inclined his head, so I asked, "How did that poison get into the bottle, do you think?"

"Anyone could've slipped it in when Merry wasn't looking. I suppose I should move this." He stashed the open bottle under the counter.

I glanced at Kristen's booth, but still no one waited there. I had a couple more moments to spare. "How did Merry end up drinking the wine instead of a customer? Maybe she wasn't the intended victim?"

"Good questions, ones I don't know the answers to." He said, looking past me, "May I help you?"

A group of young people jostled up next to me, laughing and being loud, so I said goodbye and hoofed it back to the coffee kiosk. Wondering what was keeping Axle, I texted him as I stirred the pot of chocolate.

—*On my way* was his reply.

I watched out the open hatch for him to arrive, with the chilly wind blowing in, then spotted him several yards away. He handed a man a small box, and the man handed Axle some money. I did a facepalm. Axle was selling stolen goods! I yelled, "Oh come on," but he was too far away to hear me.

When he finally showed up, I socked his arm, hard. "You're selling the earbuds. What's wrong with you?"

He jumped around to avoid another punch. "Chill out. People scalp stuff all the time."

"Are you kidding me?" I gave him a *don't be stupid* look.

"You may not know this 'cause you're clueless, but this is the kinda crap sold all the time at the flea market." He rubbed his arm where I'd poked him.

"That doesn't make it right." I gritted my teeth. "What if Ephraim shows up? Or Zach?"

Axle's eyes got big, and I'm sure mine did too. He said, "I'm outta here," and headed off at a trot. I felt like catching up to him, tearing his knit cap off, and beating him senseless with it. Not only was he doing something dodgy, but he'd also ditched me.

Allrighty then. I had to close the booth on my own. It was just like closing the store, only on a smaller scale, and I'd done that many times.

The gingerbread crowd had disappeared, and most fairgoers were headed for home. I counted down the minutes by changing my phone's screensaver photo to the famous designer shoes with red soles. Then I remembered the kiddie spy kit I bought at the Emporium and extracted the toy scope from my purse. Incredibly, I could see down the fairway all the way to the *Christstollen* booth.

The alpine man who'd yelled at me in German was in the very back, unwrapping merchandise. He was peeling stickers off the bottom of Santa figurines. I twisted the viewfinder to a sharper focus. The stickers read, *Made in China.*

That impostor! That charlatan!

And I'd purchased Santa gnomes from him, one for Byron and one for me. I'd thought they were made in Germany. Made in Germany by way of China, I guess.

This scope was incredible. I wondered where it was made.

After that, I stared at the clock. When the minute hand swept past the hour, I ran vinegar water through the coffee machines, dumped the small amount of remaining hot chocolate into a to-go cup—one last customer might stop by for a drink—then wiped down the counter and washed all the dishes. I swept the floor. I stuffed the cash in a deposit bag and forwarded Kristen the report from her point-of-sale checkout system. Then I texted Ephraim to ask if he was done with his paperwork and if he could give me a lift home, the second one that day. He texted back that he had a few more things to do, then would head over.

The lights all over the grounds blinked off as I locked up.

Jack Frier, the full-of-himself maintenance man, without a coat over his tight shirt and bib overalls, trundled his golf cart over to the trash cans. I was not about to run after him this time—no way—but he seemed to wait while I walked over.

"Here, Jack, would you like a hot chocolate?"

"Sure, thanks." He removed his work gloves before grabbing hold of the to-go cup.

He was *so* going to take this the wrong way, so I had to nip it in the bud.

"I only wanted to know the other day," I gave him a stiff smile, "about the woman in the mulled wine booth because I'm trying to help the wine vendor."

"Why do you want to help them out?"

"It's the right thing to do. We all want the market to be a success, don't we?" I pointed toward the closed-up wine kiosk. "You bought a mug of wine from her."

"Right, right. You asked me about that already. You want to know if she asked me on a date or something? You're curious about me, aren't you?" A know-it-all grin broke out on his face.

OMG. He thinks he's God's gift. Total bullshit alert. I practically yelled, "Gack, no," then tried to turn my words into a pretend cough. "Gack, gack."

"Well, she didn't. She said she felt sick." He smoothed the shock of hair over his forehead.

"Really? She said that? Did she say anything else?"

"That's all I remember."

"What time did you get your mulled wine?"

"Little after noon, I guess." He drained the rest of his hot chocolate in one gulp.

"Were any other customers there?"

"Nobody but me. She had me all to herself." He gave me a wink, crunched his empty paper cup into a ball, and made a basket into the trash. Then he made a sound like a crowd cheering.

I blew out a sigh and could see my breath in a puffy white cloud of steam. "All right. Well, Merry Christmas," I said, taking backward steps.

Cold crept through my jacket and mittens as I meandered past the other vendors finishing up for the day. They pulled their shutters closed, bid goodnight to each other, and locked up their stalls. The fire pit near the giant Christmas tree was no longer burning; now it was a dark spot with no one around. I stopped at Santa's sleigh filled with empty wrapped gift boxes and craned my neck to see if Jack Frier was still at the recycle bins. He'd vanished once again, probably afraid I'd try to trap him.

He'd given me a clue, though. Meredith complained to Jack about being sick. So, she'd already been poisoned when he purchased his mulled wine. Or was he lying about that? He could be the poisoner. He could be trying to throw me off his scent. He had the opportunity, but what about motive? There didn't appear to be one unless he was a random murderer who got off on killing people. If so, nobody was safe, but rat poison seemed an unlikely weapon for a mass murderer.

Note to self: Research serial killers to see if any used poison, like rat poison.

I tightened the scarf around my neck and kept going. I came across the Emporium, where a dim light illuminated the interior. The man stood at the cash register, and the woman wheeled in wire racks of postcards.

The man hailed me. "Hey, I have your earbuds."

"You still open?"

"Sure, let me grab them for you." He ducked below the counter.

I held out my hand to the woman. "I'm Delaney Morran. I help out at the espresso booth, Roasters on the Ridge."

She extended her gloved fingers to shake mine. "I'm Holly Jennings, and that's my husband, Frank."

"Good to meet you, Holly."

It is believed that opposites attract, which must be the case here, he in his crisp crewneck sweater and styled hair, her in a stretched-out sweater and messy-bun hair. They were about twenty years older than me, I'd guess, and as different from each other as Costa Rica and Arabica coffee beans. But they argued like a married couple, as they say, although I hoped all marriages weren't like that. I didn't want to fight all the time when I got married.

"Are you locals?" Not having grown up here, I didn't know everyone in town like the townies did.

Holly said, "No, we came up from Denver. We have space at the Denver Flea Market and this is the first year we've had a booth at the *Christkindl Market*." Her gaze ran over the goods on display in a proud way, and when her husband's head surfaced from behind the counter, her eyes lit up. *Awww.* Her face told a story. There was love in the marriage, at least on Holly's part. The mean husband had on an irritated look, but who knew? There might be love there, too, hidden beneath the scowl.

Frank set a box on the ledge. "Here's the earbuds I held back for you."

I let the straps of my purse slide down my shoulder to the crook of my arm and reached inside for my wallet. "Fifty dollars?"

"That's right."

I gave him my debit card, silently thanking the stranded family for insisting on paying me earlier. I hoped their green van made it home and they were enjoying their fresh-cut Christmas tree. When Frank passed back my plastic, he handed me the box, which I stuffed in my purse. Holly attempted to shove her arms into her winter coat, reaching behind to find the sleeve, and I caught her collar to lift the opening up for her. Frank was busy getting into his own jacket and pulling on his gloves. For once, no music sounded from the speakers, having been shut off when the market closed. The night breeze blew cold, and the chill burrowed further under my coat.

Frank led the way as Holly and I followed him to a path behind the Christmas tree lot where the gravel was littered with cigarette butts and dead, frozen weeds. The market looked so pretty from the front, especially when lit up with the canopies of twinkling white lights and garlands. The backside was not so attractive, where boxes of supplies, generators, and extension cords were concealed out of sight. In this hidden space, a nearly deserted parking lot still sheltered a few vehicles.

I halted my steps. "I didn't know about this lot. Is this where the vendors park?"

Holly smoothed loose hair back up to her bun with both gloved hands. "Yes. Didn't anyone tell you?"

"I don't normally work here, I'm just filling in."

"Next time, park here like we do." Frank rested one hand on the door of a Dodge Ram, four-by-four.

The couple said goodnight and scrambled into their truck. I cut across the pavement and waited at the corner for Ephraim as the snow started up once more. Wind whipped around the intersection, bringing with it an icy blast. Cars swished past, and I sniffed and scraped my cold nose across my sleeve, watching taillights disappear. I stomped my feet and clapped my hands and hoped my face wasn't getting chapped.

Ephraim's truck careened around the corner and came to a stop in front of me. I lifted my tired bod into his cab and shoved the door closed with a thud.

"Before we take off, let me show you something." I dug out the box and slit the taped cardboard open with my fingernail. "I bought these wireless earbuds at one of the booths for fifty dollars. Axle said, er…I mean, I found out these sell for two hundred at the stores." The tiny bud took up little space in my palm.

Ephraim shifted his gear into park and plucked the earbud out of my hand.

"Do you think these are stolen goods?" I asked. "They're name brand. Look." I tilted the box to the side for him to read.

His shoulders rose and fell again. "Probably stolen."

I handed the box over to him with the other earbud still inside. "Here, you take them. You'll want to investigate, right?"

"Yes. If they're clean, I'll return them to you. If we keep them, the sheriff's department can reimburse your money."

"Good enough." It would be nice to get the fifty back.

"Where'd you buy them?" He was probably glad to have this tip-off.

"Jennings Christmas Emporium. They have a booth here in Spruce Ridge and space at the flea market in Denver. You won't mention I was the one who informed on them, I hope." I thought about Holly and her pride of ownership in her stall. And I felt kinda bad now.

"Well, did you get a receipt?"

"Ah, no." I flushed. I hadn't even thought to do that. "But I paid by credit card."

"Good, there's a paper trail. I might need your testimony, too."

Yikes. Was I going to have to turn State's evidence? Would Holly and Frank be sent to the big house? What a rat fink I am. Desiring with my whole heart to avoid confrontation, I felt my stomach churn like milk in a frother. And then it hit me; what about Axle? Would Axle get caught up in the sting, too? If I didn't breathe a word to the sheriff about my cuz, maybe everything would work out. Yes, everything would be fine if I kept Axle out of it. I rubbed my stomach with my palm and decided to keep telling myself that.

Ephraim eased his truck away from the curb. "We brought Rory Rearden back into the station for questioning."

"Really? Did he tell you anything more about Meredith's boyfriend?"

"A few things."

Darn. Rory was holding out on me. He was in a bad habit of not telling all. "And?"

He shook his head and stared at me deadpan.

"Come on." So, Ephraim was back to cop mode and remained as silent as a Tesla's engine.

I stuck my tongue out at him. "That's okay, big guy. I'll just find out for myself from Rory." I shook off my stocking cap and threw my braid over my shoulder.

He gave the end a tug, "I love your hair down, *mi amor*." His dimples made an appearance.

There was no way I could stay mad. "Thanks for picking me up. You're a lifesaver, Ephraim. I left my Fiat at Oberly Motors. Can you drop me off there?"

"Sure, then I need to get back to the station."

The sheriff's department was probably putting in overtime.

****

The next morning, Axle knocked on my bedroom door. "Delaney, you awake? Rory's here asking for you."

I hurtled out of bed and scrambled into the clothes I'd tossed onto a chair the night before. I went to the bathroom and splashed water on my face. When I opened my door, Axle handed me a cup of coffee, the black elixir that would magically transform me into a presentable person, I hoped. Axle might be obnoxious at times, but this morning he was *the man*.

"Good morning." Rory sat on a kitchen counter stool with a coffee in front of him.

"Morning," I said back at him. I ran my fingers through my tangled mess of hair. "What's up?"

"The sheriff took me into the station and questioned me for hours yesterday." He was visibly shaken as he told me this.

"Oh, yeah. I heard you were questioned." I pulled my hair back and twisted it into my usual plait that cascaded over one shoulder.

Rory asked, "How did you hear about that?"

"Ephraim told me. Let's go in the living room." I padded in my stocking feet over to the couch and claimed one corner. I drew my legs into my chest and wrapped my arms around my knees. "So, why the interrogation? What else do you know, Rory?" *Oh boy, oh boy*, I was about to find out what Ephraim knew and wouldn't tell me. *Ha!*

Rory sat on the couch across from me and clenched his fingers in his lap. "I don't know anything. I mean, not much. Really, nothing at all."

I speared him with a laser glare. Boss the Rottweiler jumped up next to me, rested his heavy weight against me, and licked my arm. He sensed that I was irritated.

A sheen of perspiration broke out on Rory's forehead. "I swear it's not that big of a deal. Really. But Merry and I dated once, a long time ago."

I didn't see that coming. "Get out!"

"We did, but it was nothing much. Although the police are making it sound like it's important. That's why I came over. I thought I'd better explain."

"Yes. Tell me everything." I twirled my fingers in a *get-on-with-it*.

"Our parents believed we'd get married one day." He barked out a laugh. "*As if.* I mean, can you imagine her name? Merry Rearden? Rory and Merry Rearden? Too many r's. It's too ridiculous to think about. It's crazy, am I right?"

"That's why you broke up?" I laughed, but his face tightened.

"No, but it would've been reason enough."

I shot a glance at Axle that said, *can-you-believe-this?*

Rory squirmed, wringing his hands. "Will you help

me? I know you've solved other murders. You've figured out this kinda shit before."

Axle put in, "This is some crazy shit."

I took in a deep breath. "Start at the beginning. When did you date?"

"Forever ago. At least five years ago. Uh, the last year of college and right after we graduated. We both realized we didn't want to be together anymore. It was no big deal. Not a big deal at all."

I clucked my tongue. "Why didn't you come clean right away? It must look suspicious to the police that you lied about how well you knew her."

"But it was so long ago and it wasn't a big deal." He made a small side-to-side movement with his head.

"Rory, don't you see, you have a motive?"

"That's why I'm asking you to help me." His freckles stood out darker in his pale face.

"What else is there? Come on, tell all." I got the impression there was more to the story. He'd hidden their history from the police and from me. Why would he do that?

He frowned and gazed all around. "Like what? There's nothing else. Nothing more to say."

I scrunched my forehead. He was making this hard. I hated pressuring my friend, but I needed to pin him down. "What was Merry like as a person? It would help to know more about her. You know, to determine a motive for somebody else." It was a place to start, and then maybe Rory would open up.

"She really wasn't a nice person, not a nice person at all." His shoulders slumped. "I feel bad saying it. Speaking ill of the dead."

"What do you mean, not nice? Give me an

example."

"Okay, well, she'd do stuff like tell Noel one thing and me another to pit us against each other. She'd laugh when Noel and I'd get into an argument. Yeah, one time when we were kids, she tore up Noel's comic book, one out of his collection, and said I did it. Then she told me Noel ripped it himself...stuff like that. She would tattle and get him in trouble with his parents. She said mean things. She seemed to get a kick out of hurting people. Especially Noel. She always seemed to get the better of him."

"I'm surprised you two even dated if she was so mean. What did you see in her?"

"She had a nice side, too. She could be a lot of fun. And I thought she'd gotten past that meanness. But she hadn't, I figured that much out."

"So, you did grow up together. You've known her a long time." I could understand why the police had interrogated him again.

"Her folks and my parents are old friends. Their vineyard is on the western slope, but our parents had gone to school together."

I pinched the bridge of my nose. "Is there anything else you haven't told me, Rory?"

His head fell on his chest as he studied the floor, and I let the silence hang in the air for a moment or two. Finally, he said, "Her new boyfriend, he was a married man. But I swear I don't know who he was. She never said. Never told me or anyone else as far as I know, but I believe he worked at the Christmas market."

"Why do you think that?" I urged him with a *go-on* look.

"Noel mentioned Merry said she would see her

boyfriend more often after she signed up for the *Christkindl Market*. He assumed that was because they would both be spending so much time there."

A married man. That was significant information. But it didn't knock the possibilities down by much. A large percentage of the male population is married.

"I should make some notes." I pushed myself off the couch and retrieved my suspect list and a pencil. Then I refreshed all our coffees and sat back down. "Let's chart this out." I wrote the heading, *clues*, and underneath that: *Affair with a married man. Not a nice person.*

After reading the words out loud, I asked Rory, "She didn't get along with her brother, is that right?"

"No, she didn't. Not really. I'd say not." He shook his head with force.

I drummed the pencil on the notepad. "Noel told me the poison was in a wine bottle found in the trash and that the bottle was probably out on the counter and anyone could have slipped something into it when Merry wasn't looking. If Merry added mulled spices, she may not have been able to taste the poison. That's a guess, anyway."

"Good guess, Delaney." Axle thumped my head with his knuckle. *Ouch.*

I held out my notes for both of them to read: *Friday, noon, wine booth opens and maintenance man buys mulled wine. She says she felt sick. Seven to ten minutes to walk to where body found. 1:35, body found, still warm.*

Then I asked, "Who did she see between nine and, say, noon? The maintenance man's name is Jack Frier, by the way."

Axle asked, "Could he have done it?"

"He's on my list only because he had opportunity.

But what's his motive?" I looked at them both, and they shrugged. "Could he be the married boyfriend? No, scratch that," I said, already dismissing the idea. He didn't seem the type to remove himself from circulation. Although Belle, the fair organizer, had said he was "taken," whatever that meant.

I said, "These are my other loose ends. There's a booth that sells stolen goods. There's a pickpocket at large. What if Meredith was involved in a stolen goods ring or the thefts? Or maybe she just knew about them. Or maybe she knew the identity of the guy doing the pickpocketing?"

Rory expelled a breath of air. "At least you don't think it was me. Any theory that points away from me is good. So, pickpockets and stolen goods, then?"

Axle held both hands in front of him. "No, no. Forget the stolen goods angle. No way. The death has nothing to do with stolen goods."

I did a brush-off flap of my hand. "Yes, yes. Either of those things could've gotten her killed."

After giving me resigned looks, neither Axle nor Rory offered anything more. Rory soon took off, and Axle disappeared into the nether regions of his bedroom.

As quiet descended, I let the suspects tumble around in my brain. Was there a connection between the murder and these other criminals? Or was the murderer her jealous brother? Her married lover? I took a moment to seriously consider all of them.

Talk about drama.

That last one was right out of a romance novel.

Chapter 10

Who would poison someone? Statistics prove women poison more than men. Everyone who's watched *Law and Order* knows this.

Poison involved a certain amount of suffering.

Poison implied revenge or hate.

I queried serial killers who used poison. You won't believe it, but yes, it's been done. Poison is a popular way to kill people. Some of the most prolific serial killers were poisoners. Who knew?

Then I found the winery's website and clicked through all the pages. The pictures did not include any family or employees, only the vines with the cliffs in the background. I couldn't find any other social media for Meredith or Noel.

Thinking about websites, I uploaded the photo I'd taken of my red tow truck with the green van lifted on the back and added it to my website. The Christmas tree on the van's roof and the ideal family in matching scarves appeared professional, like a paid advertisement.

I included the message, "Merry Christmas from Del's Towing!"

Kristen always promoted her coffee shop, something I had trouble doing with my towing business, but I felt good about this. It felt natural.

So, on a different subject, I searched for Shannon Oberly, Byron's niece and Axle's love interest.

Here's the thing...Axle, the little twerp, wasn't going to tell me anything about the two of them, and I was his roomie and all, so I figured I had a right to know. I checked Axle's page but there weren't any pictures of him and Shannon. I didn't care if I was *creeping* my lil' cuz online. I mean, come on. Everybody does it, right?

Just then, Axle walked into the kitchen, and I slammed my laptop shut. He poured himself a coffee and said, "I'm ready to leave."

I scrambled for something to say, hoping my warm cheeks could be blamed on the furnace kicking in. I managed to come up with, "We should take Boss out."

"Good idea."

We bundled up and led Boss over to the park. My boots made crunching sounds when breaking through the snow and leaving deep impressions. Axle threw a ball to Boss, and his dog caught it several times before stopping to smell yellow spots in the snow. *Eeew.*

"Hey, you two," Kristen hailed us from across the street, then sprinted over during a break in traffic. "This snow is so pretty," she said as she came closer. She ran a mittened hand over the park bench, causing the snow to fly.

A stream of cold flakes hit Axle's face. "Hey!" He swooped down and back up with a fist full of snow and flung it at his cousin.

Kristen held out a palm. "Stop, stop!"

"Scaredy cat." Axle laughed.

"No, I want you to stop so I can get pictures." Her smile was broad, and it dawned on us what she wanted. "Christmas photo time," she said in a sing-song voice.

"Okay, Axle?" I thought he might've given up on the whole idea.

He forced a tight smile. "Yeah, sure."

Kris left and came back with a tripod for her phone, then we started up our fight in earnest. Snowballs filled the air, and even Boss joined in, frisking around, trying to figure out what all the fuss was about.

Axle plastered me with an ice-packed slush bomb, which oozed down my collar and under the neck of my sweater. Gasping and breathing hard, I gulped some air. Not that I would ever admit I was winded. "Are we done here?" I called to Kristen.

"Let's see what we've got."

We positioned ourselves around the tripod to look at the pictures. Snow on the lens made watermarks on most of the images. The others showed our faces red with effort. But the best picture was Axle stuffing snow down my coat with me looking like I'm saying the *f* word.

Kristen pitched her hands in the air, exasperated. "You guys! Time's running out. I don't have many days left to get the cards out before Christmas."

"That's it. No more." Axle brushed the snow off his coat. "Let's go, Delaney. We need to jet. Byron actually has a job for me today."

I gave Kristen a *sorry-sorry* look as I let Boss tug me along after Axle. I wanted the perfect picture for the cards, too, but we needed to accept something less than perfect or it wasn't going to happen.

On the drive to the autobody shop, Axle gave me a smack to the shoulder. "Delaney, how's the snooping going?"

"Snooping?" I gave my lil' cuz a neck-jerking glance. Had he caught me snooping around for Shannon on social media? *Uh-oh.* I would've fallen off the driver's seat if I wasn't buckled in. "What do you mean?"

"Your murder investigation. What else, brainless?"

"Oh, that. Well," I said as I settled my hands lightly on the steering wheel, "I'm not getting very far."

Axle leaned back in his seat and propped one foot onto a knee. "You'll figure it out, you always do. Self-doubt, Delaney, it's self-doubt that'll put you in the kill zone."

I shot him another sidelong look. "Did you come up with that on your own?"

"Yup." He popped in his earbuds.

I couldn't help but smile as I brought my Fiat to a stop at the autobody shop, then waited while Axle climbed out and went into the first open bay.

My phone rang—it was Ephraim calling. He asked, "Are you busy? I have an errand to run. Can I come by and pick you up?"

"Sure. I'm at Oberly Motors."

He said he'd be there in ten minutes.

I touched up my makeup in the Fiat's rearview mirror, finger-combed my long waves, and reapplied my mauve lipstick. When Ephraim's black F250, rear-wheel drive, entered the parking lot, I locked the Fiat behind me and skipped over to him in my black high-heeled ankle boots with lace-ups.

I folded myself into his passenger seat. "Where are we going?"

"Denver."

"*Ooooh-kay*. Why Denver?" I locked my door with a press of the lever.

"Thought you'd like to do a little undercover work with me."

I stared at him in open-mouthed astonishment.

"Really?"

"I'm taking a run out to the flea market to see if any more of the earbuds are for sale." His smile showcased his dimples.

"What about the homicide investigation? Seems that should be a priority."

"I have to work on more than one case at a time. You know our department is small, and everyone's pretty busy. I thought I'd step away from the homicide for a few hours and handle this myself."

I nodded. "Did you check the Jennings' booth at the Christmas market?"

"They were sold out of the earbuds."

I stared through the window at the scene flashing by and wondered if Axle had bought them out again. I wedged the toes of my boots on the dash and said, "Rory told me Meredith's boyfriend was married." I threw him a *you-heard-me-right* look. "See, I found out about it all on my own."

He grunted a laugh. "I figured you would."

"Why'd you decide to question Rory again, anyway? Did you already know he'd been in a relationship with Meredith?" The police with all their resources would always be steps ahead of me.

"Yes. We learned from the victim's family that Rearden and the victim were more than just friends."

"Humpf." It was just as I thought. I pushed with my feet into the back of the seat. "So, Rory's a serious suspect?"

"You know I can't release that information."

But I'd figured it out on my own. Rory did need my help.

Ephraim accelerated up Floyd's Hill, then coasted

down the other side of the rise past the turnoff for Evergreen and the old Chart House Restaurant overlooking the interstate. Morning rush hour had come and gone and traffic was at a minimum, so we moved along at highway speed through Golden, into Lakewood, then Denver. But traffic slowed to a standstill at the exit for the flea market.

"Too bad I'm not in my sheriff's cruiser." Ephraim chuckled, his low voice rumbling. He bumped his cowboy hat farther back on his head.

"You don't have any of those portable flashing lights you see in the cop shows?" I teased.

"I do, but I don't have a valid reason to use them."

We finally made it off the highway and broke through the traffic congestion into the flea market. Ephraim parked at the outer edge of the enormous lot, and we hiked over to the nearest row of stalls.

When he laced his fingers in mine, I asked, "Am I part of your undercover disguise?"

He waggled both our hands. "You draw attention, not the other way around, *querida*."

My high-heeled boots clacked on the pavement as I kept up with his long strides. "How are we going to know which is the Jennings' booth?"

"Got a map right here of the booth locations." He extracted his phone and brought up the schematics on the screen. "Their spot is that way." He gestured to the south.

"Let's do this," I said.

He shepherded me down the walkway past folding tables topped with piles of blue jeans, power tools, luggage, and everything else you could think of. This giant flea market was overwhelming, with so much to look at, much more than the *Christkindl Market*, and more crowded, too. There was even a Ferris wheel. I guess I'm a small-town girl now, even though I grew up in Denver.

At the Jennings' space, tables sat in front of the opened back end of a trailer that was filled with merchandise. We strolled past the heaped tables and open-air racks of clothes and stepped into the trailer organized like a store with shelves and cabinets full of tchotchke. We both searched and gave each other questioning glances, but there were no earbuds.

Ephraim said, "Let's ask."

"Let me. He might guess you're a cop."

A mischievous smile crossed his face. "Are you saying I can't do undercover?"

Even though he was dressed as a cowboy, his jacket hinted at serious biceps, and his cop-bearing was straight-up obvious. "You said I could do the undercover work. I want to help."

The sheriff eye-balled the man working the cash register, then gave me a stiff nod.

While Ephraim pretended to check out paperweights, I strode over to the man and asked, "I'm looking for some wireless noise-cancelling earbuds. Do you have any?"

"No, I'm afraid we're all out of those." He flashed me a smile. "Can I help you find anything else?" There was unabashed interest in his eyes. You know what I'm talkin' about.

I twirled a strand of my hair and smiled back to conceal my nervousness. "Shoot, I was really hoping you had the buds. A friend of mine told me she got hers from you." I laughed in what I thought was a flirtatious way.

He leaned forward, his face earnest. "I'd like to help

you out. Why don't you give me your number? I can call you if we get any more in." He sidled closer, crowding my space.

"Uh…" I felt like a heel because I was considering it, but for a different reason than what he was thinking.

In an instant, Ephraim was beside me, hooking a possessive arm over my shoulder. "Are we done here?" Was he jealous? I got a rush.

I glanced back at the vendor, who seemed disappointed. I said, "Thanks for your help."

Once we were a few yards away, I elbowed Ephraim. "What'd you stop me for? He would've called me when they got another shipment of earbuds."

"Yeah, he would've called you all right, but not for earbuds." He swung me around to look at him, with his hands on my shoulders and his face inches above mine. "People who sell stolen goods get them from hijacked trucks. Sometimes they don't even know what's inside the trucks until they open them up. They probably won't get any more. Once they're gone, they're gone."

"Oh, I see."

"I knew that was a possibility, but still wanted to look over their other stuff. I didn't spot anything that appeared stolen. We'll need to apprehend them in the act, at their source, like with a hijacked truck, and that's beyond the scope of the Clear Creek Sheriff's Department." He pulled me into his chest and enveloped me in his arms. "And I can't involve you in this any further. Even if I thought there was a chance they'd receive more stolen goods, I don't want you in the middle." He rubbed his hands up and down my back, like I belonged to him now.

"All right, I guess." What else could I say? Maybe

he wasn't jealous, just protective.

"Is there anything else you want to look at here?" He released me, and I stumbled back a step in my high-heeled boots.

"No, I'm good." I needed to buy something for Ephraim. But not with him here. And not here.

The highway was smooth sailing all the way back to Spruce Ridge. Before long, Ephraim's truck came to an idle behind Oberly Motors. He said, "I need to fill out a report on our efforts today. Sorry I can't stay for a while. Thanks for your help."

"Thanks for taking me with you, showing me how undercover work is done. Or maybe I showed you." I scooted close and initiated a kiss. A kiss he returned that made my heart race like a double shot espresso. His hands got a little fast too, until I slapped them away. "How much time you got?"

"Not enough." He blew out a sigh.

I extracted myself from his truck and closed the passenger door shut. He buzzed out of the lot, then my phone rang, and I answered it. Tanner was on the other end. "You have time for a tow? Two calls came all at once. If you could take one of them that would help me out."

"Of course. This is good timing because I just got back from Denver."

"Oh, did you go see your parents?"

I beeped the fob to unlock my truck. "No, not this trip. Hey, give me the location and I'll let you go."

He told me a Toyota Corolla, front-wheel drive, was stalled at the corner of Main and Pine, blocking the busy intersection. I understood why the call was urgent with Tanner occupied on another tow, so I cranked the engine and sped off.

A man in a light jacket and no gloves sat shivering in his front seat while traffic inched around him one car at a time. I felt the man's pain. I mean, I really felt it because I obstructed the intersection even more by backing my truck up to the front of his Toyota.

I shimmied down from the cab and walked around to the man in the driver's seat. His head was covered in dreadlocks, and he had a *fu Manchu* mustache that didn't seem to belong with the dreads. "You need to exit the car before I can move it. Why don't you get in my cab, and once I get us out of here, you can tell me where you want your car taken."

"Okay, but I need to get Buddy first." As he reached into the back from the driver's seat, he seemed as nervous as a fluttering aspen. When he straightened up, I noticed he had an alligator print scarf wrapped around his neck. I took a step away as he forced the driver's door open and hopped outside his car.

I did a double take when the scarf moved! That wasn't a scarf! It moved!

I stifled the scream at the back of my throat. "*Whaa? Whaa?*" I pointed a trembling finger out straight like a prophet of doom.

The man's hands flew to his neck. "This is my service animal. His name is Buddy, and he's harmless."

I became a blubbering wreck. "I don't want a snake in my truck."

"Buddy goes where I go. He keeps me calm."

The snake might keep him calm, but it had the opposite effect on me. A horn beeped and several others joined in, the cacophony of honks busting my ear drums. Buddy's tongue slipped out, wavered in the air, and went back in. *Ewwww!* I almost keeled over.

Was it discrimination if I refused the tow?

I squeezed my eyes shut and tried to pull myself together. The customer is always right. I was doing this job as a favor to Tanner. This was money in my bank account. This intersection needed to be cleared right now. This snake was harmless. Okay, that last one I couldn't talk myself into believing.

But, being the professional vehicle recovery specialist that I am—*as if*—I said, "Get in the truck."

After I retrieved the remote from under the dash, I hit the buttons, and the boom raised the Toyota. I white-knuckled the truck's door handle and climbed back into the cab. Watching in my side mirror, I waited for cars to pass before I eased through the intersection and gunned the engine down the street. I couldn't look at my customer. If I kept my eyes averted, then I could pretend he didn't have a deadly viper wrapped around him like a scarf.

"Where are we going?" I swear, if that snake so much as flicked its tongue at me again, I was bailing out.

"My house."

"Where's that?" My voice squeaked.

He explained he lived off Columbine Court, and I couldn't get there fast enough. I raced down Main, took a sharp left on Fifth, and a fast right on Columbine, the Toyota sailing along behind us like the wind. I reversed his Toyota into his driveway, touched the magic button on the remote, and the Toyota's tires hit the ground with a soft *pumpf*, the claws retracted, and the crossbar folded onto the truck bed. Never did I appreciate the efficiency of my Fulcan self-loader more than today.

The man handed me his plastic before climbing

down from the cab. My fingers shook as I tried to swipe the card through the reader. It took more than a few attempts. Okay, so I was more than a little freaked.

I put on a lot of bravado when I passed his card back. "Thank you for using Del's Towing. Call me if you ever need another tow." I choked on those last words and tried to keep the *thank-God-that's-over* look off my face.

My hands clenched the wheel as I pulled away, and after a block, I slid to the curb and called Tanner. "I just finished your tow for you. Thanks a lot!" My words came out in a shout.

"What's the matter, Delaney?" His voice was full of concern.

I dialed the volume back. "The guy had a snake with him. I had a freakin' snake in my truck."

"No way."

"Way." I jammed the phone between my ear and shoulder and covered my face with my hands. I took some deep, steadying breaths.

"Delaney, you still there? You okay?"

"I'm okay." *Not!* I hadn't even recorded the vehicle's VIN for my records. That part of the job had totally slipped from my mind.

"Where are you? I'm done with my tow, and I can be right there."

"I just turned the corner at Fifth and Piñon Way."

He hung up. After a couple of seconds, my heart resumed its normal beat. Even my hands had relaxed and no longer looked like claws. I glanced at my pale face in the rearview mirror and watched my natural pink color slowly return, and the determination on my face boosted me up. I *could* do this. I *would* be okay. Just another day in the life of a tow woman. A job well done. Hey, life is good. And I owed Tanner. I needed to handle this job for him without complaining since he passed work assignments my way all the time, and he'd taught me how to operate my self-loader and all.

In the beginning, he'd shown me how to work the tow boom, taken me with him on ride-a-longs, brought me to Chamber of Commerce meetings, shared his Main Street towaway contracts, and let me use his impound lot because I didn't have a secure storage site of my own like I do now. I admired Tanner's ease with his tow truck and how he handled customers. I'd had a huge crush on him at one time and pursued him shamelessly until I finally captured his heart. But not his whole heart. That's what broke us up. His job and little brother and sister always came first. Had I made a mistake there? A part of me had a little regret going on.

Crikey. Why'd I call Tanner? I was perfectly fine now. Something I learned early on about the tow business is that you never knew what to expect when you pulled up to a stranger in a car. I started to phone Tanner back when his black truck pulled in behind me. I blushed up to my ears and slumped down in the driver's seat while he climbed in the passenger's side. I'd embarrassed myself once again.

"I'm sorry I called you. I'm better now. I can handle these crazies on my own, honestly." Now I just had to repeat that to myself about a thousand more times.

He grinned. "A snake? No shit?"

"It was around the guy's neck." I swirled my hand under my chin and threw up a little in my mouth.

He had a *whoa* expression on his face. "Around his neck, huh?" Then he laughed out loud, like he was enjoying the moment. "I've seen some smokin' crack stuff before, but not that."

"I hear ya. It was a 'service animal.' " I made little quote signs.

He chuckled again, and I laughed too, slightly hysterical, until my eyes watered. I apologize to any snake lovers.

He shook his head. "I'm glad I sent that call to you instead of taking it myself."

"Thank you so much for that." I fanned my face to dry my eyes and prevent my mascara from running.

We were both smiling wide, leaning back in our seats. His sky-blue eyes studied me, my heart did a little pitter-patter, and electricity crackled between us.

But I was dating Ephraim now.

"I'm okay. I've shaken it off. Thanks, Tanner." I put my truck back in gear and my high-heeled foot on the brake.

"All right. It was good seeing you again, Laney." Tanner pried the door open. "I miss you."

I forced my eyes to meet his. "You, too, Tanner." He unfolded himself from my truck and trudged back to his own. I idled the engine until his flatbed disappeared from view, then took my foot off the brake.

Here's the deal. I'm attracted to both men. Like I'm telling you something you didn't already know.

I wish Tanner didn't affect me, make my heart beat faster, but he did. The tow man was tall and slender, with thick, dark-blond hair and heavily tattooed arms. Hotter than hot. His strength and capability were like a solid rock, an immovable mountain, which is what attracted me to him. Tanner was loyal, dated one girl at a time, but I came in second, or actually third or fourth, after his siblings and his tow company. I understood his priorities, but he left me wondering if I was important at all.

It was the opposite with Ephraim, the cowboy sheriff. I knew where I stood with him. He made it clear how much he cared about me. He was protective, interested in my life, and always told me I meant a lot to him. At the moment, anyway. Ephraim was known around town as a player who'd already run through most of the single women in the county. Ephraim may eventually leave me for another girl, but while we dated, I'd be number one. The sheriff was smart and fun and made me feel good about myself. What woman didn't want a man like that?

My past relationship with Tanner had ended. I didn't know where my relationship with Ephraim was going.

But I knew exactly where I was headed next.

Chapter 11

I breezed through the door at Oberly Motors with full bags of food in each hand and announced, "I got something for the weird files."

Byron asked, "What happened?" and Shannon looked up from the computer screen and gave me a questioning look behind her vintage wire-framed glasses. Axle rose from where he reclined on the couch and opened the bags. He sniffed as he breathed in the scent of chili dogs and onion rings.

I quipped, "I had a customer who had a snake with him. I gave the snake a ride in my truck."

Byron's eyebrows shot up, but Axle only handed a milkshake to Shannon along with one of the hotdogs. Then he passed out the rest of the franks and shakes. He took a big bite of his own chili dog and chewed.

I related the story amid appropriate gasps from Shannon and derisive noises from Axle. After swallowing a bite, Byron shook his head and said, "I don't know how you get inta these kinda situations, Delaney."

I bounced both hands off my chest. "Yay, me."

How in the world had I entered into this ridiculous business? I can tell some pretty crazy stories about vehicle recovery. When I inherited the truck, mind you, I had no experience in the car hauling industry. I knew nothing about cars. I'd never changed a tire before. Had never even driven a truck of any kind before.

Was I delusional thinking I could handle the job? If only I didn't feel like a fraud, lil' ole me driving this big truck, competing with the brawny, all-male towers in town. They'd probably think nothing of taxiing a snake around. Tanner thought it funny. Okay, so I did, too…now. *Hahahaha.* Not a big deal, remember?

I had turned into such a good con artist, I was even conning myself. I'd just have to continue to do what I always did—bluff my way through it. It's a good thing I was accustomed to humiliation.

****

The next morning, in an attempt to get serious about my profession, I took off in my self-loader, wearing my three-inch tall black Mary Jane's. Black for *all-business* today. I drove east on I-70, then west, on the lookout for stalls. Through my windshield, the mountains on the left and the valley on the right sparkled with the overnight snowfall. My phone rang as I ascended up the pass, but the caller was not phoning for a tow.

It was Kristen. "I have another favor."

"Whatever you need, just let me know. Need me to work the booth?"

"No, Axle's here helping me. But I'm low on to-go cups and napkins. We're slammed or I'd send Axle out for supplies."

"No problem. I'll swing by Roasters and pick some up. Anything else you need? Have enough chocolate for tonight?"

"Yup. Stocked up on that. Are you sure you don't mind? I feel bad asking for your help again."

"Stop. I can be there in minutes. See you then." I hung up and took the next exit to turn around.

I dashed past Guy on my way to the storeroom and came out with bundles of cups and napkins. "Sorry, I can't stay. Kristen needs these." Guy gave me a salute as I jogged out the door.

I parked my self-loader in the vendor parking lot behind the Christmas tree lot. A handy spot I now knew about.

After crashing through the crowd of slow-moving shoppers with the bags of paper goods tucked under my arms, I burst through the back door of the kiosk and spilled the supplies onto the floor. "Rudolph, the Red-Nosed Reindeer" wailed throughout the hut.

"Thank Heavens." My friend gave me a quick squeeze and release. "I was down to my last three cups, and I was completely out of napkins."

Axle and I gathered the plastic-wrapped cups and bundles of napkins and stuffed them under the counter. I could smell the fresh coffee and cinnamon with an undertone of pine boughs from the swags on the booth, which gave me a homey, comforting vibe. "Need anything else?"

"No. And thanks again." Kris gathered a deep breath and let it out with a whoosh. Axle took another order while Kris hit the dial on the espresso machine. "Before I forget, I talked to my suppliers, the baker who provides our muffins and the food service guy who delivers the milks."

"About what?"

"About Meredith Yarborough."

I enthused, "Wonderful. What'd they say?"

"They'd met Meredith on their deliveries but claimed not to know her. That's all. Sorry I didn't find out anything more. I'm not helping much."

I leaned forward on the plank that made up the counter. "No worries. You tried." I sorta knew how she felt because it seemed like a stalled-out kind of a day for me, too.

Kristen turned back to her customer to hand off a drink before greeting the next person in line.

There was only room for two workers in the crowded booth, and feeling in the way, I ducked out the door and headed to the tree lot in my high heels, slower this time since I wasn't in a rush. Dodging through the fragrant pines, I was thinking my truck might look conspicuous in the vendor parking lot, and I should probably move it.

"Hello, Delaney." The tree seller, Kane Quigley, walked up. I recognized his hooded eyes with the deep white wrinkles from squinting into the sun.

"Oh, hi, Kane. Sorry, I was taking the shortcut."

"That's fine. Just wanted to say hello. See how you're doing." That was sweet of him, one vendor to another, to be expected in this small town.

I stepped closer to him. "What about you? Are you doing okay? You know, after…that woman died…and?" I puckered my lips, and my nose wrinkled.

"And you found her in my tree lot." He shuffled his dirty work boots. "No, I'm not doing too good. I'm still bothered by it all."

Well, that made two of us. My throat constricted. "It's tough, I know."

"At least it hasn't impacted my tree sales, so I'm doing all right there." A guilty look crossed his face. "I hope I didn't offend you by saying that."

"Not at all. We still have our jobs to do," I assured him. Even after such a tragedy, everyday life doesn't stop. I was glad Kristen's booth was busy, too. "But I haven't gotten my Christmas tree yet. I'll admit it's been hard for me to think about a tree." My eyes went to the pines next to us, all perfectly shaped, and I thought about going ahead and buying one. The air was redolent with the scent. But like I said, it was hard.

Kane nodded. "I keep thinking how horrible it was. I remember she looked really sick that day, flushed and sweaty. She was clutching her stomach."

I wrenched my head back around. "You saw her? Did you talk to her, too?" Something I hadn't known. On the day it happened, we hadn't discussed this. Nor had we talked about it since.

"Just a few words. She told me she was in a hurry to get home. When the sheriff said you'd found a body, I thought at once it was her, that maybe she collapsed back there from something, like maybe a ruptured appendix. That was before the news got out she was poisoned."

I shot Kane an entreating look. "Did she say anything else?"

"No, only that she was on her way home." He made a *tsking* sound with his tongue against his teeth. "I wish now I'd called an ambulance for her, you know? I wonder why she was trying so hard to leave, why she didn't call 9-1-1 herself if she was that sick. I feel so bad about it."

"She probably didn't know how serious it was. Maybe she simply wanted to crawl into her own bed. It's not your fault, don't even think that way." I shook my head. "How soon after you saw her did Ephraim and I find her?"

"Let's see." He rubbed his chin, his sleeves falling back to expose his scratched wrists. "I got busy with a customer, a nice young lady, took her money, helped her tie her tree to the roof of her car…maybe ten or fifteen minutes, not long."

I said, "It probably wouldn't've made any difference if you'd called for help. Did you know her? Recognize her?"

"Nah." His face darkened.

"I didn't either. I wish I knew more about her…" I trailed off, and we both stared down at our toes for a solemn moment, then I chuckled, wanting to lighten up. "I ran into your wife. She seems like one busy person, bustling around in her Santa hat, showing quite the spirit."

"She certainly does. If you have questions about Meredith, just ask Belle, she knows everybody," he said, as if not wanting to talk about the murder anymore. "Well, come back soon for your tree. There's a really good selection of fresh-cut pines."

"I will." I peered through the rows but still didn't want to pick one out today.

"It was nice talking to you. Take care." He grasped my hand for a moment before I made off for the parking lot.

Driving away from the Christmas market, I went over everything in my mind, trying to get the chronology straight, but I needed to write it out. I pulled over too sharply, causing the tires to hit the curb.

My notes were in a small spiral in the bottom of my bag, so I got them out and added to the timeline, counting back the minutes as the events would have unfolded.

9:00 a.m., Kristen talks to Meredith, Axle takes her a coffee.

Noon, wine booth opens, and maintenance man,

Jack Frier, buys mulled wine. Meredith complains that she's sick.

1:10, she left booth, then it took seven to ten minutes to walk to the tree lot.

1:20, tree seller talks to Meredith, she's on her way home, she looks very ill.

1:35, body found, still warm.

Suspects: Noel Yarborough, unknown boyfriend, alpine man/Christstollen vendor, the other unknown woman in argument, and Jack Frier, the macho maintenance man.

Means: poison.

Motive: Noel wants to be in charge. Boyfriend, married, hiding affair. Alpine man, argued with victim. The other woman, also in argument. Jack, unknown motive.

I tipped my face up toward the top of the truck cab, breathing in the familiar smell of motor oil and a woodsy scent clinging to the upholstery. That scent always reminded me of Dad. I pictured him in this same seat, looking out this same windshield. Not for the first time, I wished he was around so I could ask him for advice.

If I could just figure all this out. The police had Rory on their suspicious persons list, but I couldn't believe my friend was involved. Noel or Married Boyfriend or Alpine Man were more probable. And what about that conceited Jack Frier? Don't forget him. Rory had asked for my assistance, and I'd done very little to help him. Kris needed the market to stay open, and what was I doing about that?

I turned off the ignition, pocketed my keys, and slogged the few short blocks back to the place where the answers were more likely to be found, the *Christkindl*

Market. I strolled along the well-walked path that meandered through the mounds of snow and the wooden booths. From the direction of the ice skating rink, laughter carried over in the crisp air. It was all so normal, people shopping and enjoying the holiday, like nothing bad had happened here.

The gingerbread booth displayed the winning entries, so I stopped to take them in. A typical gingerbread house out of *Hansel and Gretel*, a merry-go-round complete with tiny horses, and a barn with a rounded roof and cookie-cutter cows in the open barn door. None of these were from a kit. They were pretty amazing.

Customers lined up two and three deep at the Emporium, so I joined the crowd looking over the cheap wood-cut ornaments and plastic dime-store toys. Frank manned the cash register while Holly talked to the customers. I was just thinking how glad I was the man's business hadn't been shut down after all, when Frank said to his wife, "Are you blind? Look behind the counter in the locked case."

"They're not there."

"Where'd you put them? You're the one who unpacked the last delivery. Do I need to stop what I'm doing and find things for you?"

Holly appeared close to tears. "No, I'll find them."

Yeesh. I guess this could be a typical argument between spouses, but it was cringey all the same.

Frank threw one hand into the air. "I gotta go. You're on your own." He passed his customer some change and a bag, snatched his coat off a hook, and slammed the back door of the kiosk closed behind him. Holly took over the register with shaking hands. Her lips trembled; she was obviously upset.

Was Holly anxious about running the booth on her own? Was she distressed about the argument with her husband?

Frank came around the side of the booth and set out toward the carousel. I pushed through the crowd after him as he swept past a stall selling kites, train sets, and porcelain dolls in colorful costumes. I followed along a few steps behind, dodging couples with kids and groups of teens, hoping Frank wouldn't notice me. The show-off groundskeeper in his golf cart shot between us, and I worried I would lose Frank, but once Jack's cart crossed the path, Frank was still in sight. I half-jogged to keep up. A young woman with her face heavily made-up rushed over to Frank and flung her arms around him, stopping me in my tracks. She was the woman crowned Queen of the Festival during the opening night ceremony. I'd often spotted her with Belle, Kane's wife and the market organizer. Usually she had on her crown and sash, but she didn't today.

Frank said, "Hi, Candace, honey."

I gaped at the two of them.

What kind of marriage did Frank have? Just what kind of performance was the queen giving now? And she was engaged to someone else, wasn't she? Remember the big diamond on her finger? This was totally *ick*.

"Dad, I've been waiting for you."

Okay, so I got that all wrong. Shoot me.

The beauty queen released her hold and stepped back, exposing a little girl of about ten or so behind her. "Can you watch Ivy while I do some shopping?" She indicated with a flash of her eyes the toy booth we'd just passed.

Frank said, "Of course. Hey, Ivy, you want to ride on the carousel?"

Her face lit up, and she waved mittened hands. "Yes, Grandpa."

Granddad and granddaughter stepped into the ticket line while Candace disappeared in the crowd. I inserted myself a few people behind them. The queue moved fast, and soon we were all aboard the merry-go-round. Frank helped Ivy climb onto a unicorn, and then he stationed himself next to her. I held onto a pole near a small boy riding a horse and acted like I was with him.

"The kids love this ride, am I right?" I gave Frank a wide smile as the merry-go-round started its rotation. Ivy held on tight and squealed.

"Yeah, wish I owned one of these rides." He kept his eyes glued to his granddaughter.

Would he recognize me when he had so many other customers? In case he did, I might as well admit we'd met. "Your Emporium does a pretty good trade."

"Oh, you're the one who bought a set of those wireless earbuds."

"Right. Where'd you get those anyway? You sold them at such a good price." A little undercover work. What would Ephraim say?

"I have a supplier I buy from at volume." He pointed to the small boy riding the horse next to me. "Is that your son?"

I clutched the pole, bracing myself in my high heels, and answered, "Why else would I be riding the merry-go-round?" I laughed, my face and neck flushing a deep red in the mirrored panel on the other side of the unicorn. "So, the earbuds…I noticed you don't have any left."

"I sold out. They were a popular item."

The gizmo that cranked the horses in their fake gallop made metal scraping sounds and the organ music blared. I was getting a bit barfy watching Ivy's unicorn travel up and down, up and down. "That's too bad. I wanted another pair." Frank didn't respond, so I added, "I found something similar but they were priced a hundred dollars higher."

A crease appeared between his brows. "Is that right? Well, that figures. I let my wife price those."

The carousel ground to a slow halt, and Frank helped his granddaughter off the unicorn. The little boy on the horse thrashed his hands all around and yelled, "Mommy! Come help me!"

A woman jumped onto the platform and ran over. "I'm coming, honey."

Busted!

Frank gave me a quick, over-the-shoulder look before he descended the stage, Ivy's hand in his. I hopped off the other side and ducked into the crowd.

Was his criminal activity selling stolen goods a random operation that had nothing to do with the murder? Or was Meredith caught up in it, too? Maybe she was also selling hot goods from her mulled wine booth. Seems like such a scheme could be dangerous.

I found myself several feet from the *Christstollen* kiosk where German goods and pastries were sold. Standing behind a rack of ornaments, I kept the alpine man under observation while he rang up several purchases. His left third finger was fitted with a slim wedding band. I made a point of noticing this. First I wondered if Frank was cheating on his wife with someone who turned out to be his daughter, and now I wondered if the alpine man was cheating, too. Was

Alpine Man Meredith's married boyfriend? Think about it…that argument with Meredith and another woman could've been about their affair. The other woman in the quarrel could've been Alpine Man's wife. Use your imagination. Have you never watched *Cheaters*? I moved over to the sweet pastries to hear better. Maybe I could catch some of his conversation and he would let something slip. One could hope.

So, here I was, suspecting every married man I came across. Probably half the men working the festival were married, a statistic my mind came up with, but probably not too far off.

I circled around to the backside of the booth and found Amazon boxes thrown onto a big pile of garbage bags. No recycling here. I was thinking about gathering the cardboard to take to the recycle center when a bald, scaly thing wiggled under the cardboard. A tail. A bald, scaly tail that belonged to…a rat!

A chill slithered down the length of my spine. First a snake, now a rat. What am I going to stumble across next? A dung beetle?

The PA system crackled, then a voice blared over the intercom, "Attention, attention, please." I ran back toward the front of the booth. Everyone at the kiosk turned around and looked up, as if the voice came from the sky. The fairgoers seemed to slow their steps and fall silent all at once. It reminded me of pausing a movie with the actors' expressions fixed on their faces.

The spokesperson continued, "We have an announcement to make. The *Christkindl Market* is now closed. Everyone please proceed to the exits in an orderly manner. I repeat, the *Christkindl Market* is now closed. Everyone please proceed to the exits in an orderly manner." The harsh instructions clashed with the soft Christmas music of a moment ago.

The noise of conversations around me escalated once more as everyone turned toward the gates. I was carried along with the flow. People asked each other what was going on. Parents grasped their children's hands, and customers emptied out of the stalls. A column of people swarmed around me, pushing past me, and knocking me back against the gingerbread booth. Faces showed fear, and their footsteps an urgency to get out of there.

Was another surge of panic about to erupt? Remember, I was caught up in the hysterical throng during the market's opening ceremony. Now that the market was closing, was there going to be a similar stampede for the exits?

Watching the herd rush by, I spied a cowboy hat, high above everyone else's stocking caps. It was Ephraim, over there by the tree lot, so I inched my way between the agitated families and others sprint-running, until I reached him.

"Ephraim, what's going on?"

"I just delivered the closure order." He grabbed my elbow. "I didn't know you were here."

"Why did you have to shut down the market?" I couldn't imagine how things could get any worse than this.

"A second person was poisoned. The city really had no choice but to close everything down."

Things just got worse.

"Another poisoning!" My legs wobbled, my throat constricted, and my voice was strained.

I said, "This is a friggin' nightmare."

Chapter 12

I lowered my voice. "Who died?"

"The victim isn't dead. He's at the emergency room." Ephraim studied the crowd hurrying toward the exits.

A man, then. But who? I tried to slow down my racing thoughts. "Was it someone I know?"

"The groundskeeper." The sheriff was still concentrating on the people passing by, on the alert for danger, I supposed.

A wave of nausea rolled through me. "Jack Frier?" The man bulked up like a jock was laid up? It was hard to picture, especially because I'd spotted him in his golf cart not that many minutes ago.

Ephraim turned his attention to me and held tighter to my arm. "Yes, how do you know him?"

"I see him all the time at the garbage bins. I gave him a free hot chocolate once." How often had I looked out of the coffee booth and watched as he emptied the trash? Then the thought hit me, and I said, "Oh no, this means Kristen's booth is shut down."

He let go of me. "The closure's only temporary, just until we have a chance to search all the booths."

How long is temporary? The market was only scheduled to be open for the month of December. But it was no use complaining. I needed to look at the bright side. It's not permanent. And the bigger concern was the

160

man's condition. Was he on the verge of death?

I asked, "How bad is he? Will he make it?"

"He's been given some muscle relaxants and anticonvulsants, but the doctor thinks he only ingested a very small amount, under the lethal dose. So, he'll live. What we're worried about is other victims. We haven't determined the source of the sodium fluoroacetate yet. How is it getting introduced at the marketplace? We need to figure that out."

I was glad the maintenance man would be okay, but I still sucked in a breath with worry. Would there be other victims who wouldn't make it? And why Jack Frier? Why was he targeted?

I faced the sheriff and tucked my fists under my elbows. "Ephraim, you know that maintenance man was at the mulled wine booth the morning Meredith was poisoned. Maybe the killer believes Jack saw something. He'd denied knowing anything, but the killer might've poisoned Jack to play it safe."

"That's a possibility," Ephraim conceded.

I shifted the alternatives around in my mind, barely noticing the last of the thinning crowd scurry by. "Or, it's just the opposite. Maybe Jack's portraying himself as a victim to avoid suspicion. I wondered from the start if he was involved somehow. We can't discount that. Maybe he's the poisoner."

The sheriff's voice dropped abruptly. "You mean Frier swallowed some of the rat poison intentionally? That would be an extreme measure if he did. A cold, calculated move. Risky."

A killer who took risks. And I had chased him down to ask him questions. We'd been alone together after the market closed the other night.

The sheriff must have read the fear behind my eyes, because he drew me into his arms and circled a palm over my back.

Normally Ephraim could calm my nerves. Not now. The screaming heebie-jeebies were screaming too loud. A man, whether a killer himself or not, was in the hospital; Kristen's booth, along with every other vendor's, was closed; and a murderer—Jack or someone else—was still getting away with the crime. It was hard to get my head around that thought. At least the sheriff wasn't *poo-pooing* my theories.

"What's going to happen next?" I drew back to look at him, my voice shaky.

"You're going to leave." He pulled the collar of my jacket closed to block out the cold. "Why don't you go home and we can meet back up as soon as I'm done here. Okay?"

I leaned into his chest and his arms wrapped tighter around me. "All right."

"Where are you parked?"

"A couple blocks away."

"I'll walk you to your car."

"It's my truck and you don't have to. I know you're busy."

"I want to." He kept one arm around me as we passed under the archway and left the fairgrounds, which were silent for once without the sounds of the joyous Christmas music and happy crowd. The farther from the market we walked, the safer I felt, but I was not able to suppress the anxiety that flowed through my body. The sheriff waited as I unlocked my truck, then made me promise to go straight home before he took off back the way we'd come.

While I steered my truck down Fifth, my cell phone rang and Kristen's voice came over the line, high and shrill. "The market's closed."

"I know. I was there when they gave the announcement." I kept driving on autopilot toward Main Street, not paying close attention to the traffic.

"I thought you'd already left."

"I was on my way out." Sort of. "You know why the sheriff shut it down?"

"It's already breaking news on the internet. Here, let me read it." Kristen mouth-breathed into the phone for a couple of seconds. "Found it. It says that a man identified as Jack Frier, the groundskeeper at the *Christkindl Market*, is the second poison victim. He remains at Good Samaritan Hospital, but his condition is currently unknown."

"Wow, that's in the news already?"

"Yes, and there's more." Kristen panted into the phone again, seemingly breathless. "Jack Frier has a criminal record and was involved in a prior criminal investigation. I guess the newshounds have already dug up that information."

"Wait, I need to pull over." I shifted down and left-turned into an alley. The stench from nearby dumpsters permeated my cab, so I hit the button to snug my window all the way shut. I idled the engine and engaged the parking brake. "Okay. Tell me now."

"Frier was the subject of a prior criminal investigation, the sexual assault and murder of a young woman from Denver seven years ago. That homicide remains open. It was never solved." It sounded like she was reading from the news report.

I sat up straight and I'm sure my eyes bugged out.

How did I not know this? Because Ephraim, in sheriff mode, hadn't uttered a word of it to me, that's how. "I wonder if Zach can tell us anything more. Can you ask him?" Kristen's boyfriend never wanted to tell me anything, but he might tell Kris.

"I just walked in the door, but I'm calling him next."

"Okay. I'll let you go so you can talk to him. I'm on my way home, too. Let me know if you find out anything more."

"You know it." She disconnected.

I could hardly take in my surroundings, so I shook my head until my vision cleared and I realized where I was. In the alley behind Main Street. A Buick Enclave, front-wheel drive, blocked the brewery's loading zone. Since it was Friday, the property owner would call Tanner, not me, if he wanted the Buick moved, and it wasn't my place to touch it. Besides, we weren't monitoring the no-parking zones right now.

I drove on by, stewing in my thoughts as to why Ephraim hadn't told me about Jack Frier's criminal history. The maintenance man had been the subject of a prior murder investigation.

Pretty significant, wouldn't you say?

Understatement of the year.

I reminded myself the sheriff was just doing his job. Ephraim wouldn't fork over information if he thought it could be dangerous or put me at risk. I had to give him a break here, cut him some slack. *Harty-har.* That's a good one. I was going to call him out on this.

I dialed Ephraim's cell phone by speaking his name into my Bluetooth, but he didn't answer. When I disconnected, my truck cab felt empty.

Frustrated, much?

Yes, I know I said I was going home, but once I started it up, my truck carried me over to the building on the corner of Tall Chief Road and Bald Eagle Way, that had once housed a gas station and was now home to a wine tasting room. The parking lot was empty except for Noel's Santa Fe, front-wheel drive. I pulled in, slammed the shifter into park, and cut the engine.

When I yanked on the front door, it wouldn't open, so I cupped my hands around my eyes and leaned into the glass. Noel Yarborough had his elbows on the bar. Two people, an older man and woman, perched on counter stools. I rapped my knuckles on the glass until they turned to look.

Noel came out from behind the counter and opened the door. "We're closed, Delaney."

"I figured. But I wanted you to know there's a second victim."

He swept his hands up and down his face. "Come on in."

I followed him over to the elderly couple and rested against the counter while Noel went back behind it. He said, "These are my parents. They got home from Italy yesterday. Marge and James Yarborough." He turned to the older folks. "This is Delaney. She discovered Merry's body."

The couple swiveled their gaze in my direction, and I could spot the resemblance. Noel's dad had the same close-set eyes, his mom the same dark-brown hair, either her natural color or a really good color job. Marge's eyes appeared strained, puffy, and bloodshot.

Tears pricked my own eyes. "I'm sorry for your loss." I said what everyone says. It's so inadequate.

James said, "Thank you, young lady."

A woman came out from the door to the restroom, looking like she just refreshed her makeup with a paintbrush. I did a double take. It was Candace!

Frank Jennings's daughter.

The Festival Queen.

What the hey?

Noel said, "My parents just finished talking to the sheriff when the news came in about the second victim."

"So, you already heard." I couldn't take my eyes off Candace. "I'm Delaney Morran." I held out my hand, forcing her to take it.

"Candace Jennings." She was dressed in navy wool pants and a pink cowl-necked sweater. She must take after her well-dressed dad, Frank, rather than her mousy mom, Holly.

"We've met before. You're the Festival Queen."

"Yes." She beamed.

I wondered how well she knew Noel, but I couldn't just come out and ask, "How well do you know Noel?" No, I'd better not ask that out loud. Oops! I think I just did.

She flicked her gaze at his parents. "We're engaged."

I blinked, speechless, then remembered my manners. "Congratulations." That explained the rock on her finger.

Marge spoke up. "We got to meet Noel's fiancée for the first time today. I wish it could have been during a more pleasant time."

"You both have booths at the Christmas market. Well, your parents have a booth, Candace." The high notes in my voice were embarrassing, and the engaged couple was giving me questioning looks.

166

"How do you know my folks?" She narrowed her eyes at me, the super-long eyelashes becoming entangled.

My nose pinked up, and I hoped she hadn't seen me spying on her dad at the merry-go-round. "I, um, figured the Jennings are your parents? The Jennings Emporium booth?"

Noel's dad asked, "What's going on with the Christmas market anyway? Could these poisonings be a terrorist attack or something? A serial killer?"

I said, glad to change the subject, "I know, right? It's just awful."

Noel crossed his arms. "I wish we had more answers. But don't worry, Dad. All will be well. It will work out now that I'm running the winery."

I was surprised at this blatant statement, but his parents only looked sad.

"We need to finalize the funeral arrangements." His mom pushed herself off the stool. "We should get going, James."

He stood up and took his wife's elbow. "We'll call you when we get home, Noel. It was nice meeting you, Candace. I hope we'll see you again soon. You, too, Delaney."

Noel led his parents to the door and a bell jingled as it closed behind them.

I asked him, "You know that second poison victim was involved in a prior murder investigation?"

"What? I hadn't heard that part." Noel's voice sounded angry. He slammed his fists on the counter several times and used some creative swear words.

Candace rushed to his side. "Calm down, Noel." She clutched his arm, worry etched on her face, and she shot me an accusatory look.

I swallowed a couple of times, but pressed on. "This isn't a fluke. The police don't believe in pure chance. It must be relevant. Did that man have something to do with your sister? Is there a connection there?"

He took a step away from his fiancée and wove his arms back across his chest. "Not that I know of. His name is not familiar."

"He's the groundskeeper for the market."

His face remained blank. Candace stared into the void, too.

I asked, "Have the police updated you? Have you heard anything new?"

"Not really. But they asked me more questions when I was there with my parents. You'd think they would've already wrung everything out of me that they could. Why are the police all over me? Asking the same *f-ing* questions over and over." He pulled a rag out from under the counter and polished the wood with more energy than necessary. Candace's hands tensed and relaxed repeatedly as she kept close to his side.

I suggested, "They're probably hoping you'll remember something you'd forgotten about."

"Like a confession?" He snorted. Candace *tsked* and shook her head.

If the shoe fits. I refrained from saying that out loud this time. I asked, "So, the funeral is next week?"

"In Palisade."

Too far for me to casually drop in.

He busied himself at the sink, making clanking sounds while washing out glasses, and Candace helped put them away. His face looked mad and preoccupied, like he might have something more to say but had decided against saying it.

Pressuring him further would do no good. "Okay, then. I'm taking off."

The couple looked relieved to see the end of me.

The winter sun was low on the horizon when I parked my truck at Oberly Motors and struck out for home in my Fiat. I'd told Noel it wasn't an accident that Jack Frier was poisoned, but was it a coincidence that Noel and Candace were engaged? It was possible any two people in our little town of Spruce Ridge knew each other, especially if they grew up here, went to school here, and worked here. But Noel was not from Spruce Ridge, and I wasn't sure Candace was either. Her parents were from Denver.

Ephraim showed up at about five fifteen, when I was playing tug-of-war with Axle's Rottweiler on the living room floor. When I rose to meet him, he enveloped me in his strong arms, warming me down to the pit of my stomach.

"You're done at the market?" I asked.

"I am. But the team's still searching all the booths for rat poison. There's a lot to cover."

I hadn't really thought about how hard the sheriff's department was working on this case, now putting in overtime. "I think I saw a rat at the *Christstollen* booth. Maybe they have rat poison."

"We're checking them out along with everyone else, but there are bound to be rodents at the fairgrounds."

We sat down on the couch. I said, "I ordered pizza. Is that okay? Or are you tired of pizza?"

"Anything you want is fine by me." He looked exhausted. His eyes wrinkled at the corners, and his forehead looked tense.

"Ephraim…" I cleared my throat. How should I bring this up?

He reared his head back. "Uh-oh, I know that look." He gave my braid a tug. "What's up? Just spill it."

"Jack Frier has a criminal history. It's in the news, and you never told me about it."

He tucked my head under his chin, his right arm around my shoulder, and I could feel his breath in my hair. "Frier has a history of pickpocketing. We've had our eye on him, trying to catch him in the act."

I lifted my head. "Pickpocketing, too. Humph. I was talking about his prior sexual assault and murder."

The sheriff swiped his left hand across his brow. "Frier was questioned in that cold case because he was a witness, not a suspect. He worked near where the victim was abducted. There doesn't seem to be any connection to the present investigation."

"But this can't be as simple as bad luck. Being in the wrong place at the wrong time. Twice." My voice rose in pitch. "Too many *coinkydinks* in this murder."

"Sometimes there are coincidences. Some things do happen by chance." He shrugged, signaling the end to the information flow. Was he downplaying this important clue to keep me focused elsewhere? Jack Frier *had* to be a person of interest. No way the police weren't pursuing that angle. Ephraim might think we were done here, but I wasn't ready to let this go.

"I need you to fill in some details for me, Ephraim. Was Meredith's car parked behind the tree lot? Was she on her way to her car when she collapsed?"

He narrowed his eyes and nodded. "Most likely."

"Kristen saw Jack at the wine booth around noon. Jack told me that Meredith complained about being sick when he was there. How fast does this poison act?"

"Symptoms from sodium fluoroacetate poisoning usually occur within a couple of hours, but it can be as fast as half an hour. And I won't ask how Frier came to tell you that."

"Okay. So, it could've been Jack who poisoned the wine. He had opportunity. He could've told me she was already ill to throw me off. This is what I think happened. Jack sneaked the rat poison into an open bottle, and Meredith made herself a mulled wine from that bottle. Maybe it was nearly empty, so she tossed the bottle in the trash. She started to get sick, headed to her car, and made it as far as the tree lot. But why did Jack poison her then, and why did he poison himself now?"

Ephraim shook his head. "He didn't do it either time."

I raised my palms. "Why do you say that?" My voice came out close to a whine.

"No one would knowingly drink that deadly rat poison, Delaney. He told us he poured the wine he bought at the wine booth that day into a travel mug to save for later. As hard as this is to believe, he forgot where he got the wine, but as soon as it touched his lips, he remembered. He spit it out after only swallowing a few milligrams. Then he felt nauseated and drove himself to the hospital."

"You don't think he faked all that?"

"No."

I conceded, "I guess that idea is out." For now, anyway. I wasn't totally convinced, but I needed to revisit my original theories. "I stopped by the tasting room to talk to Noel, and I met his parents. They seem like nice people."

"I agree. But what were you doing there?" He eased back, stretched out his long legs, and crossed his feet at the ankles, as if settling in for a lengthy explanation.

"I met Noel's girlfriend, Candace Jennings. The same Jennings as the Emporium, the booth where the stolen goods are sold." This was so incestuous.

"We know about the girlfriend."

"Fiancée."

"So, tell me why you went to the wine tasting room when you told me you were going straight home?"

I cursed my pale complexion as my cheeks grew warm. "I'm hung up on the sibling rivalry angle. There's a family dynamic going on." I gave him a level look. "Was there a life insurance policy on Meredith?" He frowned; his shoulders went up slightly and fell down again. I asked, "Did you get a copy of the parents' will? Does Noel inherit everything now that Meredith is dead?"

The frown fell away, and his stony cop face appeared.

"I'm right!" I practically shouted. I drew my feet up onto the couch and sat on my heels, facing the sheriff. I gave his shoulders a playful push, my face in his face. "I'm right, aren't I?"

He leaned in and crushed a kiss to my lips. If he was trying to distract me, it worked. My fingers found the hair at the nape of his neck, and I kissed him back.

When we both withdrew, he said, "Man, do you have good intuition. I said you're a good guesser, in addition to being a good kisser, but I'm not answering your question."

Before I could pressure him into answering after all, we were interrupted by the doorbell. Our dinner had arrived. I put Christmas music on and we ate the pizza sitting on stools at the kitchen counter. Ephraim talked about how excited his nieces and nephews were to see Santa Claus at the market by the giant Christmas tree. "The fair will be reopened once the search is completed," he explained.

"Are you going back there tonight?"

"No. My family is getting together at my brother's house. You want to come with?"

"Thanks, but not this time." It felt like a last-minute invitation, and I didn't need to tag along to every event.

Once the last pizza slice disappeared, Ephraim left, and a few minutes later, Kristen stopped at my door and asked me to come over. I was glad to be able to spend time with my best friend, who'd been so busy with both the market and the coffee shop.

"You upset about the market being shut down?" I asked as I locked up my apartment and crossed the landing to the door she held open.

"Sure, but there's nothing I can do about it other than enjoy a night off."

"Ephraim told me it'll reopen soon," I assured her.

"Good. Let's watch a Christmas movie." Kristen brought two mugs of steaming tea to her living room. She picked up the remote and pointed it at her television. "Is *Christmas Vacation* okay with you?"

"I haven't seen it yet this year." I knew that movie was my best friend's favorite and she had all the lines memorized. We sat together on the couch with the lights turned off and her black-and-white afghan pulled over our laps. Clark Griswold, the main character, wanted the perfect Christmas, but all his relatives drove him crazy, turning the holiday into a disaster.

Just before the last scene, Kristen paused the movie and said, "I know what Clark is feeling 'cause I feel the same way about our Christmas picture. And I have an idea." She folded the afghan and draped it over the arm of the sofa. "Go get a pair of your shoes and a pair of Axle's, too, and come back."

I had thick socks on my feet, no shoes. "Shoes? Photos of our shoes?" When she nodded, I said, "I love it." My mind already raced to which pair would be best. Should I get my signature black stilettos or something wintery?

"The cut-off date for mailing cards in time for Christmas delivery is tomorrow." She followed me to the door where her cute brown rubber boots with plaid trim sat on the mat.

"Okay, I'll be right back." I returned in moments carrying my red high-heeled boots with the white faux fur—to go with the Christmas theme—then made a second trip for Axle's sneakers—there weren't a lot of choices in his closet. I came back, pinching his old shoes in one hand and my nose in the other.

She said, "Bleeck," and made a *pee-yew* face.

"I know, right? But you asked for it." I gave a halfhearted laugh.

Kristen positioned her brown boots, my red boots, and Axle's dirty shoes together in a row in front of the Christmas tree with shiny wrapped gifts in the background. She took several snapshots and said, "See, it's like that old black-and-white television show, *My Three Sons*. Have you seen it? It's on one of those classic channels that play oldies."

"I know. It doesn't take a genius to figure that out." I moved the shoes around, like they were climbing up a mountain of packages or trying to crawl into the Christmas stockings, and she took more pictures. Then I said, "Okay, now you need a greeting, something that makes a statement."

"What's wrong with *Merry Christmas*?"

"Lame." I swished my head side to side. "It doesn't explain the shoes."

Someone pounded on the door, and when Kristen opened it to Axle, he asked, "Whatzup?" After Kristen showed him the pictures, he said, "How about *Happy Hannukah from the Heathens*?"

Kristen said, "Heathens? No, this is a holy holiday."

"How about *I couldn't get a holiday photo so you're getting this instead*?"

"Funny, but no. Holy, remember?"

I put in, "And it should be something about shoes."

Axle ran his hand over his chin stubble. "*We three shoes from Orient are*."

"Nobody will get that." Kristen pinned her cousin with a glare.

I snapped my fingers. "*Merry Christmas from My Three Shoes*."

"Not bad. Let's go with that." Kris was satisfied because *Merry Christmas* was included. She copied the shoes-in-a-row picture to the Christmas card website and typed in the greeting while Axle and I slouched on the couch. She said, "This app mails out the cards. I already uploaded my contact list."

Axle blew out his cheeks. "It's done then? No more pictures?"

I clasped his shoulder. "No more pictures." I could tell Kristen was happy to have this task out of the way, Axle was happy not to be bothered with it anymore, and

I was happy because the shoe picture was cute and something I could include on my website since I'm the high-heeled tow truck driver.

"We need to watch the end of the movie." Kristen clicked the remote and the film resumed play.

I opened a tin of cookies from under the tree and said, "Here." Axle took a handful. Before long, the credits rolled and the Christmas lights on the Griswold house lit up for the last time.

When Clark Griswold said his final line, that he'd pulled off Christmas after all, Kristen mouthed the words with him.

Chapter 13

"When's the market going to reopen?" Cookie crumbs sprayed out of Axle's mouth.

I said, "Ephraim told me it's just closed temporarily, and it'll be reopened soon."

Kristen thumbed her phone. "An email went out to all the vendors. We might even reopen tomorrow."

"Oh, I hope so." I patted the back of my head, absently pulling some strands from the thick braid. "You guys want to go over the clues with me?"

"No. Why would you think that?" Axle gave my arm a sharp pinch.

I returned a buddy-punch, and as I got up, I gave him a light kick in the shin for good measure. "Be right back."

I went to get the notes from my apartment, and when I resumed my position on the couch, I read through my timeline.

"Hello. I'm not hearing anything new." Axle's fingers beat a drum solo on the coffee table.

"Keep up here. That's why I need your help." It was all I could do not to give him a whack on the head. Don't think I didn't consider it. "But I do have something new. Noel has a girlfriend, Candace Jennings, daughter to the couple who runs the stolen goods booth, and they're engaged."

Both Kristen and Axle were suitably surprised.

Ephraim had told me the symptoms from the poison might take one to three hours to appear, but symptoms could take as little as a half hour, so I said, "Meredith could've been poisoned as late as noon. That's the same time Jack Frier was at her booth. Funny how he got sick, too."

"That's true. What do you think happened, Delaney?" Kristen asked, obviously determined to hear me out.

I thought for a second. "Ephraim said that Jack bought the mug of wine from Meredith and poured it into his thermos to drink later. Jeez, that sounds like an alcoholic. Then after several days, he took a sip, remembered where he got it, and spit it out. That's why Jack didn't die, too."

"What's your theory?" Kristen leaned her chin in her hand with her elbow on the arm of the sofa.

"I guess Jack's story sounds reasonable, except for his criminal history and being involved in a prior murder investigation. That can't be a coincidence. I say he could've poisoned Meredith, and later he took a small sip, enough to make him nauseated."

"Why would he do something that dense?" Axle's eyes sharpened on me.

"To fake being a target of the killer." I squeezed the back of my neck, thinking. "To draw suspicion away from himself. He's the pickpocket, too, you know."

"No, I didn't know that." Kristen brought her dark eyebrows together. "I wonder what went wrong in his life that led him to crime."

"That's all you've got outta Lopez? It ain't a lot." Axle was making the most of his role as the irritating little brother.

I winced. "Ouch."

"Come on, you two." Kristen waggled a finger between Axle and me and stopped at me. "How are you going to prove Jack did it?"

"I don't know." I breathed out a sigh.

Axle glanced at the clock on the wall and made a motion with his head toward the door. I nodded since Kristen needed to get up early in the morning. I steered Axle by the shoulders across the landing into our apartment. After I locked up behind us, Boss pawed my jeans and frisked around my feet.

"I can always count on Boss. He loves me." Boss rolled on his back for a tummy rub, and I obliged. "Or at least he finds me acceptable."

Axle gave me an awkward back-pat. "Boss isn't the only one who finds you acceptable. Or at least passable."

"Really?" I almost tripped, straightening back up, and tears gathered in my throat. "That's a nice thing to say." For him. I raised my arms for an embrace, but by his stiff stance, it was clear he didn't want the bear hug, so I let my arms drop.

"You're just barely passable, carrot top." With a look that said, *say-no-more*, my lil' cuz vanished down the hall.

****

My phone dinged with a text the next morning from Kristen.

—*Market is open. I have news. Come by the kiosk for coffee.*

I rushed Axle through his second or third bowl of cereal, hustled him into my Fiat, and jolted to a stop when he got out at Oberly Motors. I zoomed away, stashed my car behind the Christmas tree lot, and sprinted in my designer knock-offs, a pair of cute cork-heeled wedges, down the fairway to Kristen's coffee kiosk.

I stuck my head in the open hatch. "Yoo-hoo. I'm here."

Kris rushed out from behind the espresso maker. "The sheriff took Meredith's brother in for additional questioning. I watched as they came and got him just before I texted you."

My eyebrows shot to the top of my forehead. "Noel? Taken in for more questions?"

"That's right. Poor guy."

"He told me the police have already drilled him many times over. They must think he did it. I wonder if he's been arrested." There went my theory about the maintenance man murderer. Or the stolen goods hitman. Or the married lady-killer.

"They didn't haul him away in handcuffs or anything. And Guy texted to let me know Rory Rearden was also taken in." Kristen pulled a shot with a loud whooshing sound.

"How does Guy know about that? Is he friends with Rory?" I'd almost forgotten about Rory, one of Kris's coffee shop regulars who was becoming one of our tribe. Rory had asked for my help, and I hadn't helped him one bit. I clapped a hand to my mouth, knowing I'd let him down.

"I think Guy learned about it from someone at the coffee shop. You know news travels fast around here." Kristen handed me a double espresso.

I reached through the hatch for the cup. The coffee aroma hit my nose, and I breathed it in. "Did anyone know why both of them were picked up?" Something was going on, and I wished I was in on it.

"No." Her expression showed deep-seated concern. "I hope they're all right."

"Yeah, me too…" I pulled my eyes away from Kristen to look over at the mulled wine booth, now closed with a padlock on the hatch. Belle stood in front, shaking her head, hands on hips. She did a one-eighty and stomped off, the long tail of her Santa hat swinging.

"Belle." I waved.

She trotted over to stand next to me. "Hello, Kristen, Delaney. I knew we needed more than one mulled wine booth."

"Can you tell me the name of that alpine man who runs the booth with the German pastries, the *Christstollen* booth?" I asked her.

"Why do you want to know?"

Because I was back to considering my other theories. But I answered, "Kris, here, is German. It's a small community. Maybe they know each other." I sneaked a look at my friend and she gave me the *silent-question-stare* back.

"Oh, well, it's Michael Murphy. You know him, Kristen?"

Kris shook her head.

"Murphy? That doesn't sound German. Maybe his mother is German, not his dad," I took a guess.

Belle said, "He's not German. He just loves all things German."

"But he speaks the language."

"That's right." Belle extracted her phone, checked her screen, and slid it back into her pocket. "Got to go. The carolers are getting ready to set up near the giant tree. Are you going to come watch? They're wearing

Victorian costumes and everything. The Festival Queen is presiding."

Kris said, "You should see that, Delaney."

"I'll head down there in a bit." I nodded at the market organizer who seemed to have everything in control. She said goodbye and set out down the fairway with purposeful strides. I asked Kris, "Why would Candace make an appearance at the fair if her fiancé is being questioned by the police? You'd think she'd be at the sheriff's station waiting for him."

"I don't know, but you're right," she agreed.

We were interrupted by two customers, and once they left, Kris asked me, "Why did you tell Belle I wanted to know about the German vendor? I don't pay attention to my German heritage. I never even think about it."

"Sorry I involved you, but I needed an excuse to find out his name, and that's all I could come up with." I explained, "Michael Murphy's a suspect."

"Another suspect? There's so many." Her eyes narrowed into sharp arrows. "Why didn't you just go over there, introduce yourself, and ask him his name?"

"I didn't think he spoke English." I gave her a palms up. "And his booth has rats."

Her lip curled.

We were both distracted when Axle swooshed by on one of the public scooters with Shannon right behind him. I caught a quick glimpse of Axle's knit cap and gray hoodie and Shannon's vintage look with her cat-eye glasses. They flew between the brew pub kiosk and the candle booth. He and Shannon must've zipped over here from Byron's. Maybe Byron didn't have any work for Axle today, and I felt bad that after I'd dropped him off

I hadn't stuck around to find out.

A police siren blared *WEE-oww-WEE-oww*. Thinking *now what*, I looked all around, sensing the sound getting closer, but in the way of sirens, the direction was hard to place.

Kristen cried out, "Look! Over there!"

I wheeled around to see where she was pointing. A Spruce Ridge police cruiser, with light bar flashing and siren shrieking, nudged down the market's main thoroughfare, and people stepped aside to get out of the way. A group of teens ran by, a dog got off leash and dodged among the runners, and several of them knocked against me in their quest to escape. The sound of dozens of feet trampling, a dog barking, and the siren echoing made my pulse rev up to heart-attack speed. I stumbled and fell to my knees.

"Delaney!" Kristen hitched herself over the counter in a flash. She yanked me up from the tarmac and together we mashed ourselves against the front of the booth. We both seemed to hold a collective breath, taking in the chaotic sight.

The teens soon forged past us, leaving overturned garbage bins and discarded paper cups behind. Glass ornaments from wreaths and garlands, which had been draped between the huts and light poles, now lie broken in places. Strings of bulbs fell and popped on the ground. The nasty smell of burning electrical wire hung in the air.

Kris asked me, "Are you okay?"

"I'm fine." To be honest, I wasn't fine. I felt shaky and scared. But I wanted to be fine for Kris. "Where'd the cop car go?"

"Let's find out."

I sped after her as she skirted the booth with the

gingerbread houses, and I stumbled into the back of her when she came to a halt.

Axle was a few yards away, on the ground, tangled up in the fallen lights, his scooter tossed to the side. Shannon stood a few feet from him, white faced, as a police officer assisted him to a stand, then placed him in the back of the police cruiser. The patrol car eased down the main street through the rodeo grounds and pulled into traffic at Fifth Ave.

A vile, bitter taste filled my mouth and my stomach felt queasy. I grabbed Kristen's arm. "Holy Crapoli! What just happened?"

Kristen said in a shaky voice, "We need to ask Shannon." We dashed over to Axle's girlfriend, and Kris took her in a hug.

Shannon gulped air. Her eyes were wide in fear behind her retro glasses.

"What was that about?" I asked her. It appeared the police were rounding up all the bad guys, but Axle had nothing to do with the murder, would never poison anyone, and didn't even know Meredith Yarborough or Jack Frier or anyone else in this drama.

"They accused Axle of selling stolen goods." Her lips trembled as she spoke.

Prickles of alarm ran over my spine. *Yikes*. This was bad. My bad. If I hadn't reported the stolen earbuds Axle wouldn't be in this situation.

I jabbed Kris in the arm. "Kristen, you need to call Zach. Right now. That was a Spruce Ridge cop who took Axle away." My head snapped toward Shannon. "Call your uncle and tell him what happened." I patted my jacket pocket for my phone, hoping I had the presence of mind not to have dropped it. Found it. "I'm calling Will."

Kristen explained to Shannon, "That's her stepdad. He's an attorney."

We all got busy on our phones, but Kris got off first and interrupted my call to Will. "Delaney, tell him Zach says Axle is going to be released soon. Will doesn't need to come all the way to town, unless he wants to."

"Okay, good." I relayed the information, and Will promised to contact the Spruce Ridge Police to let them know Axle was represented by legal counsel. I'd never truly warmed up to my stepdad and was even a tad cool toward him, a stubborn childhood habit, but I'll admit it was nice to have a lawyer in the family.

After hanging up, I said to Kris, "I hope you gave Zach a piece of your mind. What's going on with this city? Are the police crazy causing such a scene?"

Kris brushed a few stray hairs away from her face and shook her head. She looked as dumbfounded as I felt.

I asked, "Should we head over to the police station and pick up Axle if he's going to be released?"

"Yes. Zach said to ask for him, but I can't go. I need to get back to my booth. I didn't even lock it up." As Kris hastened away, she said, "Let me know what happens." She was joined by Belle and they kept walking, heads together. Belle was probably concerned about the police showing up here, too.

"I want to go with you." Shannon yanked on my arm. "And we should pick up Uncle Byron. He said he wants to come."

"Okay. My car's parked over there." I motioned behind us.

The two of us hurried to my Fiat. The Old Man was waiting in front of his closed-up autobody shop when we pulled in. After Shannon shoehorned herself into my tiny back seat and Byron plopped into the passenger side, I asked, "You're closed?" It was a Saturday, usually his busiest day.

"I don't have that much ta do." Byron shifted around to find the seatbelt. "Good thing I wasn't in the middle of a job. What are we goin' ta do about that boy?"

"I wish I knew." I couldn't get my head around what'd happened.

From the back seat, Shannon extracted Byron's seatbelt from the clip and handed it to him over his shoulder. "Thanks, Old Man, for coming with us."

Christmas lights dangled from the brick one-story that housed Spruce Ridge's police station on the corner of Main Street. We settled ourselves in the orange plastic chairs in the low budget lobby with an artificial tree decorated with what looked like ornaments hand-drawn by schoolchildren. Passing time until Zach came out, I stared at the fake Ficus tree in a wicker basket, the polished linoleum with black scuff marks, and the wall of photos of the police chiefs for the last fifty years. Time passed slowly and none of us had much to say. Finally, Zach led Axle out from behind the locked security door, which I knew opened to the bullpen of desks with phones ringing and officers typing on their computers.

Axle's knit cap was missing and his hair stood up all over. Had the police booked him? Because he did look like a really *gadawful* mug shot.

Zach remained at the front desk while Axle crossed the waiting room to join us, then the officer disappeared behind the security door. He must not want to talk to us or answer our questions.

Shannon wrapped her arms around Axle, and he returned the hug after a sideways glance at her uncle.

Byron clamped a strong hand on his shoulder and gave him a stern look, then we beat it out of there. Axle crammed into the back seat with Shannon, and Byron resumed the front passenger seat.

As I steered out of the lot, my first question was, "What happened to your hair? It smells like burned hair in here." Like sulfur. *Yuck.*

"I was shocked by the falling lights." Axle's hair did appear like it'd been zapped by a thousand volts.

"So, tell us what happened. What did the police do to you?" Shannon placed her hand on his arm.

"You know I was meeting with a guy who wanted a pair of those wireless earbuds." He continued after Shannon nodded. "When the police showed up, the guy buzzed off. I'm glad I only had two sets on me because the cops took those. Man, I've only been able to sell three, total. They're harder to unload than I thought." His words were belligerent.

I speared him with a glower in the rearview mirror. "Axle, so not the point." I was picturing him in prison garb here.

But he acted like he didn't hear me. "How am I going to flip the rest? It's not like I can put them on Craig's List."

Byron asked in his low, booming voice, "How many ya' got left?"

"I had nine, but the police confiscated two. So I got seven left."

"Wait. So you started out with twelve and sold three? Didn't you say you were pricing them for a hundred and fifty dollars each?" I did the quick math. "If you bought twelve for fifty apiece, that cost you six hundred bucks, and you've recouped four-fifty. Count yourself lucky."

Byron half-turned to ask him, "Where are you keepin' the rest of 'em?"

"The apartment."

The apartment? That was my apartment! I was harboring stolen goods. Of course I was. I hadn't thought about that before. *Duh.* "What if the police get a search warrant? Is the crime worse the more stolen goods you have?" I aimed the car for Roasters on the Ridge and my apartment above the coffee shop.

"I don't know for sure if they're stolen." Axle looked at me to see if I was buying it.

"Axle, I'll tell you when the cops will believe that. A big fat never."

Byron said, "I'm surprised they didn't search your place already. Makes no sense they didn't."

I suppressed a groan. "Right. Seems they went to a lot of trouble to pick up Axle. What was that all about?"

No one knew the answer to that. The four of us fell in line as we climbed the steps to the apartment. When we came through the door, I greeted Boss, and Axle went to his room for the earbuds.

He returned with the torn sack and set it on the kitchen counter. "Do you think Kristen will let us hide these at her place? You have her key, right? We can stash them over there right now."

My jaw dropped. "No way, you dufus. Zach and Kris are practically engaged."

Axle pursed his lips. "Oh yeah, he's over there all the time."

"That's not exactly what I meant, but that's another good reason."

Axle grumbled, "She'd help me out if she could. I

was doing her a favor. With each sale, I gave away a coupon for the coffee booth."

"No!" Lord, no. I splayed my hand across my chest. "You gave out coffee coupons with stolen goods?"

"Hey, I was just trying to do a solid for Kris."

"Some favor." I cringed because the coupons were another of my brilliant ideas. "I'll put the earbuds in my purse. I doubt a search warrant for your stuff would cover my bag. Or my car. I'll stow them in my car. But Axle, you need to figure out what to do. Talk to my stepdad." I explained that I'd phoned Will.

Heavy footsteps on the stairs followed by a knock on the door made all of us exchange alarmed looks. We froze, none of us moved, then the knock sounded again, and I screamed. Boss barked and rushed to the door.

"Delaney! Are you okay?" Ephraim was outside.

Axle hissed through clenched teeth, "Cops! They're here."

I snatched the sack and shoved it to the bottom of my handbag, then went to open the door.

Ephraim stepped across the threshold, out of uniform. So, he wasn't here on police business. "Are you okay? I heard you yell."

My bag drew my eyes like a magnet. "I was surprised. I'm jumpy, I guess."

"We were just leavin' " Byron ushered his niece out in front of him, and Axle ran out after them.

I closed the door and turned around. The sheriff's height forced me to tilt my head backward to look up. "Hey, Lopez." I was trying for nonchalant.

"Hello." His deep voice rumbled in his chest.

"What are you doing here?" *Oops*. That sounded rude. I was ready to explode in a fit of nerves.

189

"You didn't know anything about Axle selling stolen goods, I hope." He may not have his uniform on, but his cop face was on. "They ran out of here fast enough."

"Would I have told you about the earbuds if I knew?" I blushed, thinking I may have just told a lie. But it wasn't a lie; it was a rhetorical question, okay? I had an apple-sized lump of panic in my throat and stared down at my hands. "Why did the city police take Axle in? I thought the sheriff's department was investigating the stolen goods ring."

"It's an interagency operation. The Denver police are involved, too."

"You couldn't keep Axle out of it? For me?"

"It wasn't my call."

"Humpf," was the only thing I managed to say. I opened the refrigerator, pulled out two long-necked beers, and tossed one to Ephraim. He twisted off the cap and took a swig. I tried twisting mine, but my hands were sweaty and shaky, so Ephraim opened it. We sank onto the counter stools with our beers in front of us.

I asked, "Why all the drama picking up Axle at the market? I almost got trampled. Again."

His lips thinned. "I agree that was a mistake. But they were trying to catch him in the act, except his buyer got away."

I followed the condensation on my beer bottle with my trembling finger. "Why did the police release Axle? Did you have anything to do with that?"

"No, I didn't." He paused for a long moment. "But I have a proposition."

Chapter 14

I clutched the counter to keep from falling off my stool. "What proposition?"

"If Axle cooperates, the DA won't press charges. I specifically asked that he not be charged yet so there won't be any kind of a record. He's not really the one we're after."

"Cooperate how?" I focused on Ephraim's face. I liked this man, not just because he's good-looking, but because he's a good sheriff and a kind, fair person, even if he didn't share everything that was going on. At least he was talking to me now.

He snagged the bottom rung of my stool with the toe of his cowboy boot and scooted me closer. "His testimony that he bought the earbuds from the Emporium. Along with your testimony, we'll have them dead to rights."

I dropped my head in agreement. Axle and I were both going to be snitches.

The sheriff tapped the counter with his index finger. "This will teach Axle a lesson."

Axle did seem a little rebellious with his bad-tempered attitude. Maybe this was for the best after all. I asked, "Have you arrested the Jennings couple?"

"Not yet. We need Axle's cooperation first. Will Sharpton called to let us know Axle has a lawyer. So, we need to negotiate through your stepdad now. It was you who arranged that?"

"If you'd warned me you were only teaching him a lesson, I would've left Will out of it." I wish I hadn't called him now. Mom would find out and I'd never hear the end of it.

"You know I couldn't do that. Doesn't matter anyway. I'm sure Sharpton will tell his client to cooperate."

"What about the criminals who hijacked the trucks carrying the freight? Weren't you going to go after them? They would be a bigger bust than Axle."

"It's only a matter of time before we round them up. The interagency task force is working that angle." His fingers played with my shirt sleeve. "Frier was released today. There weren't any pickpocket complaints during his hospital stay. I doubt there will be any more now that he's out because he knows we're on to him."

"I'm glad for that. I heard you took Rory Rearden and Noel Yarborough in to the station for more questioning." Noel seemed the more likely suspect as the victim's brother, but Rory was probably as high on the sheriff's list since he and Meredith dated.

"We did."

"You might as well tell me about it since Rory will anyway."

He shrugged. "Okay. Yarborough told us Rearden threatened the victim after she broke up with him. Rearden denied it."

"Let me get this straight. Meredith broke up with Rory, and he threatened her? That was, like, five years ago. And he told me it was a mutual break-up."

"Evidently it wasn't. I know five years is a long time to harbor resentment, but the victim had recently started a new relationship and that could have stirred up renewed jealousy."

"Rory wouldn't kill anyone."

"Maybe so, but he said if he couldn't have her, nobody could."

I laughed out loud. "That sounds like a cliché. Come on." Although Rory often ran at the mouth and I could see him saying something like that.

Ephraim took a pull at his drink, finishing the bottle. "I need to check in at the station."

"You're not on duty, right?"

"No, but I'm going over there to see where everything stands."

We both got up. He stopped in the doorway and rested one hand on either side of the frame. "It's going to work out with Axle, you'll see."

"Thanks." I stepped up to him and brushed my lips against his. He looked even hotter in *civvies* if that was possible.

After he left, I sent a text to Rory: —*need to talk.*

He replied that he was at the coffee shop, so I gathered my coat, scarf, and mittens, slung my purse containing the bag of hot earbuds over my shoulder, and locked the door behind me. I hoofed it down the stairs to Roasters.

Guy was cleaning the roasting machines, and Sierra was emptying the trash since it was near closing time. A couple of people wearing ski jackets and bibs talked about slope conditions while retrieving their to-go cups. Rory Rearden sat at a table in the window nursing a drink, and I plopped into the chair across from him. His light-hazel eyes looked worried, and his dark-brown freckles stood out on his pale face. I hadn't seen his normally lopsided grin in a long time.

I said, "I heard the cops picked you up again."

"Yeah, and what's that about?" Anger boosted his voice. "Police brutality."

"It does seem excessive, but they brought Noel Yarborough in for more questions, too."

His forehead ridged with frown lines. "I know, I saw him there. Noel was taken into one interrogation room and I was put in another. It's like the cops are playing games, trying to pit us against each other. Like on *Law and Order*."

"Yeah, I heard Noel threw you under the bus."

"I know. That rat fink. I thought we were friends. Jeez, we've known each other since forever and this is what he does? What kind of a friend is that?"

"Listen to you. You were the one who practically denied knowing the Yarboroughs. Was there any truth to what he said? Did you threaten Meredith?"

"No. I mean, not really. Actually, I don't remember what I said. It was quite a few years ago." He was punching a fist in his hand repeatedly but said, "My feelings were hurt, but I wouldn't harm anyone, you know that. You know that, Delaney. You know it."

I'd just told Ephraim that Rory couldn't be the killer, but did I know that for sure? I wasn't that close to this frequent coffee shop customer. I didn't really know him that well, although we'd been acquainted for some time now. Was he capable of murder? I didn't know. Was he displaying over-the-top anger issues? Yes, this I did know. But he'd asked me to help find the killer. Would he encourage me to investigate if he didn't want to get caught—if he was the guilty one? No, surely not. I really couldn't believe he was involved.

He broke into my musings. "What have you learned so far, Delaney? Have you found any suspects?"

"I can't remember where we left off." I fished my notes out of my handbag, carefully avoiding the sack of earbuds, and handed the pocket-sized notepad to Rory. "Here's what I have so far."

He read down the page. "You haven't figured out who the married boyfriend is? You didn't find out anything about him? Nothing at all?"

I sat back in my seat and bit a thumbnail. "No." But I'd added the name Michael Murphy to my suspect list. The married alpine man who ran the *Christstollen* booth. Maybe he was the mystery man?

"Well, I haven't either, and I've been asking around. Nobody knows who the boyfriend was. No one's saying anything." His shoulders slumped. "The police are still focused on me, no thanks to Noel. They searched my apartment, my car, my office. They took the bottles of wine I bought when we went to the tasting room together. I told the cops I purchased those after Meredith died, but they took them anyway because I didn't keep the receipt."

"The police showed up at your office? That had to be awkward. This isn't hurting your job, is it?" That kind of police attention could be damaging. But since Rory worked for his dad, he likely had a measure of job security.

"It was beyond awkward, but my parents know I'd never hurt Merry. And they're not too happy about the police hassling me, either, so they're on my side about that. I spent all morning at the sheriff's station. Jeez, I missed about four hours of work."

I didn't bring up how often—like all the time—Rory

took coffee breaks at Roasters. Like right this minute.

He went on, "At least I'm not hard pressed with any deadlines."

"I have a question. Do you know Noel's fiancée, Candace Jennings?"

"Sure, sure. I've met her a couple of times. Seems like a nice girl. Pretty. Very nice looking." A guy would think like that.

"How did Noel meet her? Do you know when they're getting married?

"Mutual friends, I think. They don't have a date set. Noel said maybe next year. He wants to concentrate on the winery right now."

"She's the Festival Queen."

"Candace talked her parents into managing a booth at the market when Noel told her the winery was going to have one. Then she entered the competition to be queen."

Okay, so that explained a few of the loose ends, I guess.

Sierra appeared at our side. "I need to wipe your table." All the other customers had left and the dining area was empty.

"Let me get out of your way." Rory gathered his drink, then tossed his scarf over his shoulder like he was ready to brave the elements. "Call me if you find out anything new."

"Will do." I stood up to make my exit, too, but first I asked Sierra, "Do you need any help with closing? Want me to sweep?"

"Sure." She handed me a broom.

Rory took off out the door, and Sierra turned the *Open* sign to *Closed*. I shook my arms out of my jacket and hung it on the back of a chair before sweeping the floor under the tables. After that, I mopped while Sierra washed the windows. Guy counted the register and made out the bank deposit, then we collected our things and walked out the employee back entrance together.

"I'm heading over to the market to drop off supplies." Sierra pointed to her car. The back seat was loaded with sleeves of paper cups and boxes of industrial-sized bags of sugar. "You want to come with me?"

"Let me put something in my car first." I opened the hatchback and snaked Axle's bag out of my purse. I hid the bag by covering it with an old sweatshirt, relieved not to have stolen goods on my person anymore.

I climbed into Sierra's car, and we followed Guy out of the parking lot. He steered his Taurus, front-wheel drive, south toward the bank, and Sierra aimed her Chevrolet Spark, also front-wheel drive, north toward Fifth, which would take us to the marketplace.

Sierra didn't stick around the coffee kiosk, and I didn't blame her after working all day at the coffee shop. She dropped off the supplies and left, so I helped Kristen stock the booth and wait on customers. I caught Kris up on what was happening with Axle, but Zach had already told her about the proposed agreement.

She added, "And I asked Zach about that maintenance man, but he didn't tell me a thing. I guess he can't talk about it."

Not that I expected anything less.

I recounted what Ephraim had disclosed, then said, "Are you worried about being stuck with all those mugs?" The tall shelves still held more than I could count.

"Several people have been coming in with coupons." Kristen had a hopeful look as she stirred the pot of chocolate on the burner. "Besides, I can't worry about it. Worry accomplishes nothing. I just need to trust God to take care of me." She was back to her calm and serene self, and I wondered what it would be like to be so confident that everything was going to turn out all right.

A half hour before the market was to close for the night, I once again helped with end-of-day chores. The booth was easier than the store, being a tiny space. Kristen cleaned the coffee machines every night because that was the key to great-tasting brews, so while she did that, I swept the plywood floor and wiped the plank counter. Kristen left for the bank, and I stayed to wait for any last stragglers before the lights went down. Three customers showed up asking for cocoa, and since we'd already poured the last remanent of the hot chocolate into to-go cups, I gave them out for free, glad not to waste any of Kristen's drinks of perfection.

The last strains of "The Christmas Song" ended, and the lights blinked out all over the fairgrounds. I pulled the hatch closed, the rolling shutter hit the ledge, making a grating sound against the wood, and I turned the key in the padlock. As I made my way past other stalls, dark and locked up for the night, my phone rang on the company line.

I answered, "Del's Towing."

The caller said, "I need a tow. I'm stranded out on Tall Chief Road in a Kia Seltos, and you can't miss me because the hood is up."

Kris was right to be optimistic. I had a job! "I'm leaving right now, but it'll take me about twenty minutes to get there."

"That's fine." The caller disconnected.

I picked up my speed and jogged in my cork-heeled wedges to the shortcut through the Christmas tree lot. It wasn't until I reached the vendor parking lot that I realized I didn't have a vehicle parked there. I'd ridden with Sierra who'd left right away. Kristen was long gone, too. And wouldn't you know it, I was in a big hurry right now.

Should I call Kristen? She was probably busy with the night deposit. And Ephraim was at the station…but I'd walked past a scooter half a block back. That's what the public e-scooters were for, providing transportation to and from the *Christkindl Market*. I could ride one to Oberly Motors and pick up the tow truck. It wouldn't take much longer than driving over in a car.

I reversed my steps back through the tree lot. Without the strings of bulbs to light the way, the trees appeared like rows of giants with pointed heads and outstretched arms. I brushed through the clawing branches that snagged my coat and reentered the fairgrounds. None of the stall workers were around. Everyone had left. No music touched my ears. No alluring aromas tickled my nose. No scent of sugary pastries or gingerbread cookies or warm yeasty bread or sizzling sausages. It hit me that I was starved, having skipped a few meals in the craziness of the day. The ever-present pine scent lingered on my clothes, and the image of Meredith's dead body crept into my consciousness.

My feet had just trod over the spot where she'd died. My heart clenched, and fear fluttered in my chest. My courage drained away like coffee dripping from the brewer.

But I spotted an electric scooter up ahead. The last user left it propped up by its kickstand near the gingerbread booth, where the rolled-down awning hid all the gingerbread houses. I scanned the vehicle's barcode with my phone to unlock the machine, slung my purse strap across my shoulder to snug it against me for the ride, then hit the throttle. Nothing happened. I twisted the throttle several times to rev up the engine, but the engine did not fire.

A red light blinked from a gizmo on the handlebar. I checked my phone app and learned this scooter needed a charge. The app showed another a couple hundred yards away that still had power.

Okay then. I'll just walk across the marketplace and find the other electric skateboard. So what? It's spooky, dark, no lights, no music, no people. No biggie. *I could do this. I would do this.*

I didn't have much choice after all.

I ran like batshit-crazy in the brisk wintery air, my breath coming out in ghostly white puffs. Obstacles popped up in front of me out of the black expanse. Giant nutcrackers, Santas, and snowmen became apparent as I dodged right and left. Vapor rose from the huts' snow-capped roofs, appearing wraithlike and ethereal, as if disembodied spirits fled skyward into the dark. Tendrils of horror curled up my spine. My vision tunneled and everything appeared as if far away, like an out-of-body experience.

Creepy, much?

In panic mode, I stumbled into the round metal fire pit. I bounced off that and hit the railing alongside the skating rink. I rubbed my stinging hands together and leaned over to catch my breath. My teeth chattered, and

I was scared out of my wits, chicken that I am. Why didn't I bring the pepper spray I always carried with me on late-night tows?

I swallowed in deep breaths to calm myself. A little self-talk affirmation was needed here. Like…how many times had I passed this same spot, walked this same length of the market while shopping, meeting friends, taking pictures, having a good time? All in the daylight of course. But there was no reason to be scared. There was nothing different now, except it was dark, and I was alone.

Note to self: Suck it up, you wimp.

This irrational terror was all the more reason for me to solve the crime. I needed to be able to take care of myself without scaring myself half to death.

I forced my feet to move on at a slower pace. My eyes became accustomed to the dark, so the familiar shapes, rather than phantom shapes, registered in my brain. The night grew calm and peaceful with a gentle wind, and a scooter came into sight lying on the ground next to the carousel. I crossed my fingers and hoped the app was correct, that the vehicle was charged. I picked it up off the tarmac, and after activating the trip on my phone app, I twisted the throttle and it roared to life. *Thank you! Thank you! Danke Schoen!* Huh, another German word I just remembered. I hopped on and left the dark marketplace behind.

Only fifteen minutes later than the time I promised, I arrived on Tall Chief Road in a frozen state and apologized to my customer for the delay. I stomped my tall wedges and slapped the sleeves of my puffy coat but remained chilled to the bone. My tow truck was running cold, too, not having been driven in a few days. But after a groan and a whiff of hydraulic fluid, the metal claws grabbed onto the vehicle's front wheels, closed around the tires, and the boom raised the Kia Seltos's front end.

Other than trying to peer through the frosty windshield and unsticking my fingers from the ice-cold steering wheel, I hauled the car and my customer to his mechanic's shop without incident. I captured the VIN on my phone and gave the guy one of my business cards. He thanked me several times. That was my favorite part of the job, the feeling that I was helping someone. This is what kept me going.

When I crawled under the duvet back at my place, I coaxed Boss into bed with me and pulled the covers up to my chin. I drifted off to sleep, comforted by a job well done and Boss's big furry body warming my toes.

****

The next morning I awoke with dry eyes. I craved caffeine, but Roasters on the Ridge was closed on Sundays. The coffee kiosk at the market was open, though, because Kristen had made an exception to her Sunday-off rule. But that was too far to go, so I started a pot in my kitchen—not as good as Kristen's, but it would do.

Lured by the smell of coffee, Axle met me at the counter, and we bumped heads staring at the coffee pot, waiting for the last drip to drop. I couldn't help notice his hair stood up with static electricity. I extracted mugs from the cupboard, poured the black liquid, pushed a full cup into his hands, and grappled with a cup of my own. It was acrid, it was nutty, it was strong, and I threw down a long swallow like the caffeine addict I am.

"Did you talk to Will?" I asked.

It was obvious Axle had slept in his clothes. His

baggy jeans hung off his hips, and his sweatshirt looked like it could use a spin in the washing machine.

He leaned back against the counter and interlocked his fingers behind his head. "We're meeting at the police station tomorrow. I'm not supposed to admit to anything, except that I bought two of the earbuds from the Emporium."

"Excuse me?" My shoulders went rigid. "He wants you to lie?"

"No, but he said not to admit to anything else. I'm supposed to say no comment."

I drew a deep breath then blurted out, "What are you going to do with the earbuds you haven't sold?"

He dropped his hands to the counter and toyed with his mug. "I don't know."

"Well, I hid them." And he'd have to ask me for them if he wanted them back. And I wasn't giving them back. The buds were going to the Clear Creek Sheriff anonymously as soon as Axle's part in the stolen goods ring was cleared up.

I ruffled his hair, and the strands bent in the direction of my hand. I moved my hand side to side, and the hair followed my movements like a magnet. "What's with the hair?"

His fingers went up to smooth the floating strands down flat. I dangled my fingers over his head again, and the hair stood up once more.

"Is this static from your knit cap?"

He squinted one eye at me. "It never did that before."

"Maybe it's from that electrical shock you had yesterday." I laughed with a nervous quaver.

His eyes bugged out. "Can that happen?"

"I don't know. Maybe." My eyebrows must be hovering near my hairline.

"*Woah-kay*." He rubbed the top of his head—hard—and loud crackling sounds shot out while his hair floated upward toward an unseen force.

We stared wide-eyed at each other for a moment. I asked, "What are you doing today? You're not working, right?"

"I'm hanging with Shannon."

They made a cute couple, and I was glad she was sticking with him in spite of his recent problems. "Good one, Axle." We slapped palms in a high five.

"Don't press for details." He stood up and headed toward his room.

I covered my ears with my hands and said to his retreating back, "Gack, no. I wouldn't want to be grossed out."

I dragged my tired bod through a shower and dressed in a beige top, jeans, and clunky brown lace-up boots. Brown because I expected to have one of those exhausting, worn-out kind of days and I felt lower than dirt. I checked my phone, no missed calls, and my online reviews, nothing new there either. Although my least favorite thing to do, I set up my laptop in the kitchen and entered receipts into a spreadsheet, and when I was done with that, I headed to the marketplace to reward myself with one of Kristen's lattes.

The early sun shone brightly through the raised awnings of the open kiosks, and melting snow drizzled down from roofs to puddle on the ground. The market swarmed with tourists happy to prowl through the booths in such a picturesque setting. Strands of "Holly Jolly" streamed from the hidden sound system. The menacing giant nutcrackers and plastic snowmen from the night before appeared to be wishing me a happy morning.

After Kristen handed me a double espresso, I propped my butt on a stool and my elbows backward on her plywood counter and gazed across the path to the mulled wine booth. I needed to get more serious about talking to the vendors on my suspect list. I looked in my bag and took out my notes to review. *Suspects: Noel Yarborough (victim's brother), Michael Murphy (alpine man), Jack Frier (maintenance man), unknown married boyfriend, and the other woman who argued with the victim.* Two were not known to me, but three were.

I slid off my stool at the coffee kiosk and stepped over to the line at the wine stall. When it was my turn, I asked, "Noel, how are you?"

"I'm okay. Can I get you a mulled wine?"

I held up my espresso. "No thanks, I'm still drinking this." I glanced around. Coast clear. Time to put the screws on. I started with, "How are your folks?"

"They're still in shock, damn it all. Funeral is Tuesday. Maybe after that it'll seem real to them, but right now they're walking around in a daze. It's a good thing I'm running the business."

"I can only imagine how they feel, and you, too, Noel." I nodded, silent for a beat. "I lost my dad not long ago, and sometimes I still think of him as if he were alive. Your parents might feel that way, too. They might always feel that way."

Noel gathered dirty mugs off the counter and tossed them in a plastic tub, clanking the ceramic mugs together. "Merry drove me crazy, but she was my sister and grief hits at weird times. It sort of catches up. It's strange how the mind works. I know it's even worse for

Dad and Mom."

There was nothing I could add to that, so I let that thought hang between us for a moment. I asked, "Is there anything new in the investigation?"

"The police haven't said much for a while, not since the second victim. You heard that guy was released from the hospital? Seems like the case is at a standstill." He threw a metal ladle into the sink to join the mugs with a loud clatter. "Damn her for not telling me about her boyfriend. A married man. What was she thinking?"

I was used to his swearing outbursts by now. "Who did Merry date before the married guy? Maybe it's not him. Maybe there's a jealous boyfriend in her past?"

"Rory Rearden. That's who dated Merry last."

"Oh, really? Nothing in the years between?"

"Nobody serious. I can't even give you names."

"So, Rory, then." Should I bring up what Noel told the sheriff about Rory threatening Meredith? Would that only cause more conflict between the two friends? "You don't think Rory could have harmed your sister, do you?"

He blew out a sigh. "Do we really know what people are capable of?"

"Is there no one else you can think of that could be a suspect? How about problem customers? People she didn't get along with?"

"She never complained to me about anyone."

A man with a woman hanging on his arm approached the kiosk, and Noel went to help them, so I backed away and trudged the distance over to the Christmas tree lot. A selection of beautiful trees remained unsold, but my stomach recoiled at the strong scent of the pines. I waited a few minutes while the tree seller, Kane Quigley, assisted a young mom with a toddler, and when they left I said, "Hello, Kane."

He spun around and gave me a vertical sweep with his eyes. "Oh, hello, Delaney." The rolled-up sleeves of his plaid shirt revealed deep, red scratches from the pine boughs.

"Do you have a minute?"

Kane nodded. "Of course."

"I'd like to talk to you about Meredith."

"What?" His nostrils widened. "That again?"

"I just want to know if there's anything unusual you remember from the day she was found?" I pulled down my lips in a sour face and gestured vaguely away from us.

He slid a hand over his eyes. "I try not to think about it too hard."

"I hear ya. But I'm worried that the marketplace might be shut down again." A good excuse to question him, but it could happen if someone else fell victim to an attack.

He shoved his sleeves up higher on his wrists. "What? Have you heard something? Has someone else been poisoned?"

"No, I'm just concerned for my friend who runs the coffee booth at the other end of the market." I brandished a hand that way. "She still has a lot of inventory to sell."

"I'm worried about that, too. I've been selling trees, but I just got in another delivery I probably should've cancelled." He tore his gaze from me to focus on the rows of Christmas trees. We both peered through the branches beyond the Douglas firs and blue spruces, like we expected to find another body.

As unpleasant as this was, I should get to the point.

"You talked to Meredith, she said she didn't feel well and was on her way home, and…?" I prompted him.

"That's it, that's all I know." He spread out his fingers and shrugged, but his eyes widened slightly, like he just, this second, recalled something more.

"What?" I held my breath.

He adjusted his pushed-up sleeves as if taking the time to give it more thought. "After you left, I walked over to watch the police. They were trying to be discreet, but I saw them remove a bracelet from the body. They took it as evidence."

"What did it look like? Can you describe it?"

"Gold chain with a charm."

"One charm? Or more?"

"Just one."

"Can you remember what the charm looked like?"

"It was the letter 'M.' For her name, I assume, Meredith."

"Thanks for telling me, Kane." I gave him a big, grateful smile.

"Sure. Gotta go. Customer." He rushed over to help a woman steady one of the tall trees. He said, "Let me help you with this."

I'd seen similar bracelets before. Locked under glass on the counter at our favorite booth run by the Jennings couple.

Chapter 15

The purple mountains in the distance, their rocky peaks draped in white, reminded me of a beautiful image on a Christmas card. The air smelled as wonderful as a campfire at a cabin in the woods and my grandpa's cigar. Face to the breeze, I hurried past the *Christstollen* booth selling German pastries and handmade crafts but noticed the alpine man, Michael Murphy, at the counter. He was staring out at customers strolling by.

I retraced my steps to examine the hand-carved nativity scenes and the Santas with the tall pointed hats, keeping Alpine Man in my line of sight. Even though the market was busy, loaded with shoppers strolling the grounds and browsing through the stalls, there wasn't the usual crowd around his cash register, so I stepped forward. "*Guten Morgen*, Mr. Murphy." German I dredged up from somewhere.

He beamed. "*Guten Morgen.*"

"I love everything in your booth." The flaky apple strudel sprinkled in powder sugar made my mouth water.

"What can I get for you?" He spoke without an accent, but I now knew German was not his native tongue.

"You're not from Germany, are you?"

"I never said I was. I'm a high school German teacher." No wonder he knows the language.

"You ever been to Germany?"

"No, but I've always wanted to go there." He stepped out from behind the cash register.

"So what's with the *lederhosen*?"

He pulled at the suspenders and did a few steps like they do in that German folk dance. At the end, he smacked his knees and clapped his hands.

I didn't know what to say. "I'll take that nutcracker." As the alpine man bagged the wooden ornament, I asked, "Did you know the woman who was killed? The one from the mulled wine booth?"

"Ah, the *glühwein*. Yes, I remember her." He handed the sack to me. "That will be six-fifty."

I dug out my wallet. "So you knew her?"

"Not really."

"Never met up with her?"

"*Nein!* I am a married man." A cloud of anger passed over his face.

"Of course, sorry." I blushed scarlet and my cheeks radiated heat. "But you were seen arguing with her."

"That? She and another woman made a scene right here in front of my booth." He puckered his lips and his eyebrows drew together. "So rude. I told them both to leave. Six-fifty, please."

Handing him a five and two ones, I asked, "Who was the other woman?"

"I didn't recognize her. She had on a bulky sweater and her hat covered her hair. I can't tell you what she looked like, but I remember what she said. She was yelling at the woman who sold the *glühwein*, yelling something about stealing. I guess the woman had stolen something from her."

"What did she steal?"

"I don't know. If you don't mind, I have another

customer." His voice was impatient. "*Auf Wiedersehen.*"

"Thank you. Goodbye." I had a few more answers to my questions, at least.

What had I learned today? Stolen goods…bracelets with charms. Everything pointed to the Emporium. *Amiright?* Oh, yeah.

But…did I have the nerve to confront Frank and Holly Jennings? Would I be able to look either of them in the eye? I was going to testify against them. Me and Axle. Well, I might as well get this over with.

Head down, as if watching my brown boots hit the ground, I sauntered up to the Jennings' booth. Frank lounged against the plywood counter, on the alert for any customers with questions.

I had one. "Hello, Frank. I'm back." I gave him a smile.

He came to attention, straightening the boxes on the counter. "Is there anything I can help you with?"

"You had some bracelets in a glass case. They were gold with letter charms?"

"I don't know where those went to. I've been looking for them, too. I'm pretty sure we didn't sell them all, so they must've gotten moved around." His gaze darted behind him and back to the front. He shook his head and muttered, "She moved them. She can't do anything right."

"Holly?" *Crikey.* I didn't want to be the cause of even more discord between Frank and his wife. Another customer reached around me to a plastic Santa ornament, so I sidestepped and was overtaken by a crowd of shoppers. I wondered if Candace knew about Meredith's bracelet. Maybe she'd given it to her boyfriend's sister.

A tug on my elbow made me come face to face with

a handsome man, a friendly face in the crowd of consumers. "Hey, Tanner, how are you?"

His sister, Anne, and brother, Tate, were with him. Tate's eyes were glued to his phone, reminding me of a twelve-year-old Axle. Anne, a typical fifteen-year-old, clutched five or six bags to her chest with her left hand and with her right, flipped her long, straight blonde hair first one way, then the other, as her eyes scanned the crowd.

"Delaney, you remember Anne and Tate?" He glanced at his younger siblings with pride.

"Sure. Hello, there. Are you enjoying the market?" They didn't bother to answer me or even look at me.

Tanner had taken custody after their parents died within a couple of years of each other, one to cancer and one to lupus. This family had undergone a double tragedy, and I understood the depth of that pain. Anne and Tate were one of the reasons Tanner and I had broken up. Tanner hinted he didn't want kids of his own—probably because he was raising this pair already—and I thought that I might want kids someday. He wasn't interested in marriage or a deep commitment, plus his siblings always came first, as it should be.

"What do you think about that couple?" Tanner nodded his chin toward the Emporium. "When I unloaded their hut from my flatbed, he was on her case something terrible."

I agreed, "Yeah, I've heard them arguing several times now, and right in front of customers, too. It's nice you're taking an afternoon off to shop with Anne and Tate."

"Work has slowed down for now. When the market ends, I'll be busy hauling all the huts back into storage until next year." The city owned the booths and the vendors rented them each Christmas season.

"I suppose the shops on Main Street will want their towaway zones monitored again?"

"Right after Christmas. I'll let you know the exact date."

I shot him a grateful glance. "It will be nice to get back to our normal routine."

"Tanner, can we go now?" Anne whined.

"Sure, Anne." And with that, Tanner said goodbye and followed his sister to the booth of mittens and scarves. His brother trailed along behind without taking his eyes off his phone. I stared at their backs and thought how similar they looked, each of them tall and thin and blonde. They crossed in front of Belle, recognizable in the red stocking cap, and I hustled to catch up with her.

"Belle," I shouted. She stopped and turned. I said, "Your husband told me I should talk to you about Meredith."

"What's that?" She glanced at her watch. "Why would Kane tell you that?"

"I guess because you know everybody at the market." I gave her an encouraging smile. "Did you ever see her with anyone?"

"Why do you want to know?"

"Just curious since I work in the booth across from her kiosk." Her shoulders hunched up as she buttoned her jacket against the cold and looked at me with narrowed eyes. I said, "I know my question must sound weird. Except I found the body and…"

"That's right. I remember you were the one." Her shoulders relaxed. "I don't know what I can tell you. She probably talked to Kane more than she talked to me."

"Why's that?"

"He's a capable male, handy with a hammer and saw. All the women seem to come to him for help." Belle stared up at the cloudy sky with a scowl. "That's how he does such a good business, I suppose."

"You heard about Jack Frier?"

"Of course." She turned her gaze back to me and gave me a steely-eyed stare. "He's feeling better and back on the job. You know he's a married man?"

"He is?" I gasped. The muscle-bound maintenance man with an ego was married.

"I need to get going. I've been summoned to the gingerbread kiosk." Belle pushed through the crowd and receded out of sight.

Just then, as if our words had summoned him, Jack Frier zoomed down the path in the motorized golf cart he treated like a muscle car with trash bins on the back. I waved at him, but he kept going. He probably thought I waved because I had a crush. He and Belle both. I'm sure they'd discussed it.

Out of the corner of my eye, I caught a glimpse of Axle and Shannon on skateboards. Boss trotted out in front of Axle, pulling him along by his leash, and Axle held onto one of Shannon's hands. She balanced on her own skateboard, and they all wound like a train through the shoppers. Scarves billowed out behind them; even Boss had a festive scarf around his neck. They looked like they were laughing and having fun.

I know I should feel all *Christmas-y* and happy myself, with the music, the snow, the shoppers, and the sun shining in the winter sky, but it hit me that I was alone today. I didn't have family nearby, like Tanner did. I wasn't with my dog or my special someone, like Axle.

I wasn't helping Kristen at the kiosk; I wasn't busy with the towing business. I hadn't received a call for a tow this morning. I wasn't getting anywhere solving the crime, either.

Fairgoers streamed past me when I came to a stop next to the giant Christmas tree. I didn't want to do the rest of Sunday by myself. I needed a friend and who better than the sheriff?

I called him on my cell. "Hey, handsome. Want to come help me buy a tree?" Christmas was less than two weeks away, and I still needed to do this.

"I was just thinking about you. I'm off work today." His deep voice made my stomach do a flip-flop.

This was his first day off since the crime. Would he want to have anything to do with the fair—and crime scene—today? He was usually here in connection with the investigation.

I said, "I'm at the market. Right by the lighted tree and the ice rink. Is it too much to ask for you to come over?"

"Of course not. Give me ten minutes, and I'll be there."

"Okay." I hung up and slid the phone into my pocket.

Holly Jennings walked toward me, and we said *hello* to each other as we passed. Then I turned around to catch up with her. I called out, "Holly!"

She paused to wait for me as I moved in closer.

"I met your daughter, Candace, the other day. And your granddaughter, Ivy." I thought this was as good an opening as any. And Holly was not in her booth, distracted and busy with customers. Hopefully, she'd have a moment to talk to me.

"When was that?" She raised an eyebrow.

"Let's see, I met Ivy last week." It was probably less intimidating to talk about grandkids. Didn't every grandmother love to talk about the grands?

"Oh yeah, Candy brought Ivy over to ride the carousel." Her brows went up another notch. "Were you on the carousel with my husband?"

"No! I mean, yes, I rode the carousel, but I wasn't *with* Frank. I was with, uh, someone else." I blushed at the lie.

She grasped my sleeve. "Did you talk to him? Did my husband say anything about me?"

I tapped my fingers to my lips wondering how to answer her. A crowd of people surged past us on both sides.

"Anything bad?" Her chin was tucked low and she looked up from behind her lashes.

I don't think he'd badmouthed his wife in front of his granddaughter, but it was hard to remember. I said, "We were both standing on the merry-go-round, Ivy was on a unicorn, and uh, we talked about how he wished he owned a carousel. That's right. And I said it seemed like your booth is popular."

She let go of my sleeve, appearing relieved.

"Are you okay, Holly? Is there anything you want to tell me?"

"No." She brushed me off.

Was she a battered wife? I'd studied the battered woman syndrome, and I'd worked with abused women when I was employed with Social Services after college. I didn't want to overreact and imagine something that wasn't there, but I didn't want to ignore a cry for help, either. I knew from experience that women in those situations often felt helpless and refused to talk about the abuse. I made up my mind to ask Kris to stop by the Emporium and talk to Holly so I could get a second opinion.

A man's strong arms went around me from behind. "There you are, Delaney." Ephraim lifted me off my feet in a bear hug before setting me back down.

Laughing, I said, "Holly, this is Ephraim. Ephraim, this is Holly Jennings." I swung my *Christstollen* sack in Holly's direction. "She's the one who operates the Emporium."

He stole a glance her way, which I knew was more observant than it appeared. "We've met. Nice to see you again, Mrs. Jennings. Delaney, you were supposed to wait for me by the tree. Of course, I had no trouble spotting you over here." He tugged on my long red braid, and we gave each other broad smiles.

Holly alternated her gaze between me and Ephraim, then bestowed on me a quick up-and-down assessment. "Is this your boyfriend?"

My nose turned as red as the burgundy color of the mulled wine. "Uh…" I looked at Ephraim. I hadn't actually called him my *boyfriend* in front of him. We hadn't quite categorized our relationship. He was smiling, his dimples deepening as if enjoying my discomfort.

"Well, I'll let you two go." Holly whirled around on her heel.

"I'll see you later," I said when she took off down the walkway.

Ephraim gently touched his lips to mine, and I flushed with pleasure. He was my boyfriend! If I could only say it. Out loud. To his face. We held hands and walked the length of the marketplace and back, but I knew he was only humoring me. The market didn't hold the same wonder and excitement for Ephraim. I'm sure he didn't look at it the same way I did. He was probably keeping an eye out for pickpockets and stolen goods. And the killer.

Actually I was looking for the killer, too.

I looped my arm through his. "What do you want to do next?"

"Let's go back to my place for lunch. My mom gave me a pan of tamales and there's a ton of them."

"Sounds great." I loved his mom's cooking.

Note to self: Tell Ephraim's mom she should sell her delicious tamales at the *Christkindl Market* next year.

He pointed me toward the exit but paused to ask, "Wait, should we look at trees first?"

"I don't want to bother with it now after all. Let's eat lunch, and we can come back this afternoon." Bing Crosby singing "Melekalikimaka" poured from the concealed speakers as we left the fairgrounds.

But it turned out we didn't come back. Ephraim got called to assist at a pile-up on the highway. After that, the day got away from him, and I'd blown another romantic opportunity to shop for a tree with Ephraim.

****

Axle came into the kitchen on Monday morning with a necktie slung over one shoulder.

"Did you miss your head with that tie?" I asked.

He lifted his hands, spreading them wide. "I don't know how to make a knot."

A laugh welled up inside me. "I don't either, but I can do a better job than that." I drew the tie over his head and around his neck and made a presentable knot. "Your hair is still electrified. Have you tried using conditioner?"

"No, I don't have any."

"You can borrow some of mine next time you take a shower. You already took a shower this morning, right?"

Axle pouted. "Yes, why do I stink?" He raised one arm to sniff his armpit.

"No." But he wasn't wallowing in his usual aftershave and his hair was still fly-away.

He asked, "Am I dressed okay to meet with the police?"

"Is that why you're wearing a tie? Did Will tell you to?"

"Yeah." Axle had on his usual baggy jeans, though he'd put on a button-down shirt to go with the tie. I'm sure that was the best he could do. "Can you come with me, Delaney? Will won't mind and it's too bad if the police do."

"I guess I can come. I need to give a statement, too, remember?" I didn't have any calls for tows, so why not? I wasn't providing information as part of Axle's deal with the police and I didn't need Will for my statement, but why not get it over with? The cops wanted my affidavit about where I'd purchased the earbuds, and the city rather than the county was taking care of the matter since they were the ones to handle the bust.

While Axle walked Boss, I dressed in a red wool sweater over my blue-jean skirt with nude tights underneath and slid my feet into red flats. Tights for warmth. Red for power. And for Christmas, too. I braided my hair and put on a touch of makeup.

Once we were all set, I took us to the police station,

my tires crunching over the snowy blacktop, and parked next to Will's Nissan Infinity, rear-wheel drive.

I asked, "You ready?"

"*Whatev.*" Axle slammed the door after him, making my little Fiat rock. He beckoned me forward so I could proceed him through the door. Will, in a dark-brown suit and yellow tie, rose from one of the polymer lobby chairs. With a narrow briefcase tucked under one arm, he stuck out a hand. Axle glanced my way before shaking it. Will didn't ask why I was here, too, because he never seemed to be curious about things.

"Follow me." Will strode up to the intake clerk. "Please let Officer Bowers know my client is here now."

"Go on through." She buzzed the door and a click sounded.

Will went in first, and Axle and I took up the rear. Zach met us on the other side and escorted our party to a conference room.

I said, "I didn't know we were meeting with you today, Zach, *er*, Officer Bowers," as I took the chair at the farthest end of the table.

Zach flapped a hand. "I told them I'd grab this one from the docket. This won't take long. We're keeping it simple." He glided some empty forms across the table, one toward Will and one toward me. Axle's gray eyes, so like Kristen's, stared at the tabletop. It had to be awkward for Zach, dealing with his girlfriend's cousin, but Zach had on his cop face.

Will scanned the form and passed it to Axle. "Go ahead and fill out the paper as we discussed. If you have any questions about your statement, let me know before you write it down."

Axle nodded and picked up a pen, so I did, too. It

was a simple form with a place to insert contact information and empty lines to write a narrative statement. I put into a few words that I bought a pair of earbuds from the Emporium for fifty dollars and that I'd handed them over to the sheriff after I'd suspected the earbuds might be stolen property due to the bargain price. I made sure to include that it was Frank, not Holly, who handled the transaction. Would his arrest add to her stress or relieve it? They were likely both guilty so it may not matter.

I finished while Will reviewed Axle's statement. Zach handed Will a piece of paper. Will read that, too, then placed it in his slim briefcase, and we left.

Easy peasy.

Once we stepped outside, Axle swiped a hand across his brow. "I'm glad that's over."

Will said, "I'll make a copy of the agreement and mail it to you." He patted his briefcase.

Axle nodded. "Thanks, Mr. Sharpton."

I echoed his words, "Thanks, Will."

We all got into our vehicles. Will turned his Nissan Infinity out of the lot, and I turned to Axle. "Where to, cuz?"

"Shannon's meeting me at Roasters. And I think we all need to talk."

Chapter 16

I trod carefully. "What do we need to talk about?"

A grin broke out on his face. "The case, the case…what do you think? Never mind. Don't even say what you're thinking."

"What do you think I was thinking?" I asked, all Little Miss Proper.

He pointed his finger toward me. "Just start the car."

When I turned the key and backed out of the lot, I asked, "Do you need to talk about girls? The birds and the bees?" I clamped my teeth together to keep from laughing out loud.

"What?" He choked a little.

"Ax, we should talk about this. Is now a good time?"

My words were met with a grimace and an eye roll. "Nice try, but I think never is a good time."

"Just let me know when you're ready, lil' cuz." I live to aggravate Ax.

He fluttered his lips, sounding like air let out of a tire. "Things we do not speak of. Move on."

We pulled into the lot behind Roasters and observed Byron Oberly's white Ford 150, four-by-four, parked next to Kristen's Prius, front-wheel drive. I said, "Byron's here."

Axle gave me a jab to the shoulder. "How did you put that together?"

"You asked everyone to meet? Even Byron?"

He bobbed his head. "He wanted to come by after we got done at the police station 'cause he's worried about me, except I'm not the one he should be worried about. It's you. You and Kris. I'm stressing out about you two. First Kris was all freakin' about not selling out her mugs, then she's all, like, not worried about it. And I know you've been going around bugging people about that lady dying because I've seen you do it. See what I mean? You two are, like, all over the place."

I sniffed. "Oh, yeah?" Except the smug little twerp wasn't wrong.

"So, we're going to talk over your stupid suspect list."

"Well, okay. I wouldn't mind brainstorming." If Axle was interested in listening for once, I wasn't about to pass this up.

He unclicked his seatbelt. "Let's do it."

As we entered by way of the back door, I dug my notepad out of my bag, and Axle ripped off his tie. We walked through the kitchen to the seating area. Guy stood behind the cash register, but Kristen, Byron, and Shannon congregated at the large table near the picture window. Other than our group, the place was deserted, but before we took seats, Rory Rearden walked in the front door. *Wow*. The whole tribe was here except for the police officers. Officer Bowers and Sheriff Lopez were absent.

Guy called out, "You want your usual drink, Delaney?"

I answered, "That'd be wonderful, thanks," and scraped out an empty chair.

Rory said, "I'm getting one, too. Wait till I get back to say anything important. Wait for me, okay?"

I made a speed-it-up gesture. "Okay, but hurry up."

Axle explained to Byron and Shannon that giving his statement to the police was no big deal, as if he hadn't been nervous at all. Axle and Shannon held hands under the table.

Rory brought our tray of drinks over and handed them out. Double espresso for me, caramel latte for Axle, nonfat latte for himself. Everyone else already had coffees in front of them.

I ruffled the pages of my notepad and smoothed them out on the table top. "I don't have much new to add, except something the tree seller told me."

"Go over all the suspects from the top," Kristen suggested.

All eyes were trained on me. "Okay. Rory, here, is a 'suspect.' " I used finger quotes, but he pouted anyway. "Noel Yarborough is another suspect. The unknown married boyfriend. Jack Frier, the maintenance man. Some woman Meredith had an argument with at the market. About that person—"

"Wait, let's talk about 'em one at a time," Byron interrupted me.

Rory smiled with his quirky, lopsided smile and one eyebrow up. "Me first. I don't have an alibi. Merry and I dated, which I guess, proves a motive. And regarding opportunity, I don't think anyone saw me at the booth that day."

I reared back and stared at him. "Were you there?"

"No. That's why no one saw me. I wasn't there. So, no opportunity. And forget about that motive. It's lame. So what, we dated? And I had no means, either. I've never had any rat poison. So, now you can move on to the next suspect. Who's next?"

"Wait, we're not done talking about you yet. You conveniently forgot to add that you were overheard threatening Meredith."

"There was nothing to that. Nothing at all. In fact, I don't even remember saying anything like that. And it was years ago."

With his run-away mouth, how could he remember everything he said? His statement did have a ring of truth, but I asked anyway, "Did you tell her, if you couldn't have her no one could?"

"No. No, I did not." His lips were clenched in a tight line.

"But you can't remember, right?"

"I remember I never said that." His voice came out loud, causing the customer who had just entered to glance our way.

"Hold on." I stopped him. "I thought you wanted to talk about this. You wanted to go first. So, tell me, why would Noel say you threatened his sister?" I poised pen over paper. I really wanted Rory's take on that. I really wanted to know.

He stared at everyone around the table, then ripped his gaze from the others to draw a bead on me. His face turned a threatening shade of purple as he rose slowly from his chair and stomped over to the door. He said in a low voice, "Well, I know who my true friends are," before the door slammed behind him. On the other side of the window, Rory's Lincoln Aviator, rear-wheel drive, screeched out of the lot in the direction of the fair.

Whoa. Really?

We all exchanged guilty looks, but I couldn't meet Kristen's eyes. "This was my fault. I should've questioned him on my own, not in front of everybody.

225

Maybe I should go after him." I pushed my chair back. "I'll go now."

"No!" Everyone screamed in unison.

Kris said, "Haven't you learned by this time not to confront a suspect? He could be the killer."

"Rory? He's sort of a friend of ours now…" I sank back into my chair. I'd bet my last box of ball bearings he wasn't a killer, but I had to concede it wasn't impossible.

"Hey, you know what?" Axle asked.

I took the bite. "What?"

"Why not meet him in the woods at midnight with no flashlight, no weapon, and no backup, all on your own, in your pointy-toed shoes, so you can trip on a root and fall down, right when an owl hoots and the vampire…"

"I get it." I poked the air, instead of poking Axle's eyes out.

Byron tapped the table with his thick oil-stained finger. "Rory will get over it. Get back ta your list. Who's next?"

"Okay." I shook my head to clear my thoughts, then ran my finger down the page. "Next up, Noel, the brother. He claims he was in Palisade when Meredith was poisoned. I gave him a tow, supposedly the day he arrived in Spruce Ridge, providing proof as to when he got into town. Except he could have arrived earlier and lied about it. The police would've verified his alibi, but who knows? He may not have one. In fact, he probably doesn't since he's been taken in for questioning as much as Rory."

Kristen asked, "Who stood to gain from her death?"

Axle said, "Follow the money."

I raised a palm. "Exactly. And that would lead to Noel. I'm guessing he inherits the entire vineyard and operation. Someday, that is. His parents are still alive, but he won't have to share with his sister now."

"You found out about a will?" Byron asked.

I turned to the Old Man. "Yup, pretty much. Ephraim all but confirmed it. I asked about an insurance policy, too, but I didn't find out anything about that. I did hear Noel mention several times how glad he is to be running the business."

"Do you think Noel was cheesed off enough with his sister to…" Axle slid his fingers across his throat, the universal sign for croaked.

"I don't doubt it. You know how siblings get on each other's nerves." I gave him a pointed look.

"Sure do. But what about Jack Frier?" Axle asked. Shannon nodded, too.

"The maintenance man. He had opportunity. He was at the mulled wine booth around the time the poison was administered. But what was his motive?" I stared at each of them in turn. "What if Meredith found out he's the pickpocket, and he wanted to silence her? And to divert suspicion, he developed so-called symptoms a few days later."

"Yeah, but what about means? How did he get hold of the poison? Isn't it hard to get?" Shannon nudged her cat-eye glasses farther up the bridge of her nose.

"I don't know how any of my suspects would've come up with the poison. But I know how he ended up drinking it. According to Ephraim, he poured the mulled wine he bought from Meredith into a thermal mug, forgot about it, and took a sip later."

"Who saves mulled wine?" Shannon made a *pee-*

eew face. "That alone could make him sick."

"I know, right?" I turned my coffee cup around and around in my hands. "But, if Jack wasn't the poisoner, it's possible the killer tried to silence him. Maybe Jack saw something, even though he told me he didn't. Maybe he didn't even know that he saw something."

Kristen said, "Jack probably got that poisoned wine from the same bottle that Meredith did. He was collateral damage. That's more credible than a man actually swallowing poison on purpose or someone adding poison to his mug without him knowing. Anyway, what's this interesting tip the tree seller gave you?"

I beat the toe of my red shoe against my chair leg. "Kane Quigley, that's his name, said Meredith was wearing a bracelet. It was gold with the letter 'M.' "

Kristen leaned her elbows on the table. "I remember that bracelet. She was wearing it when I talked to her that morning."

"Guess where I saw other bracelets like that?" I rocked back in my chair.

Everyone stared at me.

I drew my long plait over my shoulder. "At the Emporium. The booth with the stolen wireless earbuds. And, get this, the alpine guy at the *Christstollen* booth, Michael Murphy, said he overheard an argument between Meredith and someone else about stealing. *Stealing.* Did you catch that? Meredith could've been involved in the stolen goods ring, and who knows what dangerous criminals are out there who could've killed her." I cut my eyes to Axle, so glad he wasn't selling the earbuds anymore.

He protested, "You're way off base there. That's all behind us now. The police are about to close that case, remember? We're done."

"You're probably right," I said, giving up the argument. I rubbed my eyes with the heels of my hands. "Okay then. If Meredith's death had nothing to do with stolen goods, what could it be? I don't know anything about her. I don't know what else was going on in her life."

"Well," Kristen said, "you did find out she wanted control of the family business. She quarreled with her brother about it."

"That's right. But family conflict is common. Nothing new or surprising there. And even the married boyfriend isn't shocking." I froze for a moment, thinking. "That initial bracelet could have stood for Michael Murphy. His first and last names begin with 'M'," I said, stating the obvious. "He could be the married boyfriend."

"A lot of men are married," Kristen argued.

"True. All the men I've met at the market so far are married. Being married doesn't narrow the suspect list." Heck, even that egomaniac Jack Frier was married. I mean, *dang*. "But, I think I saw a rat at the *Christstollen* booth. That alpine man could have rat poison."

"You saw a rat?" Byron's eyebrows elevated in a question.

"I saw a tail. I think." Had I really seen a rat? Was it my imagination? I threw my hands into the air. "That's it. That's all I've got. Unless anybody else has something to add?" I exchanged glances with the group, and everyone shook their heads.

A blast of cold air slapped my back when several customers burst through the front door. We all shivered and reached for our warm drinks.

Byron asked Kris, "How's yer sales goin' at the market?"

"It could be better." Kristen was amazingly relaxed about it. "How about you?"

"January is fillin' up with appointments. We'll be busy after the holidays."

I was glad for that. I glanced at Axle in time to see him give Shannon's hand a squeeze. Everyone pushed back from the table, so I got up, straightening my blue-jean skirt in one fluid motion.

Did I learn anything new? No. Did I unearth the smoking gun clue I was looking for? No. Was I missing something? Yes. I had to be.

Axle caught a ride with Byron and Shannon over to Oberly Motors, and Kristen left for the market. With no other reason to stick around, I accompanied everyone out and went to pick up my tow truck. I left the Fiat at Oberly Motors, gave the crew a wave on the other side of the open auto bay, and climbed into my Fulcan Xtruder. I hit the truck brakes at the exit and waited for traffic to pass.

Should I turn right and follow Rory to the fair? Should I turn left to follow Main Street to the highway? I cranked the wheel right, but in my mind I heard everyone shout out the word, *No!* I straightened the wheel, then turned it right again, and again the *No!* Sounded like a movie track being switched on and off.

So I turned left to search for stalled cars. But only a part of my brain was focused on work—or the lack of work. A Christmas tree would cheer me up. That was the ticket. A tree in my living room, decorated in white twinkle lights and the ornaments I'd purchased at the market. Wrapped underneath were the pajamas for Axle, the Santa gnome ornament for Byron, and the rest of the gifts I still needed to purchase, including one for Ephraim.

OMG! I needed a present for Ephraim, and there weren't that many days left. Mom would have all her gifts bought and wrapped by now.

So, I pulled a U-turn for the marketplace and blasted the radio on full volume. I sang along with "We Wish You a Merry Christmas" to drown out everyone's warnings. It wasn't likely I'd run into Rory, or the actual killer, in the crowded marketplace I'd visited so many times before.

I stowed my truck in the vendor lot and texted Ephraim.

—I'm at the tree lot to buy a tree. I really mean to do it this time. Can you take a break from work & meet me there?

Three little dots hovered in a conversation bubble, then his next text appeared

—Go ahead and pick out your tree & I can skip out for a few minutes as soon as I finish a report I'm working on.

Heavy snow fell as I crossed the distance from my truck to the opening through the pines, and "Walking in a Winter Wonderland" played from the speakers. My braid was tucked beneath my scarf and coat, but ice crystals stung my cheeks, so I pulled my scarf tighter around my neck and up over my chin. The melted snow from the warm sun earlier in the day now formed icy patches in the colder temperature, and I was glad I'd changed from my flats into the warm boots I kept in the truck. The inside of my nose frosted with the strong permeating smell of the cold pines, and I tamped down the memory of finding Meredith's body.

Pushing through the rows of trees, I evaluated each choice with a critical eye. By this time, the tree selection was picked over. My own fault for delaying.

The tree vendor approached me with the words, "May I help you, miss? Oh, it's you, Delaney. You're back."

"Hey, Kane. I'm here for a tree finally." I pointed to a stack of pines tied up with rope. "Are those for sale, too?"

"Sure are. Just haven't unpacked them yet. Let me get a knife, and I'll be right back." He stole through the trees out of sight but returned a few seconds later, a sharp-looking knife in his hand.

"Are these new ones any fresher?"

Kane laughed. "To be honest, these are all cut at the same time, probably a month ago by now. But the cold keeps 'em fresh. Just give the tree plenty of water when you get home." He sawed through the rope around the first tree, and its branches sprang out straight in a beautiful spire. It was sad that the soft green needles were destined to dry out and fall off after the holiday.

I held the next tree out with my mittened hand, while the vendor snapped the straps off. By the time he'd released all the trees from the bindings, I'd picked out the best one. "Sorry, you'll just need to tie it up again so I can get it on the roof of my truck."

"That's fine. I have plenty of twine. So, that's the one you want?" Kane nodded to the tree I still held upright. When I said it was, he told me the price. I extracted my credit card, and he wrapped the tree back up with twine.

"A friend is coming to help me." I cast a glance around. "Can we move my tree to the side or something?"

"Sure thing. I'll take it behind the booth and put a 'sold' tag on it. Here, let me show you. There's a warm spot back there where I take breaks."

He lifted the tree with ease and strode through a gap in the boughs. Compacted snow squeaked under my boots as I followed him. He leaned the tree up against the back of his hut in a small area with a tall pile of snapped branches and sawed-off trunks. A couple feet away, kindling simmered in a metal barrel, smelling like wood smoke. I could barely hear the festival music from here.

He twisted a ribbon marked 'sold' on the end of a branch. "Here you go."

It began to snow harder. I got out my phone and took a selfie, making a kissy face as I stood next to my tree with big white flakes rocketing down. I sent the photo to Ephraim and waited a moment to see if he'd text me back and tell me he was on his way. My phone screen remained blank, so I shoved it in my pocket.

"Thanks, Kane." I took a deep breath and whooshed the air back out in a cloud of steam. "I'm glad I got the tree. Now I need a few more presents, so I might head over to the booths." Ephraim's gift still eluded me. "I love coming here."

He fed a few broken bits of evergreen to the fire barrel. "You and everybody else, especially my wife. Belle cares too much about the market. She's always here, and after the fair closes at night, she works from her office on the next day's events. We never see each other."

"That will change after Christmas." I gave him a reassuring smile.

He upended two large stumps next to the fire pit and

sat on one. I took the other and held my mittened hands to the barrel, feeling frosty and warm at the same time.

"Not if last year is any indication. And the year before that." He stared at his calloused hands and gave me a sideways glance. "In fact, our marriage is on the rocks."

"It's not that bad?"

"It is."

"I'm so sorry." I patted his arm and tried to think of something to say. What would Kristen say? She always knew the right thing.

He put his hand on top of mine just as Holly Jennings came around the corner of the shed. A knit cap with a big pompom covered her head and a thick scarf wound around her neck. She wasn't wearing a coat but looked like she wore several layers topped by an ugly reindeer sweater.

I snatched my hand back. "Hello, Holly."

"What are you two doing?" Her voice was gruff. She shoved her fists onto her hips, causing her ugly reindeer sweater to bunch.

Kane went wild-eyed, like a skier caught in a snow slide. "Just taking a break. You need something?"

"He's married, you know. You're in this cozy spot with a married man." The older woman's eyes drilled into mine, and she practically spit out the words.

"What?"

"You heard me."

I gazed at nothing for a moment, then back at Holly. "I'm not with Kane, I'm dating Ephraim. You met him, remember?" Did everyone think I was a marriage wrecker? First Belle, now Holly? Good. God.

That was Meredith. She was the one going out with

a married man, not me!

"You're dating the sheriff?" Kane stood up fast and the stump fell over. "I didn't realize you were together."

"I doubt it would've made any difference to you, Kane." Holly flailed her arms around. "Men. They can't be trusted. The whole lot of them." Holly was obviously worked up about something. Her husband? Was this agitation part of the battered woman syndrome?

"Kane and I were just talking, that's all," I tried to explain.

"Yeah, what's your problem, Holly?" Kane wanted to know.

"I don't have a problem. You have a problem. In fact, you *are* the problem. You're what's wrong with the world today. You know what it's like for a wife to be tossed aside?" She answered her own question, "It's horrible. The worst feeling in the world, not to be wanted anymore. Frank used to be kind and loving. Now he's so critical, I can't do anything right. It's because he doesn't love me anymore." With her baggy reindeer sweater all stretched out, she looked the part of a deranged old lady. Not the object of love and desire.

This wasn't about me and Kane, of course. This was about Holly and Frank. I couldn't help but feel sorry for the woman. But all the same, she was bonkers.

I had a strong urge to get the heck out of there, so I rose to my feet and tried to peer over Holly's shoulder, but even standing on my toes didn't help me to see past her.

"Excuse me," I said to the woman blocking my way.

Kane put in, "I'm leaving, too."

"Yup. *Gottago*." I started around her.

"Neither of you are going anywhere." She

obstructed my exit with her solid frame.

Could I shove the old lady out of the way? No, I couldn't do that. I needed to show some respect and a little compassion.

"I don't understand, Holly. What's wrong?" I asked, wishing to be anywhere else. Low, gray clouds dimmed the sunlight, and I trembled from the cold.

"You need to know who you're getting mixed up with. Kane's a cheater." She had on a *you-heard-me-right* look. "A cheater just like my husband."

I tried to keep the surprise off my face. "Frank was having an affair?"

"That's what I've been telling you."

Was it really true? Was Holly's husband actually two-timing his wife?

With Meredith?

Was he Meredith's married lover? Maybe Holly invented the whole thing. Can you picture a young gal— or any gal—doing the deed with that old grouch? No? That's what I thought, too.

I asked her, "Did your husband ever admit to the affair? Did you speak to him about it? Confront him?"

"Talk to Frank? You've got to be kidding. I'd drive him away even more. He's just waiting for an excuse to leave me." Her eyes teared up, and she wiped her nose on her sleeve. "But I did confront Meredith. I told her to stay away from my husband. She laughed at me and called me old and ugly. She was cruel."

"Was that over by the booth that sells German pastries?"

Her jaw fell open. "How did you know?"

"I heard about it…you accused Meredith of stealing your husband. And I thought the fight was about the stolen goods ring."

Snowflakes accumulated on her eyelashes and on top of her knit cap. "Stolen goods? What are you talking about?"

"I know you're selling hot merchandise at the Emporium. The police know it, too. I gave the cops a sworn statement. They're finishing up their report now, and they have a warrant for your arrest. They're probably on their way over here as we speak." I hoped. I was totally making this part up.

Uh-oh. There went my anonymity. No secret snitching now. So much for my covert op.

A strangled laugh emerged from Holly's throat. "So, the police know about that. Well, well, well. Frank won't be happy. Too bad for him. No, that's not what we were arguing about. She denied the affair was with Frank. I'm sure my husband's having an affair, but I had the wrong woman."

"What? It wasn't Meredith?"

"No." Her eyes went to the man cowering beside me. "It's true that Meredith was having a fling with a married man, I got that part right. But not with my husband. The affair was with him." She gestured toward the tree vendor. "Meredith was having it on with Kane."

Kane gasped, and his eyes went wide. "*Whaaa*?"

I pressed my fingers to my temples. So all the married men were unfaithful. *Jeez*. She was deranged. Certifiably *coo-coo*.

Understatement!

She growled at him, "You. You were cheating on your wife. You lech. Why not admit it?"

"Why do you think I cheated?" The whites of his eyes showed.

"After Meredith denied she was sleeping with Frank, I followed her and saw the two of you together. You didn't think anyone knew about your cubby hole back here, but I discovered it right away."

I snickered, but the look of guilt on Kane's face made me ask, "Kane? You're the married boyfriend?" Mental forehead slap.

Kane's voice broke as he supplied the answer, "Yes! Yes! I was in love with her."

"You told me you didn't know her. You said your wife knew her better than you did."

Holly sneered. "Oh, Kane knew her all right."

"So I lied. Big whoop. But I was going to tell Belle the truth after Christmas, after the Christmas market closing ceremony. My marriage was over anyway."

"I doubt you were going to do any such thing." Holly's words were slow and deliberate, over-the-top angry. "You were only using Meredith. A typical man, two-timing his wife."

She yanked a gun from her pocket. It was small in her hand, silver, with a snub nose and upright trigger. Her thumb hovered over the trigger. An insane look crept over her eyes.

"Holly, what are you doing?" I shrieked.

Chapter 17

The tree vendor and I were back to the wall. Trapped by a whacko killer!

My adrenaline spiked like I'd just stepped off the edge of a cliff.

Voices of shoppers were a distant hum, muffled by the hammering snow. This was frightfully close to where Meredith met her death among the trees. If I screamed, would anyone hear me, or would Holly shoot me and Kane, leave us for dead, and escape? Where was Lopez? Was the sheriff nearby looking for me? Would he be able to find us hidden behind the hut? I tried to slide my hand into my pocket for my cell phone. Not that it would do me much good. I'm sure Holly wasn't going to accept my excuse that I needed to make a call.

She twitched the little silver gun at me. "Show me your hands."

I yanked my hand from my pocket, abandoning my cell phone. "You killed Meredith, didn't you? You had an elaborate scheme to poison her, but you're going to shoot us?" I glanced at Kane, who seemed shocked mute. "Why didn't you just shoot her?"

She *tsked*. "I didn't kill Meredith." The little silver gun shook in her hands, but before I could rush her, she steadied it in my direction, then over to Kane, who was still speechless beside me. "It was him. He killed her."

I sucked in air. "Kane?"

Kane said, "No freakin' way. I didn't kill her. I loved her." He spun toward me. "It was Delaney. She's the murderer." He pointed his finger at me.

I barked a laugh but realized he wasn't joking. "Really? Me?" I bounced my hands off my chest. "Why me? I didn't even know her."

"You were the one who found her body. Isn't the person to find the body the number one suspect?"

"In the movies, maybe, but this is real life." I narrowed my eyes at Holly, but she kept her gun aimed at Kane, who was still pointing at me. I had accused Holly, Holly blamed Kane, and Kane cast aspersions on me!

"Mom?" Candace stepped into the dim circle of light from the smoldering barrel. "Mom, what's going on here?"

I said, my voice amazingly calm, "Your mom killed Meredith. And now she's threatening to shoot Kane. And me."

Candace glanced sharply at her mother, whose feet were planted in a shooter's stance and the gun was pointed at Kane. When Holly pulled back the hammer and aimed the little pistol directly at his heart, Candace yelled, "Don't shoot, Mom, don't shoot. Please put the gun down. You're ruining everything."

She shouted back, "How am I ruining everything? Why is everything always my fault? Why do you and your dad gang up on me? Can't you take my side for once, Candy?"

Candace countered, "I'm getting away from you, and I'm taking Ivy. Now that Noel has the winery, we're going to move away from here, far away from you. Noel's going to buy me a nice house, we're going to live a nice life. Away from you."

"I don't understand. What did I do that was so wrong?" Holly's face crumpled.

"Well, just look at you." Candace gave her a disgusted glance. "Clean yourself up, for God's sake. Put the gun down and quit acting like a crazy, paranoid old lady." She laughed with a few hysterical notes. "Maybe that's where I get it. Will I really be able to escape all the hate, all the craziness? Have I turned into...you?" Her laugh scrunched into a frown and a tear ran down her cheek, making a rivulet in her perfect makeup. "I just wanted a better life for Ivy. And look what happened. Look what I did. What kind of a mother am I?"

I was stuck in the middle of a family dogfight with a senile old woman, a hysterical beauty queen, and a cheating husband. And the senile one had a gun. And me? I was laughing one second and the next second, fighting the panic gripping my chest. My legs were wobbly, my teeth were chattering, and I was losing it.

Hang on. Just hang on. No irrational terror was going to take control of me this time. Now the sky wasn't black and spooky. Now the market wasn't closed and empty. There were people all around us—except, we kinda were in a shadowy, secluded spot.

I took a few seconds to compose myself. Then the truth struck me like one of Axle's slush bomb snowballs, cold and clammy and completely by surprise.

I asked, "What did you do, Candace? What would make you a bad mother?"

"What do you mean?" Her voice quivered, and her beautifully made-up face showed strain, like a mask was about to crack and fall off.

"Tell us what happened. Go ahead, be honest. Do it

for Ivy," I prompted her.

Holly said, "Candace, honey, what happened? What did you do? You can tell me."

"Nothing," she protested.

"Come on, what is it?" Holly urged her daughter.

"Will you put the gun down if I tell you?"

"Yes, yes. What happened?"

Candace's shoulders sagged in defeat. "I took an almost empty bottle from the wine tasting room, added the rat killer to the bottle, and brought it to the booth while Merry was setting up." She had an inward look; you could see her thoughts drifting back. "I figured Merry wouldn't taste the poison because of the strong mulled spices."

"Did the maintenance guy see you?" I asked.

"No. He never saw me. Nobody saw me." She wrung her hands together, her eyes on her mother, her gaze burdened and troubled. "I didn't intend for that man to end up with any of the poison, Mom. I didn't. I thought the bottle was empty when I left. I didn't know Merry made that man a drink with it. Of course I didn't drink mine. I dumped it out."

Jack Frier really did come along afterward. He was an innocent victim after all, innocent for the murder, that is.

"Where did you get the poison in the first place? Ephraim said it was illegal," I wanted to know.

She flicked a dark look over to me. "Mom's not the only one who knows where to get illegal stuff."

I blurted out, "I never guessed it was you, Candace. But I did think that Noel had a motive, and if he has a motive, so do you since you're engaged."

"What's Noel's motive?" She scrunched her

forehead.

"The same as yours, I imagine. To control the entire winery. Once you got married, your future and your daughter's future would be secure with a man who owns a successful business. Totally owns it without interference from his sister."

A small sliver of fear passed over her face. "Noel knows nothing about what happened to Merry."

"I doubt the marriage will go forward once he finds out." I glanced at Holly, who still held the gun.

Candace's panicked gaze flew to her mother, then her face crumpled, and she broke down sobbing.

Holly swung the pistol at me. "Noel won't find out."

My muscles seized up, and Kane tensed next to me.

She said, "I'm sorry I failed you, Candace, but I'm going to make it right now. No one is going to know, especially the police, because these two aren't going to be around to tell them."

The deadly weapon could go off any moment.

I forced myself to take a step forward. Kane must've had the same thought because he pushed me aside, then made a grab for the silver pistol. Holly fought for control of the gun, which suddenly pointed at me!

The sound of *pop, pop, pop!* went off, loud. Three little puffs of smoke escaped from under the hammer.

Was I shot? I patted myself but didn't feel anything. Maybe I was in shock.

Holly may have a little silver pistol, and all I have is a bit of redheaded spunkiness, but I rushed at her anyway. The gun flew out of her hand when my shoulder went into her gut, and she sat down hard on the wood pile. She started to heave herself up, but I caught the back of her ugly sweater in a vice grip while she strained away even harder. Her sweater broke from my grasp, and I feared we were going to topple like bowling balls, when Candace suddenly came to life and made a run for it.

Right smack into someone.

A big guy in a cowboy hat.

Lopez!

Ephraim caught Candace in a tight hold and clamped handcuffs to her wrists. "You're under arrest for the murder of Meredith Yarborough."

I didn't realize how out of breath I was until I gasped, "How long were you standing there?"

"Long enough to hear this woman's confession." He had a strong hold on Candace's elbow.

I flushed, breathing in and out fast. "The gun went off. Holly could've killed me." I rubbed my arms up and down, but I wasn't bleeding anywhere.

Ephraim tugged Candace toward the trees. He said, "I knew it was a toy gun. There's a whole bin of them at the Emporium. You three wait here. I'm taking Ms. Jennings to my patrol car, and I'll be right back."

Kane said, "A toy gun? That was a toy gun." We gave each other *can-you-believe-it* shrugs.

Holly elbowed herself off the woodpile and dusted off her backside. "It's a cap gun. I didn't plan to kill anyone. You see, I just wanted to scare you, Kane, and make you suffer for your affair."

"Humpf." He stomped off after the sheriff.

"Hey, we're supposed to wait here," I shouted after him, but he kept going.

I collapsed onto one of the tree stumps in front of the firepit and shook the snow off myself. "Holly, you really scared me." My fingers were numb, and my toes, too, and not only from the ice cracking under my feet. It was from fright. In my panic, I hadn't recognized the familiar sound and smell of the cap gun.

"Sorry." She picked the toy gun off the ground. "Are you okay?"

"Yeah," I fibbed. Actually, I think I peed my pants. "I can't believe you tried that trick with the gun."

"I can't believe you suspected me of murder."

"Well. Gun." I pointed at the fake weapon.

Suddenly Holly looked totally shattered. The appliqué reindeer hung loose from her sweater, the hair in her bun fell down, and she dropped onto the other stump, her thighs gaping open.

I folded my hands together and tucked them between my knees, then ducked my head down for some deep breaths. "I'm sorry about your daughter."

She didn't say anything to that.

"Did Candace buy an initial bracelet for Meredith, do you know?"

"Meredith bought it for herself. Frank sold it to her. That's when I caught her flirting with my husband. Kane was trying to pick you up, you know. He's slime, just like Frank."

"You're probably right about Kane, but it's possible you're wrong about Frank. What if he's not messing around? Why don't you talk to him? You could go for marriage counseling."

"Maybe, but I suppose the sheriff's going to arrest me when he comes back."

"I suppose so."

****

It was evening by the time I'd returned home and explained everything to Kris and Ax. The three of us were gathered at my apartment when Ephraim finally showed up with my tree. Axle found the song "O Christmas Tree" by Nat King Cole on his iPad, then the two men strung the lights. I went to get the boxes of ornaments from my closet, and when I returned, Axle had taken off his knit cap and his hair stood on end with static electricity.

I asked, "Have you used any conditioner on that hair yet?"

"Yes." He dove for his knit cap and shoved it back over the top of his head.

I hoofed it to the kitchen for the Roasters on the Ridge souvenir mugs I'd accumulated from the market and filled them with hot chocolate. We hung the red and silver balls, the potpourri ornament, and the Santa gnome ornament I'd kept for myself. The other Santa gnome was wrapped up for Byron. Ephraim, the tallest person in the room, positioned the angel topper on the tree's crown. The nutcracker stood at attention on the sofa table.

My friends sat around for a long time, listening to music, laughing with comic relief when I retold the story of the toy gun a few more times. Finally, after we wound down, and after I assured Ephraim I was fine and he took off, I asked Kristen, "Can you come with me to shop for Ephraim's gift? It's only eight, and the stores are open until nine."

"Sure. Guy's at the Christmas market booth until closing, so I'm free. Where are we going?"

"Not the market. I've looked at everything there ten times over. We're going to the mall."

Kristen's lips turned up in a delighted smile. "Let me grab my purse."

I asked Axle if he wanted to come with us, but he

declined my invite. His words, "That's a no-go."
    My response, "I'm crushed."
    I'd thought of a fantastic gift for Ephraim.
    One that would totally surprise him.
    And you, too.

Chapter 18

My friends came by my apartment on Christmas evening.

The weather was perfect, a crisp Colorado winter night.

The turkey was in Kristen's oven at her apartment, but she was sitting in my kitchen on a counter stool beside Zach. A few feet away in the adjoining room, Axle reclined on the couch in his hoodie next to Shannon in a similar hoodie. Byron placed presents under the tree, his knees snapping as he stood back up. Boss chewed on a bone, his gift from Axle. A pan of potpourri simmered on the stove, steaming up the windows with fragrant, moist heat. Ephraim had his arm around me on the couch.

It was a cozy setting right out of a Christmas movie.

Kristen said, "Good news. Guy sold the last of the ceramic mugs last night. Just in time, right before the market closed for the year."

"How about the dated ornaments?" I asked.

"Those were gone a week ago. Great ideas, Delaney." She beamed at me.

I breathed a sigh of relief and admitted, "I was worried."

"Me, too, at first. But then I prayed about it. As it turns out, the murder wasn't bad for business, just the opposite. Everyone came by as an excuse to gossip. It had to be divine intervention to turn around something as bad as that."

"Hmmm." I shrugged. It was just like my friend to see the bright side in everything, even murder.

Axle had a Christmas playlist going. Kristen set her phone in front of my tree with the timer on, and we all mugged it up for the camera. When she turned off the timer, I made a *gimme-gimme* gesture, and she handed me her phone.

"Oh, no. You won't believe this." I chuckled.

Kristen's dark eyebrows arched. "What?"

"These photos are great. They would've been perfect for the Christmas card, but it's too late now." I laughed. "They're *so* perfect."

"Perfect? Not likely with Axle in them." Kristen laughed as she stood and stretched her arms over her head. "I'm going to check the turkey. Be right back."

Muttering, "These *are* perfect," I tapped the screen to enlarge the image, then swiveled the phone around for the others to see. "I'm framing this one to put on my wall." Axle's and Shannon's eyes were closed in laughter, and Axle's hair stood on end. That one may not look perfect to anyone else, but it did to me.

As I fiddled with my earlobes, the silver earrings with dangling stilettos and red gemstones for bows brushed against my neck.

I hid my smile thinking about the gift bag I had for Ephraim, tucked out of sight, and all the other presents under the tree we planned to open after dinner. I'd filled his bag with paint sample chips, a gift certificate from the paint store, a coupon for a weekend of painting I'd printed myself, and a framed picture of the two of us. I couldn't wait to see the changes in his townhome. It would be fun to help him decorate and that was my gift to him. My present for Kristen was a sterling silver necklace with a cross. As far as Axle's gift, he'd opened his pajamas the night before but had still slept in his clothes. Oh well, good intentions and all that.

Rory had given us two bottles of wine from the Yarboroughs' vineyard. He'd gotten over being mad. Noel had decided to continue with the tasting room after all. It would keep his mind occupied now that he was no longer engaged to be married. I'd exchanged gifts with Mom and Will on Christmas Eve as per our usual tradition.

Axle's gift for Shannon was tucked in a stocking hung in the doorway. It seemed they were definitely a couple now, and he wasn't denying his crush anymore. Byron and Axle were laughing together at something Shannon had said. *Ahhhh.* It gave me a warm fuzzy.

"Anyone want to sing Christmas carols?" I asked the group.

They all stared at me in total disbelief.

"You want to get a breath of fresh air?" Ephraim tugged on my hand and inclined his head toward the door.

"Sure." I weaved my arms into my coat sleeves, wrapped my scarf around my neck, and drew on my mittens. I put the leash on Boss, and we descended the steps after Ephraim.

His words floated back to me in the silent night. "I want to thank you for your help with the case. But don't tell anybody I said that. You can't be part of an official investigation, you know. We hadn't found Candace's connection until her confession."

"I know, right? I was focused on Noel myself. Holly and Frank were suspicious because of the stolen goods.

And the pickpocket, Jack Frier. Even Rory…"

We proceeded a few more steps to the parking lot, and Boss sniffed around the snow.

I asked, "So, you never prosecuted Jack for the thefts? You never got any of the money back?"

"No. He told us he planned to move to Denver after the market closed. The Denver police are aware of him. And, he mentioned without admitting to the crime that his near-death experience, as he called it, made him turn over a new leaf. I hope it did."

Jack Frier had escaped the law, but Candace Jennings was at the county lockup, and her dad had been arrested, too. Holly was at home with Ivy and was not going to be prosecuted for selling stolen goods or threatening us with a toy gun. Neither Kane nor I wanted to press charges against her. After turning in the remaining earbuds anonymously to the city police, I had made a call to the Health Department to check the fairgrounds for rats, but the fair had come to an end by then and they'd never gotten back to me.

"So, you didn't mind my help?" I teased.

His dark eyes softened, and he hugged me to his chest. "No. In fact, we make a good team, *es mi novia.*" I now knew this meant "my girlfriend." I'd looked it up. So, the boyfriend-girlfriend thing was on.

When snow began to fall, we both stared skyward, awed by the twinkling tree that blazed from my window. Boss, having completed his business, sat on my foot. I couldn't hear the music with my ears, but I heard it in my mind. The Christmas song was stuck in my head, "I've Got My Love to Keep Me Warm."

I snaked my arms around Ephraim's neck and snuggled closer to him.

This *was* my best Christmas ever.

~~*~*

I hope you enjoyed *Friends Come to Call*.
Please consider leaving a review. For links of places to leave reviews, see my website at:
http://www.karencwhalen.com/newbooks/

A word about the author...

Karen C. Whalen is the author of two cozy mystery series, the Dinner Club Murder Mysteries and the Tow Truck Murder Mysteries. The first in the dinner club series, *Everything Bundt the Truth*, tied for First Place in the Suspense Novel category of the 2017 IDA Contest. Whalen loves to host dinner parties, camp, hike, and read.